Baklava, Biscotti, and an Irishman

By

Kathy Aspden

CONTENTS

Blue Shoe Publishing
PO Box 487, Barnstable, MA 02630

www.BlueShoePublishing.com

ISBN-13: 978-1533022004

ACKNOWLEDGMENTS

This novel was the work of angels. I didn't have a plan. Instead, I had characters who made decisions in the night, forcing me out of bed to write it down while it was fresh in my mind. My job as the author was to stay out of their way and let them tell their tale. *Baklava, Biscotti, and an Irishman* was most definitely a character-driven story.

In deference to the realness of my characters, I chose to use locations that actually existed. I picked out restaurants they would have liked, and houses located on the streets where my characters would have lived. Although the businesses, hospitals, restaurants, churches and landmarks are real, all the characters and their situations are the product of my imagination and my dreams. Any resemblance to people, living or dead, is coincidental and unintentional.

I want to thank Suzanne Glover, Bob Bevis, Tom Sgro and my daughter, Jocelyn DiGiacomo, for their invaluable insight and encouragement as my first readers; along with my editor, Heidi Sullivan, for adding wisdom and skill to my vision. A forever debt of gratitude goes to the talented Jule Selbo, who pushed me to finish my first screenplay and see myself as a writer. I have received much-appreciated camaraderie and support from fellow writers, including Vincent Sgro and Sandra Bolton, along with Kathi Driscoll and Tim Miller (my friends in the 'hood).

I would like to thank my husband, Bill, and our daughters, Casey, Jocelyn and Sara for adding color, humor, in-laws, babies and love to my life; and my mother, Barbara, for being the most colorful of all.

To Christine Merser, and her staff at Blue Shoe Publishing: I'm humbled that you saw what I saw in *Baklava, Biscotti, and an Irishman.* Your guidance made it possible for my dream to become a reality.

DEDICATION

This novel is dedicated to my nana, Mary Celli, and my father, Raymond Bragg. Their strength of character and commitment to family created the foundation for a life of endless possibilities. Their angel work can be read in these pages.

There is a phenomenon that happens when two people meet. It's the moment when their futures become set. One soul, with a pre-planned agenda, recognizes another soul, with its own agenda, and remembers exactly how they were meant to fit into each other's lives. Nothing can be done to take back that tiny millisecond when one soul recognizes another.

It was like that. It was that rapid, that breathtaking, that devastating. And it was too late. His soul had recognized hers and there was no turning back.

PROLOGUE

2015

NEA MAKRI, GREECE

COSTAS HAD CONTEMPLATED taking a run, but he wasn't wearing his trail shoes. "No sense maiming myself," he muttered, scanning the jagged coastline of the Mediterranean. This was so different from the sandy beaches he ran every day at home. Running had become his obsession. His sanity had come to depend upon it.

Being apart from Julia after going through so much together was killing him; likely killing her too. She had been furious when he told her that he wanted to come here alone. He couldn't blame her. Europe had been her idea.

Maybe that was my plan, some relationship-killing distance before I start school in the fall.

He had no choice, really. How could he separate the stark reality of his life from the body of fiction that he had been told, with her looking on as a witness? If Julia saw the truth, she would never let him live the lie.

No matter what his original motive, this solitary trip had been what he had needed to do: visit his grandparents, backpack through the mountains of Greece and put away some of the grief over his mother's death - and her revelation. But he also needed answers. There were only three people who could give him those answers; none of them still alive.

Costas thought about his mother's letter, still unopened in his backpack, along with her ashes, waiting to be spread. *Running has become my obsession.*

The essence of his life had come down to two choices: go home and forget about what she had told him just days before her death, or take the next step and find out the truth. *Running has become ...*

It was time to stop running. He had three days left to make sense of it all before the next chapter of his life: Tufts School of Medicine in Boston,

Massachusetts. Classes were scheduled to start on September 2nd, his twenty-third birthday.

Where do I begin?

PART I
1972
NEA MAKRI, GREECE

NINETEEN-YEAR-OLD Teressa Giannopoulos was furious. She had assumed that her father was going to be the biggest obstacle to her happiness. All Greek fathers were. It was the stuff of legend. But getting into the University of Athens should have made him ecstatic. Teres was making it easy for him - a college close enough to take the bus, with no fees or tuition. But, no, her Papa wanted to ship her off to a one-year program at the Jewelry Design Academy in Florence. *It is not going to happen!*

After the latest of ten arguments, she had grabbed the first bike in the shed; her brother, Nicky's. The seat was so high that Teres could only touch one pedal at a time with the toe of her sandal. It didn't matter. It was all downhill to the beach, where she was going to scream a piece of her mind into the wind. She planned to discharge a complete tirade against her father, and his profession. If Teres had to look at one more Parthenon pendant necklace or ridiculous charm of the great Athena she would vomit. She was *not* going into the family jewelry business!

As the wind and the speed began to have its calming effect, Teres let go of some of her anger. Tears of frustration filled her eyes. *Let the wind wipe them dry*, she thought to herself, flying effortlessly down the mountainside. She knew this mountain road better than she knew the landscape of the home she had lived in all her life. There was a large hole in the pavement just around the bend. Every year the roadwork department fixed it. And every year it wore away again from the rain pouring through the century-old ravine down the side of the mountain. Teres readied herself to go slightly into the road to avoid it. She rounded too wide. "I was blinded by my tears," was what she would later say to Danny, in halting, thickly accented English, as she lay there bleeding.

*

Daniel David Muldaur, Danny, was stationed at the US Naval Communications Base in Nea Makri, Greece. He was career Navy, having joined straight out of high school rather than let fate decide if his draft number would be pulled. As the chief medic attached to a construction battalion, his days were spent giving antibiotic shots for venereal diseases, pills for throat infections and generally patching up his group of dryland sailors after fistfights and construction mishaps. Everyone called him "Doc." But he wasn't a doctor. He was just a guy who had signed up for a clerical position, but through the Navy's infinite wisdom had been trained as a medic. Danny liked his work, especially at this base in Greece. He knew that he was one lucky man to find himself situated five thousand miles away from the horrors of Southeast Asia for his last tour of duty. As wartime posts go, it was a gift.

By the time he landed in Nea Makri, he was well known and respected enough to warrant a measure of latitude. Higher ranking officers considered him a peer (some with the misconceived notion that he was a physician) and he was privy to a great deal of secrets, both military and nonmilitary. At thirty-nine years of age, Danny could honestly admit that he must have a guardian angel. His service record was clean. He had only two months of duty left before he hit twenty years in. Then he'd be out, with his health intact, a government pension and nothing ahead but open possibilities.

Danny had never been married and, up until Greece, had never been in love. Sure there were a few women who had held his interest for a time, but at the end of the day he didn't love any of them enough to put up with the work and the restrictions of a relationship. He thanked his lucky stars that none of them had gotten pregnant. He had seen it happen dozens of times to other guys. Then they were stuck making the decision to abandon the woman and child in the country of conception or bring them back to America - a war trophy of sorts. Danny figured that the only thing more difficult than a wife was a wife from a foreign country. All of that changed when he met Teres.

*

What a shitty day, Danny thought as he shifted to second gear to accommodate the steep incline of the road. There had been two easily avoidable accidents at the site of the new communications tower that his Seabees were building. The first had resulted in a broken collarbone when one of the guys walked in front of a beam that was being transported by crane. The second was when the driver of the crane, rattled by his part in the injury, stepped on an unsecured board which flipped up, hit him in the head, and knocked him unconscious. Danny couldn't believe it when he saw the second stretcher come into the infirmary just one hour after the first. He had left them resting side-by-side, reliving their misadventure. He was happy to have their bad day behind him and the open mountain road ahead of him.

With an elevation barely above sea level and a vast mountain range as its backdrop, Nea Makri was beautifully isolated from the rest of Greece. Danny had come to love everything about the little city, nestled as it was into the coast of the Petalioi Gulf; one of the smaller gulfs that flow in from the Aegean Sea. Because it was a great place to explore, he took any opportunity to drive his convertible, a 1960 VW Karmann Ghia, through the village and mountain roads. The little car was surprisingly comfortable for a man of his stature. For Danny, there was something obscenely freeing and powerful about driving a tiny car up a big mountain. It was almost like being on foot. He was a great, bad driver. He had driven in enough left-side-of-the-road countries to be grateful that the Greeks drove on the right. It made the pastime of sightseeing an effortless pleasure.

The Karmann Ghia didn't sound like it would make it up the hill, but it always did. With over 200,000 miles on the odometer and on its eighth owner, the little car owed nothing to anyone. It had been passed down from one Navy sailor to another for most of its life. Danny already had a list of men willing to buy the car off him when he was ready to pack it in. He was really going to miss this car. The Karmann Ghia was a treasure. Its simple engine design made it the kind of car that an idiot could fix, and Danny was no idiot. Within two weeks of buying it from the last guy (for the bargain price of three hundred dollars) he had the car running like a charm. This was why when his prized possession coughed and sputtered a bit, he took his eyes off the road and looked down at the tachometer; worried about the transmission. A moment later Danny looked up, just in time to hit her.

*

The girl was knocked out cold, of that Danny was certain. He hadn't hit her hard. The steel bumper of the Karmann Ghia had barely grazed the front tire of her bicycle. That tap led her to spin out at the exact moment her loosely-planted foot slipped off the pedal and got caught between the spokes of the bicycle's front tire. The momentum of her trapped foot caused her body to catapult over the handlebars and slap viciously to the ground. The entire event took a matter of seconds. In just a few seconds more, Danny had vaulted out of the offending car and was assessing the young woman's injuries.

Her forehead was split open, deep into the hairline of her raven black hair. She probably had a concussion, maybe even a broken neck. Her foot was bloodied and most likely fractured.

Think! Think, stupid! What do you do next? For reasons he couldn't fathom, Danny was paralyzed. It wasn't the slow-motion version of a disastrous dream, but something close. He was floating through it, not in a detached way, more like an intensely *attached* way. He was part of the blood coming from her head. He was thrown from the bike with her. Danny was confused. Was it possible that he, too, had hit his head when he swerved the car? She moaned.

"Damn. Damn. Damn." With her thick accent, Danny thought she was saying his name.

How does she know my name? Later, when it was too late for him to not be in love with her, he would realize that "damn" was her favorite curse

13

word. Teres opened her eyes and brought her hand up to touch her bloodied scalp. She looked right into Danny's eyes and said, "I was blinded by my tears."

It was like that. It was that rapid, that breathtaking, that devastating. And it was too late. His soul had recognized hers and there was no turning back.

*

Two months later they faked a pregnancy, endured her father's wrath and were married in the Greek Orthodox Church of Saint Nicholas. Six days after the wedding they headed home to Quincy, Massachusetts and their new life.

1992

SCITUATE, MASSACHUSETTS

"HOW, BY THE mother of Christ, did it come to this?" muttered Danny as he watched the dark yellow stream of urine squirt spasmodically into the toilet, then stop. It was probably an enlarged prostate, or worse: cancer. There wasn't a chance in hell he was going to tell Teres about this. She was constantly hounding him to go to the doctor's. If he had to hear about one more article she'd read on how to stay alive, he would kill himself.

Danny concentrated on not concentrating too hard on the task of urinating. *Just relax. Let it flow... let it flow...* "Ahh. Finally." As he felt his bladder empty, he again made a mental note not to breathe a word of this to his wife and to keep the fan on in the bathroom when nature called. The idea of nature calling was enough to get Danny's blood pressure up. For him, nature calling used to be about sex. Somehow, when he first heard the saying, he assumed it was horniness that was calling, not taking a whiz. Either way, both of those things had become a pain in the ass for him now. Poor Teres. She had already heard enough crap about his penis to last a lifetime.

He was forty-five when he had the first problem with his erection. It scared him. Truly terrified was a more accurate measure of his fear. To fall in love with a woman who liked sex just as much as he did was like winning the lottery. So when the unthinkable happened, not even six years into their marriage, Danny was devastated.

What kind of guy can't get it up for his gorgeous, twenty-five-year-old wife?

He had snuck out to the doctor's office; not their doctor, the doctor of a friend. The physician had examined him, reduced his blood pressure medication and then told him that most of his problem was in his head. He was trying too hard. He had a classic case of performance anxiety. Eventually, it cured itself. Teres had been amazing. She assured him that it was not uncommon or anything

15

to be ashamed of, having read all about it in her Anatomy and Physiology book, *most likely the morning after it had happened.* Prior to that incident, Danny thought that giving his wife a class about the human body was like giving bank codes to a white collar criminal: no good could come of it. She was already ten times smarter than he was and interested in everything. But Danny rarely said no to his wife. Whatever Teres wanted was what he wanted to give her. And what he *really* wanted to give her was good sex, which he had managed to do for most of the nineteen years of their marriage.

But lately, there had been no sex. *Lately,* meaning the six months since his surgery. Even though his body wasn't quite up to the arduous task of sex, he took his time to see that Teres was satisfied. It was enough for him, making her happy. But after a while, she didn't want that. She said it was too selfish, satisfying her and leaving him hanging. Little did she know that he felt no real urge for sex. He was on so many pills that he was definitely not being left hanging.

No use thinking about this right now, Danny decided as he walked out of the bathroom. He made a beeline through their bedroom and to his favorite chair in the sunroom. As he watched the sun slip down behind the white fence of the pool enclosure, Danny thought about how much he loved this property. It seemed strange that he, a man with absolutely no roots for most of his life, could fall in love with a house. He knew part of the reason he loved it so much was that Teres loved it. Its Grecian-inspired style reminded her of home. Danny laid down on the cushioned chaise and wondered, for the one-millionth time, how he had gotten so lucky. This home, their friends, their successful business were all because of her.

Where is she, anyway? Even when she was on the road for the day, Teres usually called him if she was running behind. Something was up. She was absent-minded, less talkative. He was probably worried over nothing. Knowing her, she was busy concocting a plan that she would spring on him, maybe a trip. His sixtieth birthday was coming up in a couple of weeks.

Sixty years old. The thought of it made Danny want to slit his wrists.

*

Teres looked at the clock on the dashboard: 7:45. Glancing at the speedometer, she saw the needle coming up on 80 mph. *All good.* In just a couple of miles she would be turning off Route 3 South and onto Washington Street where she would be less likely to run into a speed trap. Teres knew the chances were good that if she got pulled over she'd be able to talk her way out of it, even without the company car. Being on the road so much had its consequences. *I can't believe that I had ever been terrified to drive!* It had taken her forever to learn. Danny's initial attempt to teach her had gone badly, almost deadly. After years of intentionally suppressing the memory, Teres let herself think about the first time she had gotten behind the wheel of Danny's little blue car...

1973

HOUGHS NECK, MASSACHUSETTS

THE DAY HAD begun with promise. Danny drove them in his newest, used Karmann Ghia to a coastal neighborhood of Quincy called Houghs Neck. He chose that particular area because it reminded him of Greece. It was a village-like community with a rocky coastline that was surrounded by Hingham Bay, Quincy Bay and Rock Island Cove. The locals called it The Neck and Danny had spent a lot of time there as a child.

On a Saturday morning in early winter, Houghs Neck was asleep. There had only been one car to pass by them on the narrow bridge-like road to the water. The ride to The Neck was always beautiful. It paid to take the long way down Quincy Shore Drive, past Wollaston Beach and hug the shoreline to the other side of Sea Street.

Danny was excited to show off one of the city's more appealing areas to his wife. He had packed a little brown bag of foil-wrapped English muffins with peanut butter. And they had stopped at Harry's along the way and grabbed a couple of coffees to go. Teres would only drink the coffee from Harry's. To Danny, it was burnt, thick and you could smell it from forty feet. But he knew that for Teres, it was a reminder of the Turkish coffee that she was used to having in Greece. She told him that she wasn't a heavy coffee drinker, it was more the nostalgia of a cup of coffee that was so strong and had so many grounds floating in it, it could have been boiled in a cezve rather than dripped through a filter. Regardless of its taste, Danny liked the way it made her smile when he pulled into Harry's, because she knew that he only did it for her.

Teres seemed anxious to get behind the wheel. She hardly took a moment to look around them as Danny pulled off the side of the road by Rock Island Cove. He killed the engine and his wife jumped out of the car and bolted for the driver's side.

"Teres, wait. I thought we'd drink our coffee, maybe take a walk along the water. It's so beautiful here. I wanted to show you..."

"Stop showing me things!" Teres whirled around at him as she spat out the words. "I know what beautiful things look like! I left a world of beautiful things at home!"

Danny was stunned. He felt blindsided by her revelation. Teres began to run toward the water. He got out of the car and ran after her. She was fast and he was out of shape. "Stop, Teres! Tell me what's the matter?"

"Leave me alone," she yelled back, "Let me walk the beach without you telling me how!" Again, Danny felt the confusion and nausea of her epiphany. In the six months they had been married, Teres had never acted anything but happy and excited about their new life together. His mind immediately acknowledged, then rejected, the idea that her happiness could be an act. She had loved him enough to lie and defy her father. She had loved him enough to leave everything behind, her family, her friends, the comfortable life she was born to. *Maybe she...*

Suddenly, he couldn't see straight. It wasn't his water-filled eyes or the wind. It was that a hollow tunnel had formed in his line of vision, a tunnel that was growing smaller by the second. It was accompanied by the worst pain he had ever felt in his life. The pain emanated from the left side of his breastbone, like a violent indigestion, then spread like wildfire across his chest and to the shoulder and neck of his left side. His ears became incapable of hearing any sound outside of the body to which they were attached. As his tunnel of vision closed down, Danny wondered abstractly if he was getting a tooth infection. Then he blacked out.

*

When Teres began to run, she usually didn't stop any time soon. And that morning, running from her husband, was no exception. Danny was driving her crazy. She suspected that it was the kind of crazy every new wife feels, times ten. Her adjustment to her drastically changed life was completely wrapped around him. She was in his world and he was killing himself to make her embrace it. It wasn't normal. She came from a family where she was loved, adored even, but not considered more important than she was. For generations, the women in her family had to fight for everything - they were used to being told no. But for Greek women, no wasn't no. It was the beginning of cajoling, pleading, using your wits and even your sexuality, to change the mind of the man who stood in the way of you getting what you wanted. It was more than a strategy; it was a way of life. And unless the man was too harsh, or the situation too dire, it was mostly fun.

Teres had been good at this game. She knew, even on the day of the bike accident, that she would have eventually been able to change her father's mind. Oh, it would have taken everything: crying, not speaking, losing a few pounds. But in the end, her Papa would not have been able to see his precious daughter so miserable and would have made a compromise that looked like he wasn't giving in, when he actually was. Teres suspected it would have involved continuing to work at Giannopoulos Family Jewelry (even the name was an assumption of pressure) and taking university classes at night. It was a deal that she could have lived with, a foot in the door, or actually out the door. Eventually, those night classes would have turned into taking a class that wasn't offered in the evening and the beginning of full-time day school with only weekends at the shop.

This life with Danny was turning out to be much harder than the control of her father's house. It was a combination of indulgent love and *still* not really getting what she wanted.

For instance, Danny loved Greek food. One Friday night, he insisted that they go to a local Greek restaurant. Teres didn't want to go because they were trying to save money. Their goal was to use Danny's VA loan to buy a house in the spring. They were anxious to get out of their small, rundown apartment on Sea Street, which sat next to one of Quincy's most notorious dive bars: Joe's Hofbrau. Every night, the noise from the bar and its surrounding parking lot seemed to get louder, making it impossible to enjoy either open windows or sitting on the porch. They were putting aside as much money as they could, from Danny's weekly paycheck, toward a down payment. *Why would we waste our money on eating out?*

Teres was a great cook. If she had wanted to make souvlaki and moussaka, she would have bought the ingredients and made it herself. But instead, she was sitting in Helena's Greek Restaurant, working desperately hard not to criticize the meal. Her criticism wasn't because the food wasn't good. It was because the food wasn't prepared exactly as they made it at home in Nea Makri, or in the restaurants in Athens for that matter. In Teres' mind, she was just saying what she knew to be true, "American food is your territory. Greek food is mine." But when she saw the wounded look on Danny's face, Teres felt a stab of pain no amount of father-daughter fights had ever induced in her. This was going to be tricky. How could she say disagreeable things to this man, whom she loved so much, without feeling as though she was being a bully?

Teres was not accustomed to men who didn't fight back. Greek men used their wounded looks so manipulatively and routinely that it wasn't to even be considered - much like a Greek woman's first tears during an argument. Danny was different. His desire for her happiness was so complete that it was plastered all over him like Anteros, the champion god of unrequited love.

So, Teres ate the baklava that her husband brought home for dessert, even though baklava was ridiculously sweet and was never her favorite. And she drank the bitter, burnt coffee from Harry's because she had told him it reminded her of the Turkish coffee from home (which she hated). And, in general, she began changing her reactions from the feisty Greek ones of her youth, to the reactions of a woman who would never hurt a man who loved her so much. And this change took its toll. Sometimes, it made her run.

*

When Teres finally stopped running and turned around, Danny wasn't behind her. This surprised her. He normally didn't give up on trying to figure her out, which was a problem in and of itself. But she was also surprised to realize how disappointed she felt. Yes, she had told him to leave her alone, but she hadn't expected that he would. More curious than upset, she began to walk back to where the car was parked.

From a distance, she could see the car. Even with its low profile, it stood out more than it should have. It was the clear blue of a coastal Greek villa. That's what Danny had said when he bought it, one week after their return to the States. How could she see the car and not be able to see Danny? She decided that maybe he had walked the beach in the opposite direction. Teres quickened her pace, and then she saw him.

He was lying on his side in front of a pile of quarry stones that were designed to stop Houghs Neck from flooding during the New England winter storms. He appeared to be crumpled up, like the abandoned marionette doll of Teres' youth. She screamed his name. By the time she reached him she was screaming for help in two languages, at the top of her lungs, to no one. Her screaming roused him and he began to mumble incoherently.

Getting the semi-conscious Danny back to the car proved to be nearly impossible. He was big, six feet, two inches and all of it coated with a few extra pounds garnered by his recently military-less life. He kept saying that he was fine, but then passing out again as soon as he tried to stand. Teres was hysterical, which made Danny, during his moments of awareness, slur, "Izz okay," like a drunken sailor from the Quincy Naval Shipyard. Teres didn't know what to do. No one was in sight. She couldn't carry him, and she wouldn't leave him to go get help. She propped him up against the rocks and looked back to where the car was parked, then made a decision.

When she reached into his Navy-issue peacoat pocket and grabbed the keys, Danny must have realized what she was going to do because he made his biggest effort yet to get onto his feet. "No, no, no, no, no… you don't know how to…" Boom. He was down again. Teres left him where he fell and looked around to assess the situation. She judged that the car would probably fit between the cement pillars of the walkway. The beach was mostly rock, and what wasn't, would be hard enough to drive over after last night's freeze. She took one more look back at him and ran for the car.

What Danny didn't know was that this wasn't Teres' first attempt at driving. Sure, she didn't have a license. Her father had felt it unnecessary for a woman who lived so close to town to drive when there was a perfectly good bus system. But she had driven before. The boy's name was Tommy. He had been the son of one of the Naval commanders at the base. He was eighteen, a year older than she at the time. Tommy had spent the summer trying to get Teres to be interested in him. She wasn't. But she was interested in the fact that he had a car. Twice he had let her drive. Twice she had made a mess of it. One of those times the car had stalled going up the mountain road. It had rolled backward, and almost off the side of the hill before Tommy managed to jam his foot between Teres' legs and onto the brake. She hadn't wanted to drive again any time soon. But she was going to drive now.

*

Even half-conscious, Danny could hear the gears of his precious baby grinding like a washing machine with a bad bearing. The sound was killing him worse than the chest pain. He almost wished that he would faint again. He wanted to tell Teres that he was sure that the crisis had passed. The "Doc" part of him knew he was probably having a heart attack. The "Danny" part was still in denial.

His father had died at forty-three of a heart attack, his grandfather at fifty. *Leave it to me to be an overachiever.* He could hear his car coming closer. *Way to go, Teres*, was his fleeting thought just before he heard the crunch of the Karmann Ghia's low chassis going over the jagged rocks. His "Ugh," was not from the pain. He closed his eyes. When he opened them again, to his utter astonishment, the car's front bumper was right in front of him, its engine-filled trunk facing the water. Teres jumped out, intent on getting him in.

It might have been euphoria from the lack of oxygen, or perhaps the first of many out-of-body moments this heart attack would produce for him, but Danny clearly saw what was going to happen *before* it happened. It was different than guessing something was going to happen and then watching it unfold. As Teres came near him, he shut his eyes and saw the car roll backward, take on speed from both the slant of the shoreline and weight of the rear engine, and then plunge into the icy water. All of this happened twice, once with his eyes closed and the second time after he opened them. Danny felt his chest tighten again, the lightheadedness returned. He almost rolled over to take a nap in the sand, done with the scene before him. But just before he checked out, he saw Teres head for the water and toward his slowly drowning car. It shocked him into action.

*

It wasn't the dread of ruining Danny's prize car that made Teres run into the ice-cold water. It was the desperate thought that she still needed the car to get her husband to the hospital. She was up to her waist, with her body across the hood, when she felt Danny grab her from behind. She gasped when she saw his blue face.

"Oh my God, Danny! Get out of the water! You are going to die!"

Teres slid off the hood of the car and into his arms, pulling them both under water. Somehow they struggled back to shore and fell to the frozen sand, shaking and clutching each other. Danny began to laugh uncontrollably through his chattering teeth. Teres was too scared to wonder if he had gone crazy. They laid there, panting and hugging with no next move in sight.

*

Danny tried to tell his wife how funny it would be for him to die on the beach of a resort community in the United States, after surviving twenty years in the Navy. But, he couldn't make his lips move. Other than the numbing cold and the shivering, he felt okay. The icy water had probably shocked his heart into a normal rhythm. *But now, what?* Then he heard a siren in the distance. His body relaxed. He pulled Teres' head against his ineptly beating heart and assured her that help was on the way.

*

The doctor considered the heart attack a mild one, a warning he called it. Danny continued to refer to it as "the worst case of indigestion I've ever had." He was put on medication to lower his blood pressure and advised to watch what he ate and increase his physical activity. At the end of six days in the hospital, on his fortieth birthday, he returned home. He still felt a body-dragging tiredness that his bravado couldn't entirely mask. But Danny wasn't the one with the problem. Teres was.

*

When they returned home from the hospital, Danny's fun-loving wife became all business. In a span of six months she had changed from being a young war bride from a foreign country, to the commander of an army of one.

Gone from the apartment were any foods that Teres considered counterproductive to Danny's health, which was pretty much every single thing that he liked to eat. There was no more pizza, chips, bread or butter. A six-pack of Pabst Blue Ribbon Beer had become a rare find in the refrigerator. Chicken was the new steak. And then there was the exercise. Danny was grateful that pushing him outside to run in the snow wasn't an option for his wife. But to his horror, the Jack Lalanne fitness show was. Every morning, after a healthy egg-free breakfast of Special K cereal, skim milk and fruit, Teres turned exercise guru, Jack Lalanne, onto their state-of-the-art nineteen-inch color television (a purchase Danny had loved up until this point). They did the workout together. Danny hated it. He couldn't wait to get out from under Teres' command and back to work. *Thank God they're holding my job.*

Danny had been reassured that his corpsman job, in the emergency room of Quincy City Hospital, would still be there even though he was one week shy of his three-month probation. His boss was a fellow veteran. He had told Danny that he planned on dragging his feet to fill the vacated position, but added that Danny should "hurry up and get his ass back to work." The job had been an easy fit. It was basically the same stuff that he had been doing in the Navy. He liked most of the people in his department and it looked as if they liked him; some maybe a little too much.

In the Navy, a man didn't wear his wedding band for one of two reasons: either he was worried about his finger getting ripped off if the ring got trapped in a piece of equipment, or he was worried about missing an opportunity for a roll in the hay. Danny wasn't worried about either of those things. But he was having a hard time getting used to wearing jewelry on his hand. For the first few weeks at his civilian job, he left his ring on the nightstand by the bed. It drove his wife crazy in one way, and his coworkers crazy in another.

Danny had no illusions about his appearance. He hadn't exactly been a slave to maintenance and the sun had taken its toll on his Irish skin. But he was easy-going, tall, passably good-looking and apparently the *new meat* in the ER.

The unattached nurses and unit clerks flocked to him like squirrels to a bird feeder. It was something that Danny had gotten used to in the service, but annoyed him now that he was married. Three weeks into the job, he put his wedding ring on for good. He was surprised to find that he liked the idea of women knowing he was somebody's husband. It gave him the freedom to tease and joke without having to worry about it leading to the next move. Being content with one woman was new for Danny. There was a cocky relief to it.

If the sight of my wedding band is a disappointment, wait 'til they see my wife!

Yes, the job was good and hanging onto it while he recuperated was nothing to worry about. But potentially losing his spot in the hospital's inhalation therapy program *was* something to worry about.

Quincy City Hospital was considered a specialist in pulmonary care and they had a topnotch program to prove it. This year's class was filled to capacity. Danny knew that he had only been added on because of his status as a veteran. In one year's time, he would be a respiratory therapist. The best part of the deal was that his Veterans' VEAP benefit would be picking up the tab. He was excited to get started. He just had to get this little heart attack thing behind him - and behind his wife.

*

"No, Danny! It is too soon." Teres pulled his warm, searching hand off her breast and wriggled away from the hardness of his rising enthusiasm. It had been weeks since the heart attack and more than a few attempts at sex. Danny was finally pissed.

"Jesus, Tee, I'm fine! If I can do all of those fucking pushups you're forcing on me, I can sure as hell handle doing a couple leaning over you!" He whipped the covers off and stood up, towering over her. "Don't you want to have sex with me anymore?" he bellowed, more loudly than he had intended.

27

Whether it was the volume of his voice or his crude reference to their lovemaking, his wife began to cry.

"You don't know! You are not me! I cannot just…"

The crying accelerated. She was babbling in Greek and Danny wasn't getting much of it. As usual, her tears deflated him and broke his bruised heart. More to the point, both his anger and his erection were now gone. He climbed back into bed and held her.

"Teressa, just tell me. Slow down and stop crying. What are you trying to say?"

Danny waited as Teres sucked down a few more sobs and took a breath. Nothing prepared him for what flew out of her mouth next.

*

"I want a baby!" She blurted, with sloppy, spasmodic force. "I know that our pregnancy was not real, but telling my family about losing it made it real. I am sad about a baby that never was!" Teres couldn't believe that she had chosen this moment to charge into a conversation that she had been strategically planning in her head for days.

She knew that it was unfair of her to spring this on him now when he had so much to deal with between work, school and a heart attack. It was not part of their plan, *her plan* to be exact. School, a house of their own and then perhaps a baby. *That* was the plan they had talked about. But it all changed last week, when she went to see her doctor.

*

Because Teres had never been on birth control pills before, her doctor had written the first prescription for six months, requiring that she come back for a blood pressure check and chat before he wrote it out for an entire year. When she walked into the office for her follow-up appointment, prepared to say that she was fine, grab her new prescription and go, the room was filled with women of every gestational size. All it took was for one adorably pregnant girl to make the mistake of smiling in her direction, and Teres began firing questions at her that bordered on harassment.

"How far along are you? Is this your first baby? Do you have names picked out? How old are you?"

Beth was twenty years old, eight months pregnant with her first baby, and hoping for a girl, who she would name Catherine after her mother.

She is me, if I had really been pregnant! The thought rocked Teres.

Up until then, she and Danny's pregnancy ruse had been a means to an end. Without warning, it became an undefinable loss. For six days she had obsessed about having a baby, an idea with which Danny was iffy at best.

And now, seeing the panic-stricken look on her husband's face made her cry harder.

*

"Okay, okay! We'll figure this out, Teres. Just don't cry! You know I can't stand it."

"I never cry!" his wife shot back at him, causing Danny to roll his eyes because he knew that she believed it to be true.

"Oh, baby, you were crying when I met you." And he hugged her tighter thinking about the crying at the beach, and at the hospital, and because he didn't eat the salad with the cooked chicken on top. His girl knew how to cry. But this was different. *A baby so soon? I'm just getting used to a wife.*

"Okay. Let's talk about a baby." Danny whispered in her ear, "It seems a little opposite of what you want if you won't let me have sex with you." The kidding quality in Danny's voice was meant to lighten the discussion of a topic that Danny had successfully avoided for all of his adult life. It didn't work. Teres wailed louder.

"I can't have a baby like a trick with you! I would never have a trick baby. You have to be…"

"What's a trick baby? Like pretend?" Danny was confused. He knew that Teres had decided that it was not wrong to deceive her father with the pretense of a pregnancy *only* after they had consummated their love and created the possibility of a baby.

"A trick baby!" she cried at him, "Where the woman gets pregnant and the man has to be a father even if he doesn't want to! I cannot do that to you!" She sounded mad. The only thing that Danny had figured out for certain about Teres, was that every emotion she experienced led to anger. If she was frustrated, she got angry. If she was hurt, she got angry. If she felt insecure, she got angry. And the list didn't end there. He tried to view all of this anger as part of her passionate personality; a good thing. His own anger already had no place in this relationship. She had enough for both of them.

"What makes you think I don't want to have a baby?"

"If a man is forty and doesn't have a child, it is because he doesn't *want* a child!" she shot back, as if his absence of offspring was a deficit to their relationship, rather than an advantage.

"Teres. Did it ever occur to you that I was waiting for you? You're right. I didn't want children. I never loved anyone enough to want something permanent, let alone a child. I want one with you." *Wait? Did I just agree to a baby?*

And just like that, Danny realized that he wanted to be a father. In ten minutes, he had gone from wanting to get laid, to wondering what Teres would look like pregnant. "Let's have a baby."

Danny cupped her face toward his in order to kiss away her tears. He was ready to begin the amorous job of creating a baby, his key player already up for the task. The sigh from his lips went from "Ahh" to "Ow!" when Teres punched him back with all of her strength and spat out, "No! I will not have a baby with a man who is about to die!"

Teres' behavior over the last few weeks suddenly became crystal clear. *She thinks I'm going to die!* His wife had not only become the worst drill sergeant that he ever had, but she had also begun pulling away from him emotionally. *She's protecting herself - like a man would.* Every guy knew that the best defense was a good offense. *Well, baby, you have become pretty offensive.*

"I'm not going to die," he said, trying to sound convincing.

"You do not know that!" Teres shot back. "People die all of the time! They die when you least expect it! They die… at the beach!"

"Babe. I'm not going to die, not under your watch, anyway. I'm taking my meds. I promise to take care of myself. I'll eat the salads, exercise every day, maybe join the hospital's softball team. I swear I'll stay alive long enough to raise our trick child and be a pain in your ass."

"And you promise this on your life?"

Danny didn't bring up how ridiculous that was. He made an X on his chest.

"I cross my heart and hope to die."

*

And just like that, with very few words and a lot of tears, Teres got Danny to agree to all the things she had been nagging him about. And her desire to have a child became his idea. There was nothing conniving or manipulative about it. She hadn't even known she had done it. It was just the Greek way.

1992

SCITUATE, MASSACHUSETTS

ANTICIPATION AND DREAD were a strange combination of emotions to experience simultaneously. Teres had finally identified those two feelings as the primary emotions she felt every night, driving her 1992 Lincoln Town Car home to the dream house she and Danny had built in the coastal town of Scituate, Massachusetts. Once she put a name to her emotional milkshake, the flavor wasn't so bad. She imagined that a lot of spouses drove home with equal parts of anticipation and dread as their first cocktail of the evening. *But never us.*

Most of the important things in her and Danny's life were of equal parts, or at least that was the intent. After years of essential marital negotiations, they had become good at split decisions. Their home was a classic example of that. Unlike their old house on Wallace Road, this structure was a collaboration of their unique tastes. From the outside it was all Danny, a substantially sized New England style colonial. Like most colonials, it stood tall and stoic, almost defiantly on the lot. The front clapboards were painted a gray that was slightly darker than typical (darker, at least, than her husband thought it would be when he had picked out the little paint chip sample under the fluorescent lights in the paint store). The real wood shutters were black and the trim, white. Hardy winter-immune bushes dotted the landscape. A bank of Leyland Cypress trees, which had seemed so far apart when they were planted seven years ago, created an impenetrable border along one side of the property. In the summertime, the huge rhododendrons, a magnificent red maple and the annual flower beds made the house look more cottage-y, less foreboding. But this was winter and the house looked like the fortress that it was.

The inside of the Muldaur mansion belonged to Teres. It wasn't as though Greece knocked you over when you came through the front door. It was more of a subtle transition that gradually went from New England foyer to full-out Grecian pool area, complete with stone pillars and statues. Danny had balked at her desire for statues. Teres informed him that the statues she had chosen were "Greek-New England" statues; four life-sized Goddesses that represented the four seasons: Winter, Spring, Summer and Autumn. *What could be more New England than that?*

Teres pulled into their long driveway, hauntingly illuminated with the onion lanterns she and Danny had handpicked at an iron shop on Cape Cod. Thinking about picking out those lighting fixtures always put Teres on the verge of tears. It had been a perfect day. They were down to the final details of their house construction and had decided to go to the Cape and kill two birds with one stone: visit Danny's childhood friend, Frank Sullivan, and check out authentic onion lanterns. It was a good day for everyone. Later that summer, when Danny heard that Frank had died, he was less devastated and forever grateful to Teres for suggesting the visit. Teres tried to forget that the main reason she had suggested they visit Frank was to get Danny to drive her to the lighting store in Sandwich. She hated Cape Cod traffic. And, once again, she hated herself for being selfish.

What a horrible, wonderful memory. It made her feel worse. She was already feeling so guilty that she was unable to calm herself down. Maybe she needed to see a doctor. *A doctor is the last thing that I need.* But it was what she wanted: a doctor who could fix everything. Teres sensed that her internal conversation was heading in a dangerous direction. As she drove her car into the garage, she concluded that the only thing she could do was to clear her mind and turn her thoughts to Danny.

With the garage door's descent officially shutting out the world behind her, Teres wished that her first evening cocktail of anticipation and dread would soon be followed by a bottle of red. But even that nightly pleasure would have to be a thing of the past. She got out of the car, squared her shoulders, and readied herself to greet her devoted husband. Until she had a better plan, it was the only thing she could do.

*

Danny was always happy to see his wife walk through the door. It was the best part of his day. And he loved hearing her holler his name from the kitchen as though she didn't know that he would be camped in his favorite chair in the sunroom. His wife had a lot of versions of his name: Daniello, Danny Boy, Daniel Davide. But, when Teres needed or wanted him, it was always Danny and he loved how it sounded on her lips, *the same as the word "damn."*

1973

QUINCY, MASSACHUSETTS

THE PUSH WAS on to buy their own home before Teressa's father and mother came from Greece to visit. Danny was sure that if Teres' father, *Big Nick the Greek*, (a name he only said in his head) were to actually see the shithole apartment his daughter had been living in for the past ten months, he would punch his new son-in-law in the mouth, chloroform his only daughter, and drag her back to Greece. And Danny wouldn't blame him.

It was June; the traffic at the German bar next door had picked up considerably. The parking lot that separated their apartment building from the Hofbrau only made things worse. Parking aside, its biggest function was to serve as the "let's take this fight outside" venue. Some nights Danny and Teres laid in bed and laughed at the loud conversations they overheard. Other nights they stayed awake and wondered at exactly what point they should pick up the phone and call the police. His wife definitely made the best of it. She even invented a game. Late at night, they would lean on the windowsill and silently count the number of "f" words coming from the bar. When the stove timer went off, each of them would write down their number and see if they matched. If the numbers matched they rewarded themselves, sometimes with sex, sometimes with food that wasn't on Danny's diet. Years later, whenever they heard somebody use the *big swear word*, as Teres referred to it, they would look at each other and say, "That's one…"

Danny had to hand it to her. Even when her mother, Katharine, had requested photographs of their new life, Teres had artfully taken pictures of pots of geraniums on the barely-held-together front porch, along with a view from the kitchen window of a majestic weeping willow, the only tree on the small grounds of the apartment building. She then staged some newlywed-like images of a meal that she had prepared, placed on a table set for two featuring a water glass of purchased daisies. With only her pictures to go on, even he'd have thought the apartment was amazing. All of the other photographs she had sent to her mother were in the nature of him, standing proudly in front of the Karmann Ghia, and her, eating a giant Hoagie sandwich at the beach. There were no snapshots of the nicotine-coated walls, or the peeling ceiling paint that sometimes fell in pieces when the people upstairs stomped their feet, or the disgusting little bathroom, improved only marginally by his wife's seven hours of scrubbing. In a relatively short time, the new Muldaurs had become the consummate liars to their family in Greece. They had made no mention of his heart attack, Teres' difficulty signing up for college or their inability to find themselves pregnant: infertility being impossible to explain to a mother who had assured her daughter that as sad as her miscarriage had been, "at least she knows she can get pregnant."

The three-bedroom, one-bath house that they found on Wallace Road in West Quincy was more house than Danny had ever envisioned owning. The truth was that Danny had never actually envisioned himself a homeowner. His parents had been renters. Their parents had been renters. At one point in time, Danny's great-grandparents had owned a three-decker in the city. It had somehow ended up in the hands of an in-law, who later rented parts of it out to family members over the next two generations, keeping the beautifully renovated top floor for his side of the family. Danny had grown up on the second floor: a mishmash of rooms connected by a bathroom in the center. It was the worst of both worlds, having to listen to the commotion above you and still "keep it down" for the family below you. Neither of his parents had lived long enough to make it down to first-floor living, which usually happened every time the second-floor residents were too old to climb the stairs.

He was surprised by how excited he was at the prospect of being a homeowner. But his excitement was minuscule compared to Teressa's. She was beside herself and could talk about nothing else. They had discovered the little bungalow-style house themselves, during one of their Sunday afternoon drives. After randomly driving around for weeks looking at properties and neighborhoods, his wife had decided that it was time they educated themselves about Quincy neighborhoods and schools. Her research began by first finding a Greek Orthodox church.

*

Teres was no different than many other young Greeks, she had a love-hate relationship with the restrictions of church and family. In Nea Makri, her life structure had been built around her faith. When she was a little girl, Teres thought that the Greek Orthodox Church of Saint Nicholas was named for her father. She had no reason to think otherwise. His family had been a part of that church for generations. Nicholas Giannopoulos was on every Saint Nicholas decision-making committee, from paint crew to choosing the next priest after Father Adelino Mitsopoulos passed in his sleep. All eyes of the community had been on Teres and her brother, Nicky, for their entire lives. Teres hadn't stepped foot in a church since coming to America. She knew how tightly their communities were woven and she dreaded the prospect of being the newcomer. As it turned out, she was pleasantly surprised.

Saint Catherine's Greek Orthodox Church was less than five minutes from their apartment. Teres made the leap back into faith at the end of March, four weeks before Holy Week. She knew that a lot of lapsed parishioners came back to church during the holiest of seasons, so she would likely be in a more anonymous setting with the other sinners. She had also decided that she would feel like less of a fraud if she did not attend the Orthros before the Liturgy. *There is no point in looking too devout.*

*

"Ο Χριστός είναι ανάμεσά μας," Teres' face lit up. "Christ is in our midst!" She hadn't realized how much she had missed her native tongue.

"Αυτός είναι και πρέπει να είναι: He is and shall be," Teres replied, in both Greek and English, to the greeter in the doorway of the church. *This really is a Greek church!* The outside didn't resemble any Greek church Teres had ever seen. All shingles and multi-gabled, peaked roof, its absence of archways and domes initially made it difficult for Teres to accept it as a Greek Orthodox Church.

The inside of the church was different, too. It was not nearly as ornate as her beloved St Nicholas. Although they were beautiful, only a few of its Icons were made of marble. Teres saw that the others were vividly painted Frescos from the Byzantine and Hellenistic periods. *And they have benches for everyone!* At Saint Nicholas' there had been just a few marble benches along the outer walls of the large sanctuary room. They were used mostly by the old and the sick. Everyone else stood for the entire three and a half hours; except for the extremely devout who prostrated themselves or knelt on the hard marble floor. At this church, most people remained seated once the Divine Liturgy began. The service was said in both Greek and English, and it was music to Teres' ears.

After the Liturgy, the congregation retreated to the big hall for coffee and donuts. Just as Teres had hoped, it was filled with families taking advantage of an easy, and free, breakfast for their children. Teres recalled, with a wave of homesickness, how many Sunday services she had suffered through, knowing at their end she and her friends could run around the big hall and its grounds, playing tag (and later flirting with all the boys) under the watchful eyes of their parents. She decided that she had best hurry up and approach someone before her eyes filled up with nostalgic tears and she would have to flee. The woman she had in mind was holding a baby girl and scolding a three-year-old boy in Greek. She didn't look to be much older than Teres. As Teres began to make her move, she felt a tap on her shoulder.

"You're new." Startled, Teres turned and knocked a paper coffee cup out of the tapper's hand. The coffee splashed over both of them. *Damn!*

"Oh! I am sorry!" Teres got down on her knees and began to clean the coffee with her used, donut-crumb-covered napkin. She was dabbing at the hem of the woman's long skirt and apologizing in Greek, when the woman pulled her up from the floor by her shoulders.

"Don't you dare worry about this," she laughed. "It's my fault for scaring you. Look at me. Like most old Greek women, my clothes are indestructible and depressingly dark. I'm Martha Bertakis."

When Teres looked up, she saw that Martha Bertakis was neither old nor drab. Her long, brown-tweed maxi skirt was the latest style. Her chunky-heeled Frye boots matched the leather and suede of the hobo shoulder bag slung across her chest. Martha's dark eyes were lined with just enough black eyeliner and barely crinkled at the edges from thirty-eight years of a good life in the sun. Her black hair was piled on top of her head in the type of planned, unplanned heap that Teres' had never been able to master. *She is beautiful!* Teres was immediately in awe of this woman.

"Yes. I am new. New to not spilling coffee, being graceful and new to this church," Teres said with an embarrassed laugh. "I just moved here from Nea Makri at the beginning of this past Autumn."

Martha linked her arm into Teres'. "Ah. Then you will need a good friend." In that gesture, Martha became Teres' first real friend in America. She was likable and easy to talk to. Teres learned that Martha's comfortable demeanor was partly due to the fact that St. Catherine's was her second home. She had been a secretary at the church for nine years. Her husband, Bemus, was a stoneworker. The company he had built up from nothing, ten years ago, dealt in imported marble and local granite. The Bertakis were second-generation Americans and appeared to be well respected in the Greek community. Teres hung on Martha's every word.

For over an hour they sat at St. Catherine's and talked about schools, neighborhoods, Greek communities, homes and husbands. Teres learned more in that short time than she had learned over the past six months. She now not only knew where she should be looking for a house, but more importantly where she should *not* be looking. Martha offered to take them on a neighborhood-by-neighborhood tour. *Oh, Danny would really love that,* Teres thought, sarcastically. *I can't even get him to use a realtor.* Teres assured Martha that although her husband didn't know the neighborhoods of Quincy from a family-man perspective, he knew the area well. Martha settled for writing down streets and areas for them to search. They exchanged telephone numbers and made plans to get together for coffee, agreeing with humor not to go to Harry's.

*

"Martha says that a lot of Greek families send their children to Catholic school because there are no Greek schools. St. Agatha School and St. Mary's are so close to Wallace Road."

Danny could feel his patience wearing thin. Not only was he already sick of hearing what Martha had to say about everything, he was also tired of planning for a baby that they had yet to conceive. He took a deep breath. At this point, even a deep breath had to be done discreetly, its implied sign of his opposition all too obvious to his wife. He wasn't up for another session of tears or worse, temper. Teres was like a volcano lately. Her parents were coming in two weeks. The veteran's loan for the house was stalled. Danny had his doubts about whether the money even existed. It was, after all, the government. Everything they owned was already packed up in the apartment. And alongside those packed boxes were the bags and cartons of newly purchased things they would need for the place that they were buying. *This is not the orderly, simple life that I imagined.*

They should have been in the house weeks ago. Teres had already informed him that she had no intention of moving into somebody else's "filth and color choices." The minute they passed papers, she planned on removing the old wallpaper from the dining room, kitchen and master bedroom (a room they called the master bedroom because even though it didn't have its own bathroom, it was one foot wider than the other two small rooms). And then every square inch of the place was getting a new coat of paint. The paint had been purchased, colors too bright in Danny's opinion. The cans were taking up residence on the corner of their porch, as there was no room left inside the apartment.

The porch didn't have a lock and his wife was terrified that somebody would come in and steal her paint, trays, rollers and brushes, as well as the old wicker furniture she had found at a yard sale a couple of weeks ago. He and Teres had fought over her buying outdoor furniture for a porch they didn't own. Teres won. Every night, Danny had to push an old Hoosier cabinet, which Teres had turned into a potting bench, up against the wooden screen door. He had screwed a padlock to the outside, *which anyone with a screwdriver could remove,* for when they were not at home during the day. It was, in Danny's opinion, a lot of work to go through for somebody else's old furniture and six cans of paint whose colors he didn't even like. But Teres had confirmed it with Martha that their current neighborhood (if you could call their busy street a neighborhood) was one of the worst. *That little piece of information, I already knew.*

"Babe. We have plenty of time to figure out where we're going to send little TB. And the Furnace Brook School is great."

"Stop calling him that. It hurts my feelings and reminds me of my lies to my mother." TB or *Trick Baby* was Danny's latest reference to the offspring that his sperm seemed unwilling or unable to produce. When Teres continued speaking, Danny feared he had gotten her started.

"And a public school named after a furnace machine doesn't seem like a very good school. Schools should be named after great philosophers or great men."

Danny stopped himself from retelling Teres about the history of John Winthrop and the famous ironworks furnace of the 1600's. They had just finished their dinner of Italian subs and potato chips, a meal way off his wife's healthy-eating food list, purchased from the pizza place across the street. Maybe with some wine and a little luck, tonight would be a night of passionate lovemaking. Danny wasn't going to blow it with a fight about private school versus public school. *Thank you, again, Martha Bertakis: who I haven't even met and is already a pain in my ass.*

*

The Muldaurs moved into their newly painted, adorable house during the first week of August, exactly a month to the day *after* Teres' parents returned to Greece.

When Danny realized the loan was not going to come through in time, he completely panicked at the idea of Big Nick seeing Sea Street, let alone the apartment they had been living in. Teres, on the other hand, knew that both of her parents would understand, even admire, their humble beginnings. Danny didn't buy his wife's most recent assurances. Instead, he took what was left of their savings and rented a small house on Cape Cod for the ten days that his in-laws would be there. Teres was furious.

*

"You are out of your mind, Daniel Muldaur! This is stupid! We will make do. My parents will not care!"

"Your parents won't care because they'll never know."

What is he thinking? Teres looked at her husband as though he had lost his mind.

"They are not idiots! They know we live here, in a city called Quincy! They send me mail! I send them pictures! My father is not a man easily fooled."

"I'm not talking about acting like we haven't lived in Quincy. I'm saying we tell them our lease is over, our stuff is in storage. We'll say that we're closing on the house in just a few weeks and in the meantime, they'll never have to see the horrible apartment I've been keeping you in." Teres had no idea that he felt this way. The apartment had been such a fun joke between them. She wrapped her arms around his big frame.

"Danny! You haven't been keeping me in a horrible place. I love this awful apartment. It's our first place. This is the place we will laugh about in our old age."

"Which'll be next week, for me," her husband mumbled. Seeing him like this made the tears well up in her eyes.

"Danny, please! Why are you so upset? Everything is going well. We are good. My parents will see that. They will see how much we love each other and know that I am fine." Teres' voice was low and soothing, the tone you would use to talk to a wounded animal. Her voice didn't have the effect of calming her husband. It was quite the opposite. He began to rant loudly.

"You want to know what Big Nick is going to see, Teressa? He's gonna see an old man, with a job - not a business, not a legacy - who can't even buy his wife a house, let alone knock her up! You're not in college and you're not pregnant! I haven't given you anything! He is going to see a man who is just too set in his ways to be trying at this late date to get a life. God! If he ever finds out about the heart attack…"

"Enough! Stop this!" The loudness of Teres' command made him stop talking.

"Teres, I'm sorry."

"No. You are not sorry! Maybe, yes! Sorry for yourself! So you hate this stupid life we are making here in stupid Quincy, with our stupid apartment and your stupid job and our baby-trying? This isn't enough for you? I am not enough for you? You, you... old man!"

*

His wife's voice had risen to a screech. Her arms were flailing. Her hair had fallen out of the loose bun on the top of her head. She looked wild, crazy. Danny had no idea what a banshee was, but the word came into his mind. He couldn't remember why he was so upset. *How does she do this to me?* He began to laugh.

"What?" she screamed. "What is so funny?"

She fought him off when he tried to wrap his arms around her. He kept trying, all the while saying, "I'm sorry. I love you. I love our awful life. I'm an asshole and you're married to an old asshole. I'm sorry, baby. I'm just a jerk." And finally, "It's just that your father scares the shit out of me."

Danny felt Teres stop struggling. He was surprised to see that when she looked up at him, a smile had crept across her face. "You are not alone, my sweet man. Big Nick scares me, too."

He wondered for the millionth time why he always resisted telling her how he felt. *We're on the same side. She gets it.*

Danny picked up his wife, kicked his way through the boxes and rubble of the living room and laid her down on the awful bed that came with the apartment. As he made love to her, slowly and passionately, he knew this was different than their lovemaking had been in the past. The intensity Danny felt was born of the conviction that he was exactly where he wanted to be: in a hellhole of an apartment, as long as it was with Teressa Giannopoulos Muldaur.

*

In the end, they lied to her parents again and enjoyed a wonderful visit. Danny drove Teres and his in-laws all over Quincy and Boston in the sedan that Nick had rented at Logan Airport. They saw the Plimoth Plantation, Plymouth Rock and the Mayflower. Teres loved Faneuil Hall Marketplace and the view from the top of the Prudential Tower. Danny asked the realtor for an extra viewing of the house they were buying. And while Teres and Katharine talked about decorating and gardening, he and his father-in-law discussed things like window replacement and heating systems. Nick deemed the house "a keeper."

On the Cape, they sunbathed at a different beach every day and dined at waterfront fish shanties at night. One day, toward the end of their vacation, Danny dropped Katharine and Teres off to spend the afternoon at Race Point Beach while he and his father-in-law went deep-sea fishing out of Provincetown. The ocean had been rough enough to induce seasickness and Nick vomited half on and half over the side of the boat. They didn't catch a single fish. The men got their second wind upon returning to the dock, and decided to hit Commercial Street and grab a sandwich and a beer at the Governor Bradford. By the time they came back to pick up their wives, the ladies were burnt and the men were half-baked, telling fabricated stories about the fish that got away. It was on that day Danny and Nick became more than relatives, they became partners in crime. As far as Danny was concerned, it was worth spending every last penny of his savings. He had never seen his wife happier.

Danny finally realized that this was what he wanted most in the world: to see his beautiful, laughing, passionate wife happy. If Teres was happy, he was happy. It seemed such a simple concept. But for an only child, who had spent a lifetime worrying solely about his own needs, consciously wanting someone else's happiness was indeed a revelation.

1992

SCITUATE, MASSACHUSETTS

"DANIELLO?" TERES SANG out, knowing full well that he was in the sunroom. She threw her handbag and briefcase onto the upholstered high-backed chair at the kitchen counter and flicked on the switch to the recessed can lights above the breakfast bar. Her walk through the gourmet kitchen and adjoining family room included turning on three more lights. It drove her crazy that her husband could sit there in the dark. Sometimes, she didn't get him at all. Why would anyone sit in the dark? The question itself suddenly bothered her: to sit in the dark, to be in the dark or to pretend to be in the dark were three different things. Which one was Danny doing? Was he pretending to be in the dark? Did he really know everything that was going on?

"Teres. You're home." Danny's smile said it all. *He doesn't know a thing*, Teres reconfirmed to herself for the millionth time. "I was waiting for you so we could decide about dinner." Deciding about dinner was like a funny joke. Danny didn't cook. What he was really saying was, "Are we going out, have you planned something to cook, or is it a cheese sandwich night?" Tonight would be a cheese sandwich night. *Or maybe salad*, she thought, trying to remember if she had enough bits and pieces in the fridge to throw together a halfway decent salad. She went over to give her husband a kiss on the top of his head.

"How was your day? When did you get home?" Teres asked, even though she knew the answer to both questions. Danny had left work at four o'clock, the same time he left the office every Tuesday. But this was the nature of their relationship. They were nice people, saying nice things to each other, at the end of their nice days. *Or at least Danny is a nice person.*

Teres patted his shoulder and moved to make her way back to the kitchen. He grabbed her hand and brought it to his lips.

"Is everything okay, sweet girl?"

Her stomach churned and flipped. She knew that if she wanted to talk, come clean, now was the right time. Anything said after this moment would be a lie. Teres willed herself to open her mouth, let it all spill out and take whatever fate was due her.

"You look a little tired. Are you feeling okay?" The moment had passed. What would have been a confessor's session had turned into a husband's moment of concern.

"I am fine, Daniello. You're right, though. I am tired. Let's go to bed early tonight, okay?"

*

"Sounds like a plan, Tee." Danny's stomach settled down. Whatever was wrong with his wife wasn't going to be discussed tonight. His anticipation and dread were put to bed for another day.

1973

QUINCY, MASSACHUSETTS

DANNY AND TERES Muldaur had finally settled down to the nuts and bolts of living together. Their house was decorated with a combination of yard sale finds and purchases picked up after weeks on layaway. To Danny's dismay, Teres was always bringing something home. Their basement became filled with chairs that "just needs a coat of paint" and a couch "that would be a 'piece of pie' to reupholster." His wife's energy was limitless and at times made him feel depressed and even older. She was up half the night sewing curtains (at first by hand and later with the used sewing machine she bought through the want ads) then using the leftover material to quilt potholders and placemats. Every day there was something new.

*

"Look what I did today while you were at work!" Teres' beaming smile of accomplishment greeted him at the door.

Danny looked around. For the life of him, he could not figure out what was new. Everything was new as far as he was concerned. He dropped his car keys on the table and walked around his wife and into the kitchen, searching for the new mystery item. *Nope. Nothing there,* he thought to himself as he walked into the living room. *Was that pillow always there?* He knew that it probably was and to guess it as new would be a disastrous move.

"Danny!" He turned around to face his unintentionally angered wife. She shook her hair and pointed to her face. "Bangs, Danny! I cut myself bangs! Do you like them?" Danny hesitated for just a minute. It wasn't that he didn't like her new look. It just wasn't that much of a change. Teres' hair was dark, curly and wild. Every day it looked different. His hesitation was just a hair too long.

"You hate it!" And just like that she stormed into the bathroom and slammed the door behind her. Danny grabbed a diet cola from the fridge and sat down at the kitchen table to contemplate his next move, which had better be the right one or his night would be ruined.

"Babe. It's hard to see anything but beautiful when I look at you. You know me. I don't know fashion. I just know you always look great no matter how you do your hair." Even as he said it, he knew it wasn't true. When it came to Teres' hair, Danny had his preferences, which he was smart enough to keep to himself. He loved her hair down and softly framing her face. He loved it wild in the morning or after making love. He wasn't a fan of the tight ponytail she pulled it into when she was cooking or cleaning. And she owned a wide, white leather headband, with a peace sign carved into the front, that made him cringe.

There was no response from the bathroom. Danny listened harder and heard crying. He got up and softly knocked on the bathroom door.

"Hey. You okay?" He tried the doorknob and was surprised to feel it turn in his hand, locking the door behind her being the norm for this kind of event. He slowly pushed open the door. Teres was sitting on the toilet seat, her head was cradled in the nest of her arms, which were crossed and resting on the edge of the sink. The massive expanse of her new hairstyle was flowing over both arms and into the square white marble basin. She lifted her tear-streaked face to look at Danny.

"I got my period today."

"Oh, Teressa. I'm sorry, baby." Danny pulled his wife up from her sad throne and hugged her while she renewed her crying. "You were late. I thought that this time we were good? We'll figure it out. You just have to relax, it'll…" Before Danny could get the word "happen" out of his mouth, his wife was back to furious.

"Relax? That is what I should be doing?" Teres flew past her husband and out of the bathroom. "Maybe you are relaxed because you don't want a baby!" Once again, Danny acknowledged to himself, with a little Navy pride, how well his girl could throw a stone.

"Teres. Of course I want a baby. I'm just saying getting so upset is not gonna help the situation," again, a wrong word choice by Danny.

"Situation! We are in a situation?" Teres ran to her bedroom. Danny had been home from work for less than ten minutes and they were already on room number three for their fight. *We haven't made love in every room of this house, but we sure as hell have fought in them all.* Danny followed her to the bedroom and stood silently in the doorway. Done thinking he could console her, he tried a new tactic.

"What do you think we should do?"

Teres reached into the top drawer of her bureau and pulled out a letter. "I got this in the mail from my mother. It is the name of a doctor in Boston and the money to pay for it."

"Tee, we have insurance and you've got a doctor, already."

"I know, but this money and this letter says to me that even my mother thinks it is time for us to get some help with this *situation*." She spat the offensive word like a bullet from a gun. "It has been more than a year."

"You're right. It sounds like a good plan," said Danny, dreading everything about the prospect of fertility testing and medical intervention. Maybe a miracle would happen and they would end up pregnant next month. But for now, agreeing to see this doctor was his only choice. "Okay. Let's call their office tomorrow." And Danny lamented, once again, that a simple life was no longer in the cards.

*

"You were fourteen when you had the mumps, Mr. Muldaur?" Dr. Ruff was getting to the point quickly. Danny looked over at the diplomas on the office wall, partly to avoid looking in the other direction at his wife. Ruff, too, had been in the Navy. It was something that should have bonded them, but it didn't. Dr. Peter Ruff was turning out to be the enemy.

"Yes. I was fourteen, but just on one side." *It sounds like I just admitted to being fourteen on one side,* Danny thought weirdly. "I only had the mumps on one side," he unnecessarily reiterated.

"And, you've never heard that having the mumps at that age could cause sterility?"

Lie, lie, lie! You stupid fool! was what Danny's brain screamed, but his mouth said, "Well, I knew it was a possibility… but it was such a mild case… and I was hoping, praying really…" Danny could feel heat coming off the woman beside him. Teres had stopped hanging on to Dr. Ruff's every word and had turned to look at Danny, while backing away from him at the same time. Dr. Ruff continued to speak as though he didn't know or care about his part in the drama unfolding on the opposite side of his desk.

"It appears that in your case, the mumps may have been a problem, Mr. Muldaur. A low sperm count, under five million…"

Five million! That sounds like I hit the jackpot. What's this jerk talking about?

"…when the average number it takes to conceive is normally in the range of twenty to forty million. On top of that low number, I'm afraid motility is also an issue. The tails of most of your sperm are bent which doesn't allow them to swim straight, upstream so to speak…"

"You knew about this?" Teres' voice was a low, accusatory growl. "You knew about this mumps thing? Danny, did you?" Her voice was reaching a more normal get-ready-for-the-fight-of-your-life decibel level. For reasons Danny couldn't imagine, the louder, more Teres-like fight tone wasn't scaring him as much as it should have. He was still wrapped up in the ailing numbers of his sperm.

"So, you're saying it's gonna be tough going, but not impossible to get pregnant?"

"No, Mr. Muldaur, I'm saying that it would likely be a miracle to conceive a child with a sperm analysis such as yours. You are not dealing with one problem. You are dealing with two. And we haven't even gotten the complete report back on the percentage of sperm with abnormalities."

"Abnormalities! This is bullshit! You don't know what you're talking about!" Danny stood up and towered over the doctor's desk with a height that looked larger than his six feet, two inches. Some part of his passive personality was smart enough to figure out that if he ever wanted a future with his beautiful wife, he had better rage over this bad news like a raving lunatic. Yes, the mumps thing had been nagging at him all along, well before he met Teressa. It was the tiny speck of information in the back of his mind that was never going to become real, unless he pushed it into the front of his mind and out his mouth. Now, some asshole doctor had done that for him.

"Mr. Muldaur, please sit down. I know this is distressing, I deal with these situations…"

"Situation? You're calling us not becoming parents a situation?" The line sounded faintly familiar to his own ears. Danny looked down at Teres. She was staring at the doctor, no tears or expression on her face. Danny guessed that she had stopped comprehending anything after the word "miracle." The anger left him and was replaced by an overwhelming sadness. He sat down and put his arms around his wife. He wanted to say something comforting to her, perhaps even profound or perfect.

Teres put her head down against Danny's chest and patted his large thigh with her small hand. Then she said softly, "It's okay, my sweet Daniello, we will figure this out, together."

His beautiful wife's warrior-like strength had crushed his heart again. Danny knew that he would have done anything he could to take back that horrible day. Or perhaps it was another day that Danny wanted to take back, a day twenty-seven years earlier, when he had kissed a girl for the very first time. He wouldn't know until that moment in Dr. Ruff's claustrophobic office how important his first innocent love would be to his future. Her name was Laura: the girl with the mumps.

*

"There will be no baby, because there was never a baby, because a baby with my husband is impossible and I have never been with anyone other than my husband." Teres practiced saying this true thing to herself. She envisioned telling it to her mother, who would then tell it to her father. Her vision went no further than that. *Would their disappointment in me be so great that they would take back the newfound love and respect they felt for Danny?* Teres couldn't bear that. Her husband was suffering so much already.

*

Danny had told her that he would do anything that she wanted him to do: tell her parents himself, not tell them at all and act as if they were still trying (which he knew would make things worse) or tell them part of the truth. The "anything she wanted" also extended to their becoming parents. Danny suggested adoption, foster parenting (an idea he hated, but would consider), or finding a sperm donor so Teres could have her own baby. But the notion of someone else's sperm inside her body had repulsed Teres to the point where she told Danny "to never bring up that immoral idea to me again!" This actually turned out to be the only portion of the "no baby" conversation that gave him any solace. He wasn't certain he could bear watching Teres' body growing larger by the day, with another man's baby. But he was so scared she would leave him, that he was putting everything on the table; everything but the option of divorce. He just couldn't bring himself to offer his wife an option that would set her free, but kill him.

He had wanted to say it, do the right thing for Teres. After all, it was his damaged sperm. "Teres, I won't blame you if you leave me. You're young, beautiful. You should find a guy your own age, get remarried and have babies. You'd be a wonderful mother," were the words that Danny practiced in *his* head. He couldn't say them. *Does that mean I love my wife too much or too little?* Thinking about it made his head feel like it was going to explode.

*

One night, two weeks after the appointment with Dr. Ruff, Teres and Danny finally made love. Danny spent their lovemaking pushing thoughts of crooked sperm out of his mind, their bent tails flashing before his eyes with expected unexpectedness. Teres was searching for a more sexual, loving mantra than the one she had been using for the past year, "Maybe this time. Maybe this time. Maybe this time," always said in rhythm to Danny's thrusts.

After it was over, they both began to cry. They held each other tightly as they sobbed. Danny told Teres that she should leave him. Teres told Danny to "Shut up and never say such a thing again!" Danny gratefully added that to the ever-growing list of things he should never say to his wife again. They talked about what to tell her parents. Teres wanted to tell them it was her fault. Danny pointed out that because her parents thought that she had already been pregnant once, it would make them work even harder to find the right fertility specialist for their daughter. Their conversation always came back to the original lie.

In the end, they settled on a part-truth. They would tell Nick and Katharine about the bad sperm analysis, making the defect the reason she lost the "baby that never was," and then say that they were advised to never have a baby because of Danny's condition. That would stop her parents from waiting to hear wonderful news every month. If, by some miracle, Danny's circle-swimmers did manage to crash the party with one of Teres' eggs, they would happily cross that bridge when they came to it; perhaps with another lie. They cried some more, both of them wishing their first baby had been real. But, at least they were in it together again, Danny and Teres against the world.

*

Ten days later, Danny's final medical report came in. Dr. Ruff announced, in his disconnected, emotionless voice, that Danny's sperm were severely abnormal and strongly suggested that he have a vasectomy, rather than risk a deformed child. The Muldaurs' latest mutual fabrication had turned into the truth.

Teres took this new revelation better than her husband. She accepted, with a fatality born of generations of Orthodox devotion, that since they had lied about one of God's most miraculous gifts, she and Danny had gotten *exactly what they deserved.* She would bear it bravely, and did so until she received the letter from her mother.

Katharine wanted them to know that she and Nick suffered with them and prayed for Danny and Teres' strength and happiness. She also enclosed a handwritten poem:

My Beloved Parents

Please don't forget your vision
Of the mother you planned to be,
Even though my dear, sweet face,
You never got to see.

I know to be my Daddy
Would have given you such joy,
Whether I turned out to be your little girl
Or your sweet baby boy.

To parent one of God's angels,
That you'll see only in your dreams,
Still makes you "Mom" and "Dad",
No matter how that seems.

So just remember, precious ones,
To always hold me dear.
Because even here in Heaven,
My parents, I am near.

*

Teres broke. Danny cradled his rock of a wife for five hours of unrelenting hysterics. Just as he decided he should take her to the hospital for a sedative, Teres stopped crying. She silently disengaged herself from Danny's arms and got out of their bed. Danny looked on, fearfully and equally silent, as Teres reread her mother's crumpled, tear-stained letter. When she was finished, she smoothed and refolded the paper, then tucked it into the bottom of the mother-of-pearl jewelry box that her father had given her as a wedding present. With one turn of the tiny gold key in the lock of the iridescent nacre shell box, Danny watched Teres shut away the portion of their life that included the dream of motherhood.

1992

SCITUATE, MASSACHUSETTS

DANNY DIDN'T WANT to wake Teres, but he really had to pee. She was sleeping so soundly tonight. The minute they had finished their salads, Teres had told Danny to come to bed. Once in bed, she scrunched herself into a tight ball on her side, tucked her head and shoulders into Danny's armpit, and pulled his other arm, along with the satin damask quilt, over her body. Then she passed out. This was the version of *Sleeping Teres* that Danny referred to as the "I'm exhausted and I need the comfort of your body" version. His wife was extremely selfish about her sleeping comfort. For twenty years, she had used his body in any manner that suited her, in order to facilitate her own sleep. On some nights, it was more of a "you stay over there and don't smother me" directive. But most nights were spent like this one: with his wife's ample bottom tucked between Danny's low belly and bent thighs, especially in the wintertime. It had taken ten years of marriage for Danny to finally convince Teres to wear socks to bed since she also had no problem using him as a foot warmer.

This wife of his was such a mixed bag of contradictions. She worried about every little thing concerning Danny's health and well-being. Yet, she couldn't care less if she ruined his sleep by acting nasty just because he had moved his arm out from under her head when it began to go numb. "I'm putting you first - after me," was Danny's joking way of interpreting Teres' selfless-selfish behavior. But, lately, he could see that she was exhausted and he was going to hold out with the pee problem for as long as he could.

Danny had to admit that his wife worked harder than he did. She always had. Even when he supported her in the beginning of their marriage and later, while she was in school, she simply put more effort into their lives. Once they started the ambulance company, she *really* turned into a workaholic. The drive that his girl-of-a-wife had was beyond anything he had ever experienced. Danny used to think that if something was too difficult or had too many

57

obstacles, it was a sign that it wasn't meant to be. He remembered the first time he mentioned his 'not meant to be' theory to Teres. It was when they were faced with a licensing issue for the business, before it had even gotten off the ground. She was furious.

"Not meant to be? You're saying this is not meant to be? When did you become a spiritual philosopher on what is meant to be?" What had followed was an hour-long tirade on the value of perseverance and going after your dreams, along with a mini-history of her family's struggle to build a good life out of nothing. Although, from what Danny remembered during his conversations with Big Nick, the Giannopoulos family came from generations of fine jewelers. *How much of a struggle could that have been?* But in the end, as always, Danny watched in awe as his determined wife plowed through every stumbling block. She actually seemed to love obstacles. The more difficult the challenge, the more insistent she was that they do it. That insistence, along with a little help from her precious Papus, had indeed given them a very nice life.

*

It was toward the end of 1979 when Teres' beloved grandfather, Papus, died. She and Danny had been back to Greece only once in the seven years since their wedding. Papus had never been to America. Papus and Yaya were the original owners of the hillside villa in Nea Makri. When Nick, their only son, had chosen a wife, George and Ana had moved from the big house into a small cottage on the property which had once been used as the housekeeper's residence. As a child, Teres had spent every day with her grandparents while her parents worked in the jewelry store. George was as opinionated as his son, but never with his Teressa. In his eyes, she could do no wrong. It was Papus who had advocated for Teres and Danny when she announced that she was getting married to an American soldier who had gotten her pregnant. Papus' faith in his granddaughter was so complete that it was enough to convince his son to accept this new development with potential joy, instead of distrust and hatred. Teres couldn't imagine a world without Papus in it.

1979

NEA MAKRI, GREECE

DANNY BOOKED THEIR flight to Nea Makri the minute he heard the news of Papus' death. It was a 12:35 a.m. red-eye flight, which was taking off from Boston in just six hours. Teres was surprised that they were leaving so soon.

"Danny. We can wait a day or two. Neither the Trisagion Service or the funeral can be held on a Sunday. We have time. What about your shifts at the hospital?"

"It's covered. I know how much you loved Papus, and Yaya. Your family's gonna need you. We'll spend the extra days getting to know your brother's girlfriend. Your dad said Nicky was going to pop the question soon."

Teres' heart melted again for this big bear-baby of a man. He knew what she needed even when she didn't know. She reached for his face and pulled him down to her lips. The kiss was sweetly tinged with desire. Teres pulled back, wondering how her emotions could have swung from sadness about her grandfather to lust over her husband in less than a minute's time.

"In my psychology class we learned about sexuality and grief. Apparently it is an acceptable way to get comfort…"

She waited while Danny registered her meaning and then checked his watch. He closed the lid to the suitcase and slid it off the bed.

"The packing can wait," he said seriously. "What kind of husband would I be if I refused my wife a little comfort in her hour of need?"

*

Papus' burial was Danny's first taste of a Greek Orthodox funeral. It was impressive. George Giannopoulos had been as much involved in the Church of St. Nicholas as his son was, perhaps more. Hundreds of mourners attended the Trisagion Service, held right at the Giannopoulos home the night before the funeral. The solemn atmosphere of the wake was different from what Danny was used to. The waking of Doctor Michael O'Donovan had been his most recent bereavement experience; an event that half the city of Boston had attended, while the other half directed traffic for the occasion. It was one of the best social engagements of the season. Some of the good doctor's closest friends got so drunk on toasts of Irish Mist Whiskey that they could barely attend the funeral the next morning.

Teres' grandfather's wake was nothing like that.

*

"Ἅγιος ὁ Θεός, Ἅγιος ἰσχυρός, Ἅγιος ἀθάνατος, ἐλέησον ἡμᾶς."

"Holy God, Holy Mighty, Holy Immortal, have mercy on us," Teres whispered the Trisagion Prayer into Danny's ear. "It's said three times and then the Lord's Prayer." Danny could barely remember the Lord's Prayer in English, let alone Greek. His wife had become increasingly religious over the past six years. Danny sometimes wondered if she went to Saint Catherine's because of her friendship with Martha Bertakis, or if she were still praying for the miracle of a child, which would indeed be a miracle since Danny had reluctantly taken Ruff's advice and gotten a vasectomy.

Χορηγήσει το αναχωρημένο υπόλοιπο εις τον κόλπον του Αβραάμ, Ισαάκ και Ιακώβ. Χορηγήσει αιώνια ανάπαυση, ω Κύριε, η ψυχή σου αναχώρησε υπηρέτη, Γιαννόπουλος Γεώργιος και κάνουν τη μνήμη του αιωνία.

"The Priest is sending Papus' soul off to rest in the bosom of Abraham, Isaac and Jacob, and asking that he be eternally remembered," Teres again whispered.

She must be giving me the CliffsNotes version, Danny thought to himself. He almost laughed when he remembered Teres' confusion over CliffsNotes.

"Everybody keeps telling me to get these notes from Clifford. I do not even know a Clifford, except maybe the Big Red Dog?" His wife's delightful misunderstandings were one of the many highlights of knowing her.

"I could write a book," Danny muttered under his breath, knowing he could never write a book. He could hardly stand to write out his patient notes at the end of his shift. He hated writing.

"Shhh," Teres whispered, more loudly than Danny's mumble, "It's almost done."

After the service, everyone gathered under the stars of the perfect fall night. In a mysteriously orderly, but unorganized fashion, Papus George was eulogized. While some of the stories brought tears, others brought peals of laughter. In the silver shine of the moonlight, Danny watched the various emotions play over his wife's face. He knew that he had never met a more beautiful woman, inside or out. Under a canopy of Greek constellations, Danny again thanked God, or whoever was in charge of this life, for the gift of his wife.

*

Teres felt Danny's stare and turned to look up at him. His rapt expression puzzled her. She smiled, as his face turned back to normal and then assured him she would recall all of Papus' funny stories for him once they were alone. Even as she said it she knew there would be no storytelling once she and Danny reached the privacy of her childhood bedroom. An unspoken message had passed between them, letting her know that a little more husbandly grief counseling was in order before tomorrow's funeral.

*

The next morning, Danny watched each mourner approach the open casket and put their face close to the deceased. *Are they kissing him?* The thought of kissing Papus on the lips, alive or dead, was disturbing.

"Do I have to kiss your grandfather?" Danny whispered to his wife.

*

Teres tried to hide her amusement at her husband's American-born discomfort over all the kissing that Greek men do. She wanted to say something that would make him even more uncomfortable, but opted for being kind. She had watched her husband smile, and make every effort to comfort her and her family. She knew how much work it was to be the language outsider. *He's been a saint.*

"No, Daniello. There is a holy cross on his chest. Just pick it up and bring it to your lips. Papus knows you love him."

*

Later, Danny would wish he had just kissed Teres' grandfather on the lips. At least then he wouldn't have dropped the cross awkwardly back down and watched it slip between the dead man's neck and the satin-sheened lining of the casket. As he fumbled to reach into the crevice and grasp the crucifix of Jesus, he lowered his head so close to Papus' face that it looked like a kiss. The gesture, not real and definitely not intentional, brought tears to the eyes of both Teres and her parents. Danny decided to let the truth pass untold since it had made them all so happy. *Great. Now I'm lying in church.*

More prayers were said over the body of Papus at the graveside. By now, the concern over his immortal soul was not an issue and the prayers were being made to wish him "memory eternal." His recently-closed casket was anointed with dirt, oil and flowers. It appeared that everyone was to have a hand in the burial of George Giannopoulos. The hundreds of mourners each passed by with a handful of dirt. Danny doubted if, by the end of this procession, a shovel would even be necessary. He looked over at Teres' grandmother. Yaya hadn't said one word since they had arrived from the United States. She was shrouded in black, a thick veil pulled away from her face, like a bride who had just been handed over to the groom for marriage. Her normally animated expression was so worn from grief, that it was difficult for him to believe that she was only seventy-two years old. She had been married to Papus for fifty-seven years. Now he was gone. *How do you get over that?*

*

Η ζωή μου έχει γίνει.

Ana was fifteen and her husband, thirty, when their families formalized their arranged union. On top of a young wife, George had gotten the beautiful hillside pasture, where he later built their seven-room villa, and five head of cattle in the bargain. It was a good deal for both families. An affluent family of village jewelers had married into an affluent family of landowners. Ana had known from the time she was ten years old that she would one day be George's wife. The thought was never upsetting. She loved jewelry and grew to love George.

It had been a good life: friends, family, security. She watched all of it being covered over with dirt. Like it had never existed.

My life is done.

*

The strange thing about Yaya's silence was that before her husband had died, she never shut up. She had ranted on and on about every little thing Papus did. Most of her rants ended with the words, "You stupid old man!" Looking

64

back, Danny would have to admit that hers was the loudest form of worry he had ever heard: "Don't put that child on your shoulders! You're going to break your neck, old man!" or "Fine! Have another piece of Vasilopita! You won't even live to see the New Year, you stupid old man!" To see Teres' grandmother so shrunken and purposeless made Danny wish (for the hundredth time and for as many different reasons) that he and Teres had a child to place in Yaya's arms. Teres' crying shook Danny out of his thoughts. He pulled her into the shelter of his oversized embrace and they walked away from her grandfather's grave.

*

The Makaria, or mercy meal, was attended by all. Nick and Katharine had decided that with so many mouths to feed, they should have the meal outdoors, between their fall gardens. Mourning and fasting being synonymous, the meal's main course was fish. That was where the "fasting" aspect of this post-funeral meal ended. The food was traditional, abundant and delicious. Katharine had arranged to have the meal catered by their friends, John and Athena Pappas. The Pappas family had owned their small restaurant by the water in Nea Makri for twenty-three years. Even with the outdoor seating, the tiny little taverna held only fifty people, but it was constantly filled. Its coastal location made it a favorite spot among both vacationers and locals. But the business' real value was in event catering. The Pappas' little Prytaneion Taverna put out over two hundred Makaria a year and catered just as many combined parties and wedding celebrations. It was Prytaneion that had catered the impromptu wedding of Teres and Danny.

*

"I expected to see three babies in your arms by now," Athena Pappas said to Teres as she walked by with another trayful of Paximadia, the delicious anise and cinnamon biscuit cookie that Teres loved better than baklava.

Even after six years, the topic never failed to take the air out of her lungs. Teres had, in the past, used a variety of different responses to that question (or statement in Athena's case) and had found none of them adequate. It was apparently also Teres' job to assure her well-intentioned inquirers that it was "okay" and they needn't apologize for their curiosity. But it was not okay. *None of this is okay! Not Papus' death, or Yaya's silence or the children running underfoot, being chased by mothers with baby-filled arms.* Today, finally, it was not okay. Teres ran from Athena and her deliciously prepared mourning treats. She was barely able to control herself long enough to reach the privacy of the grassy area behind the shed.

*

The conversation between Danny, his brother-in-law, Nicky, and Nicky's girlfriend, Irene, was quickly going in the wrong direction. It may have been the Metaxa brandy liqueur and not the language barrier that was responsible for Danny's ill-thought-out opening line.

"I heard we're going to be in-laws," Danny said to the girl who had not yet been asked for her hand in marriage.

Nicky gave his brother-in-law a look that clearly said, "Shut up, you fool!" And knowing his future fiancée didn't speak very much English, he translated Danny's comment into, "Ο γαμπρός μου σκέφτεται ότι είναι πολύ όμορφη. My brother-in-law thinks you're pretty."

Irene smiled, embarrassed, and replied in her native Greek that Danny was handsome, as well, if a bit tall. Which Nicky translated into, "My girlfriend thinks you look like a giraffe."

Danny laughed loudly. Irene laughed, too, even though it was clear she could not figure out what was so funny.

Athena Pappas flew into the middle of the laughing trio. She said something quickly to Nicky and then turned to Danny. With stumbling English that was much better when she was not upset, she said, "I'm sorry. Your wife need you. She is behind the small house." She patted his arm and pointed to the shed. Danny took off running.

He found Teres sitting on a large pile of firewood. "Teres, sweetheart, are you okay? Is it your Papus? He lived a good, long…"

"It is so unfair, Danny." There was no anger in her words. Her overwhelming sadness was always more difficult for Danny to witness than was her rage. "All we did was tell one stupid lie and now I can never have a baby. This punishment is more than I can bear. Look at all of those babies!" Teres waved her arm towards the field where the children were playing. Danny was momentarily puzzled and needed a second to catch up. He sat on the pile of logs beside her. He pulled her downcast chin up to look at him.

"Teres, you don't honestly think that us not being able to have a child is a punishment, right? It has nothing to do with that. What happened to me began way before I met you. Hell, it happened before you were even born."

"We lied before God and we were punished."

Danny was shocked that she truly believed his sperm problem was something they had brought onto themselves.

"No," he crooned into her hair as he rocked her back and forth in his arms. "Teres look at me." Danny forced her to meet his intense stare. "We're good people. You're a wonderful woman and you'd have made an amazing mother. It's just something that happens sometimes. It's nobody's fault."

"It's fate, Danny. Everything is fate," his beautiful, sad wife said, with a finality that was unarguable. Danny decided he would let it rest for now. He would just hold her and rock her and wish, again, that one of those children in the field were theirs.

*

"My father put this aside for you on the day you were born."

Big Nick held a wooden box with an ivory carved lid out to Teres. It was intricate and ancient. Teres assumed that the box *was* the gift until she lifted its lid and saw the two small satchels resting on the velvet lining of the box. She opened the first satchel and her breath caught in her throat when she beheld the cameo wrapped inside.

"Oh, Papa! I have never seen this before! Where did this come from?" Teres held the cameo into the light of the lamp on the desk. As she did, Nick reached into the desk drawer and took out a jeweler's loupe so that his daughter could better view her new treasure's intricate detail.

"The Three Graces! I have never seen one so beautiful! Did Papus carve this?" Teres gave the loupe to Danny so he could get a closer look at the carved brooch. Nick sat down in his favorite chair: large, comfortable and made of Italian leather. He put his feet up on a square upholstered stool, whose worn needlepoint covering was stitched by his mother in the early years of her married life. Both Teres and Danny could see he was poised to begin a long story. Teres refilled their glasses from the open bottle of Xinomavro, the spicy red wine that was a favorite of her father's. She smiled as she remembered their trip to the vineyard in Nemea, where the grapevines were tied into the shape of a basket to protect the precious grapes from the wind. She was ten years old. The vines' arched architecture made her think that a wedding was taking place. She had spent an hour running through the rows, looking for the bride, while her father stood and talked to the viticulturist. Since that day, Teres and her family served Xinomavro wine for every special occasion and always referred to it as wedding wine. When the vineyard owner heard this story, he created a version of the wine that he named "Γάμος κρασί" or "Wedding Wine." The delicious blend became so popular, that Nick and his family hadn't paid for a bottle of wine in years. Nick's sudden smile was evidence that he and his daughter were experiencing the same memory. He put his glass down and leaned back, hands folded, and began his story.

"My grandfather, Nicholas Giannopoulos, Nico, was born on May 14, 1853, exactly one hundred years, to the day, before your beautiful Teressa was born." Nick directed his oration to Danny, knowing this part of the story was already familiar to his daughter. "In fact, Papus wanted to name my little girl Nicole, after his father…"

"Mama hated the name Nicole!" Teres clamored, never tiring of the story of her birth. "It reminded her of her bossy cousin!"

"That is true, and we also hoped to someday have a son who we would name Nicholas. Nicole would have been, well, too much of a good thing. So we named you Teressa, after your mother's mother." Danny began to wonder if there were only fifty names in all of Greece, everyone being named after someone. Big Nick continued.

"Your great-grandfather was an amazing sculptor. He studied in Milan under the great sculptor, Adolfo Wildt. His work was well regarded both here in Greece, as well as in Italy. He put his large marblework completely aside when he fell in love with cameos. There was something about creating a miniature masterpiece out of a conch shell that spoke to old Nico's heart. Although I never knew my grandfather to be a seafaring man, he said he was pulled by the mysteries of the sea and the treasures buried beneath its surface. It was Nicholas who founded our family's jewelry business. With the help of Adolfo Wildt, he learned about gold and other metal works." Nick gestured at the box. "Teres, go ahead and open the little silk bag."

Teres picked up the other little purse. It felt like it was empty. She pulled open the drawstrings and tipped it upside-down into her hand. Out fell a single perfect gold band.

"That was the first piece of gold jewelry your great-grandfather ever made."

Teres examined the small thin band under the magnifier. "*MDCCCXCI*" was stamped on the inside of the ring. The letters worn, but oxidized to a deeper tone over time.

"What does the stamp mean?" Teres grabbed a pen and paper from the desk to write down the letters.

"Not necessary. I know those symbols like my own hand. It is 1891, the year your great-grandfather, Nico, got married. This was his bride's wedding band, and now it is yours. I should have given it to you when you married Danny." Nick sent an apologetic glance toward his son-in-law. "Papus wanted you to have it, but I refused...'

Teres hurried over to hug her father.

"Σ ' αγαπώ, ΠΑΠΑ, I love you, Papa. I am so happy to have this now." Teres put the tiny gold band on her left ring finger, above her half of the matching carved gold wedding bands that she and Danny had picked out from Giannopoulos Family Jewelers on the day before they were wed. The band fit perfectly.

*

Danny watched the exchange between his wife and her father and felt the slight pang of his family-less heritage. A family was one more thing he hadn't known that he had needed until his wife had given him hers. Loving Teres had meant loving her family and, thank God, they loved him back. Just as Danny was feeling like this moment could not be more perfect, he saw a cloud drop over his wife's face. Like the switch of a light, something had clicked in her mind and changed everything. Teres took off the band, put it back in the bag and handed it to her father.

"I can't take this. You need to give it to Nicky. He is getting married and Irene should have it." All of this was said with Teres' own brand of irrevocability. She had made up her mind.

Nick rose from his chair, astounded at his daughter. "What are you saying? This is crazy! Papus wanted you to have this. After all that I have just told you… how could…"

Danny knew where this was going, and was surprised that his father-in-law didn't. "Teres, honey, your Papus wanted you to have the ring. Wouldn't it be bad, maybe disrespectful, not to take it?"

"Danny! It is stupid for me to take something so precious that I can never pass down!"

Well, there. You've said just what I thought you were going to say. He felt weirdly impressed that he finally knew his wife so well. She had been a tough nut to crack and he experienced a little misplaced pride over the fact that he had seen this coming before her own father had.

"Teres! Don't say that. You make my heart ache. The ring is yours. Do with it what you want." Big Nick looked crushed.

"Wait. Let me tell you why this ring should be yours!" Nick suddenly said with excitement. "There is a story about my grandfather that I should have already said to you."

Danny pulled the defiant-looking Teres down to sit on the sofa, half on top of his lap. "Tee, let's just listen to what your father has to say."

Nick began. "Your great-grandfather was a man who had vowed never to get married. All of his passion was to be his art. When he was nearly thirty-nine years old - quite old for a man to fall in love for the first time," Nick smiled at Danny, "he was traveling to Athens to deliver a cameo that had been commissioned by a government official to give to his wife. Ten miles outside of the city, his carriage broke down. He knew that this cameo was meant to be presented that evening during a fancy birthday celebration. Nico also knew that he could have easily walked the distance in plenty of time. But he felt that traveling on foot would make him look like a commoner and he was charging quite a sum for this brooch. So he unhitched his horse from the wagon and using the backboard he pulled himself astride the saddleless horse, an animal unused to carrying the weight of a man on its back. It didn't turn out to be a good idea. Or maybe it did." Nick's eyes sparked at the intrigue he was creating in his storytelling.

"As you would guess, Nico did not make it all the way to his destination - close, but not all of the way. Shortly before he reached the man's villa, his horse was spooked by some children playing alongside of the road. When the confused horse reared up, your great-grandfather fell backwards and somersaulted off the beast's huge, carriage-pulling rump and slammed to the ground."

"When he regained consciousness, a beautiful vision was before him. She was the exact face of Thalia, the most beautiful of the Three Graces, which Nico had created on the cameo tucked in the leather bag inside of his vest. He was astounded, and mystified. He would later say he had experienced a type of amnesia, or a spell. He had forgotten everything: his own name, the fact that he was a sculptor and a jewelry maker, and also that he had vowed to never fall in love. The living goddess, Thalia, knelt before him and Nico was paralyzed by her beauty."

"The woman's name turned out not to be Thalia, but Talia. She stayed with him until somebody came with a carriage. Nico then insisted he be taken to the government official's home before being treated for his broken leg. Talia laughed and told him it was her home, too, and the cameo was for her mother."

Teres was mesmerized by the story. "Papa, what happened to the woman? Your Yaya was not named Talia."

Teres couldn't see that Danny had gone white behind her. This walk back into time was inducing the strange déjà-vu effect Danny had experienced so many times since meeting his wife. History was repeating itself. And why was it *his* history? *Maybe Nick's making this whole thing up to get Teres to take the ring? This family loves a good story. Wouldn't she already know about her great-grandparents?*

As if in answer to his question, Teres' father said, "This story does not have a happy ending, which is why it was never told to you as a child."

Danny wasn't sure he wanted to stay for the ending. Teres, on the other hand, looked excited to hear the rest of the story. "Continue, please Papa. I cannot believe I've never heard this before!"

"Talia's father, Alexandros Zaimis, was an important man. He and his family had been leaders in the overthrow of the Ottoman Empire during Greece's War for Independence. Alexandros, himself, was a mere boy when he took part in the Epirus Revolt in 1854. Although the revolt was not considered a success, his efforts were rewarded after the Ottomans were no longer in control. Alexandros became part of the people's government whose power increased as the Monarchy became less powerful. A life of protection and government power was all that Talia had ever known.

But, when the star-crossed lovers met, under both a spell and the feet of an errant horse, they knew they had to be together. Nico was brought to the Zaimis home to recuperate. Although their affections for one another grew deeper each day, they dared not tell her father. Talia was promised to the son of another government official. The wedding was scheduled for the eve of Talia's fifteenth birthday, in just one month. Talia suggested they run away. Nico would not hear of it. He had a plan."

Danny was nauseous. *Why couldn't she see where this was going? They're gonna lie to their parents just like we did.* Danny knew that there was no stopping this story - or its aftermath. Resigned, he tightened his grip on his wife.

"At a public dinner, Nico decided the time was right. He told Alexandros about his undying love for Talia. Alexandros was furious. He banished Nico from his sight and ordered his men to take him away. As the men came for him, Nico yelled, "It is destined by the Gods! Look at the cameo that hangs from your wife's neck! Before I ever met her, I etched my love for Talia into the perfection of the shell! It was a vision from my dreams that your daughter be Thalia, the Goddess of Beauty!" Nico proclaimed this destiny, as he pulled a glass from his coat pocket and gave it to Alexandros so he could better see this miracle.

Alexandros took the magnifying glass and walked over to his wife's lovely neck. He bent down to closely examine the oval cameo that hung from a velvet ribbon, threatening to fall between her pale breasts. The three Goddesses had each been etched with very different faces. And with complete certainty, the face of Thalia was the very same face as that of his daughter, Talia.

"It is true!" Alexandros shouted. One by one, the guests and dignitaries took the glass from Alexandros and after close inspection, proclaimed it to be true. The last man was Anecto Simitis, the man Talia was to wed. He took the glass from the previous witness and gestured for Maria, Talia's mother, to remove the necklace. Disbelief flooded his face as he held the cameo behind the glass and up to the light of the chandelier. He became furious.

"It is a lie and a trick!" Anecto screamed into the crowd. "The real cameo has been replaced!" Everyone held back to see what would happen. Anecto walked up to Nico and declared, "With the help of her family, you have dishonored my name and I can only assume deflowered the beautiful *Thalia!* You can keep her. She is nothing but a whore!"

Nico felt a madness come over him. He dropped the crutch from under his arm and pulled away from the men who held him. As he grabbed Anecto by the back of his shirt, the rage became larger. "You have no right to even look upon Talia, let alone be wed to her!" With that, he smashed Anecto in the face with his fist, knocking him unconscious to the ground. The crowd cheered.

Alexandros realized that there was only one thing to do: believe in this miracle and welcome his new son-in-law into the family."

The relief on Danny's face was mirrored by the romantic excitement on his wife's. She leapt off his lap. "That was a beautiful story! Papa, I thought that you said the story didn't end happily?"

"It doesn't, my sweet girl. You see, one year later, the beautiful Talia died while giving birth to a baby boy. Nico's heart was broken and he never created another piece of art again. Two years went by, during one of Greece's worst depressions. No one was buying art or jewelry. Alexandros saw that his son-in-law's malaise was growing deeper by the day, so arranged for Nico to marry the daughter of a man who he had fought with during the war. With a small son to raise, no money and no spirit, your great-grandfather married Barbara, the woman that you knew as my grandmother. Eventually, the recession ended. Barbara proved to be a good business partner, as well as a loving mother to your Papus, George. It was Barbara Frangos who saved our family."

Teres was silent for a moment. Then she reached into the carved box. She took the tiny ring out of its purse and put it on. "It feels right to wear this. It is a ring of love and joy and the sadness of loss." Teres turned to meet Danny's eyes. "These are things that I know, as well."

Danny wrapped his arms around his proud, but heavy-hearted, wife. As he buried his face in her hair, he knew that she was going to be fine. He was going to be fine. They had each other. He glanced up through the tangle of Teres' curls just in time to see a single tear run down the side of Big Nick's face. It glistened in the light like the glint of Teres' little golden band. Danny had never felt more a part of anything than he did at that moment. No amount of military camaraderie had ever given him this sense of belonging. Without realizing it, a tear of joy and loss escaped his own eye, and he made a solemn vow to protect his wife and be a credit to the family she had given him: a vow that Danny never broke.

1980

QUINCY, MASSACHUSETTS

THE MULDAURS HAD been back in the States and immersed in their lives for six months when the letter from Greece arrived. It came by special delivery and the return address was from the law offices of Basagiannis and Partners ~ Athens, Greece. Teres waited until Danny got home from work to open it. The check fell out first: Ten thousand dollars made out to Teressa Giannopoulos Muldaur.

Also enclosed was a brief letter from the attorney explaining the estate and then a personal letter from Papus. Teres read the page written by hand in Greek, while Danny read the legally translated version in English:

> *My Dearest Teressa,*
>
> *If you are holding this letter, it means that I have passed from this great world. Is it funny to say that I am sad for your loss? But know that I have had a wonderful life, filled with all of the things a man could want: a devoted wife, children, grandchildren, a beautiful home ~ and a business that has made it possible for me to leave you this gift.*
>
> *My only wish is that you use this money to follow your heart. It is not money to pay a bill, or keep in an account to collect a meager interest. It is money from my heart to yours. It is dream money.*
>
> *Please don't forget your loving Papus. I am here, in the Heavens, holding you in my heart and watching over you.*
>
> *All of my love, Papus*

"Holy shit! Do you think your father knew about this?"

Teres was too stunned to answer. She held tightly to the letter as though she were hanging on to her grandfather himself. Her hands were trembling and her heart racing. The words *"follow your heart"* were repeating themselves in her head. *What does that mean?* Teres thought to herself, between the repetitive chanting of the phrase. She read Papus' letter again. Then she began to cry.

"I don't want this money. I want Papus to be alive! I don't know what to do!"

"I know, baby, but he's not alive. And it looks like he sent you another piece of his love. Just breathe. This doesn't have to be figured out right now, or any time soon. You can just put the check in the bank until you decide what it's for."

Teres looked confused. "Papus said not to put it into the bank…"

*

Danny began to laugh. *There's my girl*, he thought to himself. Everything for Teres was so cut and dried, black and white and completely literal. A thing was either right or wrong. "I think Papus meant that you shouldn't save this for a rainy day. You should use it for something you really want - a dream."

Teres carefully folded the letter from the attorney, and along with the check, put it back in the envelope. She then put the envelope in "the special place" reserved for paperwork that she and Danny considered important: the top of the refrigerator. She kept the handwritten letter from Papus and went into the bedroom. Danny knew the letter was going to be tucked into the mother-of-pearl jewelry box. As he watched her walk out of the kitchen, he could almost hear the discussion in her head. His wife would be lobbying for a practical use for the money: pay down the mortgage, perhaps buy a more dependable car. He knew that she would be afraid to follow the one dream that truly spoke to her heart, having a baby. Danny wasn't going to let her fear or guilt stop her from having her heart's desire. He also knew how stubborn his wife was and that he most assuredly had his work cut out for him.

1992

SCITUATE, MASSACHUSETTS

DANNY'S ARM WAS seriously numb. And he had another raging case of indigestion which lying on his back was only making worse. He began the slow, step-by-step work of untangling Teres' hair from his armpit so as not to yank it when he disengaged himself and got out of bed.

Teres' sleepy, dissatisfied grunts at her husband's shifting were familiar and soft enough to give Danny the impression that she would stay asleep while he went into their pink marble bathroom to relieve his aching bladder. Necessity had made him a master of the bedroom escape.

The brightness of the bathroom light and the hum of the exhaust fan woke Danny for good. Maybe after he got this spurt-by-ridiculous-spurt of peeing done, he should just go back out to the sunroom and try to fall asleep again. He would have to sleep sitting up, the indigestion was killing him and making him chuckle at the same time. *God, she's a stubborn woman.*

Apparently, raw green peppers have a lot of vitamins. At least that's what Danny heard every time he left a few of them on his plate. So most times he just ate them with the rest of the healthy salad even though they always gave him severe heartburn. *Teres the Jailer,* he smiled to himself. What a fury she had flown into the one time he had actually called her that out loud.

"That's what you think of me? That I am a jailer of you? You think I like worrying about you? I'll give you a news report, Daniel Muldaur! I wouldn't have to worry about you if you worried about yourself! You are a big baby! Who tells me to eat good or go to the gym? I just want you to be healthy! And, okay. No more! You worry about yourself. I'm done!"

His wife had taken her sweet time getting over that comment. She even signed a few messages to him as *Your Jailer*. "I am going to the store to grab fish for dinner. I know you want steak, but I am *Your Jailer*." At least she had signed those notes with the same loosely scrolled heart at the bottom that accompanied all of her written messages to him. *Ugh*, he really needed to find an antacid. A bad case of indigestion always reminded Danny of his first heart attack, a performance which he did not want to repeat. Heartburn, heart attack, heartache: it had all become the same thing over the years. He absentmindedly rubbed the scar that ran down the center of his chest as he opened the narrow bathroom linen closet, hoping that the box of little pink triangles would jump out at him and give him some relief.

Teres was beyond organized. Every shelf had a plan. The bath and hand towels, along with the washcloths, were meticulously folded to maximize the space on each shelf. Three of the shelves in that closet each housed four black sturdy baskets. They fit perfectly onto their designated shelf, creating a two-basket by two-basket square. It had taken his wife months to find the perfect baskets for her new bathroom, which was the reason Danny never opened the closet: twelve baskets with God knows what in them. It had become much easier to yell, "Teres, can you get me a new razor blade (shaving cream, deodorant, bandaid…)." But the indigestion was getting bad and he didn't want to wake his wife. So, like a soldier going into battle, he was charging into her perfectly-organized closet.

The front basket contained first-aid supplies. *When was the last time we needed an ace bandage?* Danny wondered to himself. Behind that basket was the winner! It contained aspirin, antihistamine, cough syrup, and two kinds of Pepto-Bismol, the liquid and the tablets. Danny carefully put the first-aid basket onto the bathroom counter. As he pulled the medicine-containing basket to the front of the shelf, something hidden behind it caught his eye. It was a purple and white cardboard box with the words e.p.t. Early Pregnancy Test. *What the hell?* Danny pulled the little box out of the back of the closet and into the light. He decided it must be something that Teres had kept from their first year of marriage. *Did they even have pregnancy tests in 1973?* It looked new and the box was open. Only one of the two original test kits remained. He held the box under the light above the bathroom sink and squinted to check for an expiration date: October 1994. Danny's head began to spin. *What was Teres doing with a pregnancy test?* He suddenly leaned over and, as quietly as he could while clutching the offending box, he vomited into the open toilet.

*

Danny's burning indigestion had now been replaced with a grinding pit in his stomach. After returning the pregnancy test to its hiding place and reorganizing the closet, Danny had retreated to his sunroom sanctuary. He chose the rocker/recliner instead of his comfortable chaise with the throw that Katharine had knit him for his birthday. That chaise was his relaxing chair, his sleeping spot. There would be no resting now. As Danny rammed the rocker back and forth, his mind raced through a thousand different, more palatable but not as plausible, reasons for the presence of that intentionally-hidden purple box. In his heart, he knew that there was only one explanation, with perhaps two outcomes. His wife had taken a pregnancy test because she was pregnant or she had taken one and found out that she was not pregnant. Either way, somebody else's undamaged, unneutered sperm was involved. Danny tried to dress it up with a few possibilities that included deception, but didn't include another man: artificial insemination, a test tube baby? His options were limited. *Jesus Christ, what have you done, Teres?*

A wave of nausea washed over him. He knew that he should go to the kitchen and take his morning handful of medication. The pills were supposed to be taken with food, which made taking them this morning impossible. His stomach would reject anything he tried to eat. The pills were the least of his worries. His body ached with the unwarranted remorse that Danny suspected was a product of both fear and guilt. He had been selfish to marry her. Anyone could see that a woman as vibrant and full of life as Teressa deserved to be a mother. It was he who had been the weak link in their attempt at parenting. Maybe his shoddy sperm were nothing to feel guilty over, but the adoption disaster was definitely all on him. No matter how many times he tried to tell himself it had all been for the best, he knew that by "all for the best" he meant all for the best for him. He should never have given up, especially after how long it had taken him to convince his wife to use her grandfather's money to adopt a child.

1980

QUINCY, MASSACHUSETTS

PAPUS HAD BEEN dead for exactly one year when Teres finally took the envelope off the refrigerator. Danny, along with the lawyer (whose title meant nothing to Teres) had told her the check would expire six months from the date of issue. She ignored them both. The two men eventually stopped trying to convince her that the money should be in the bank.

"What if somebody breaks into our house and steals the check?" Danny had asked her one day.

"Then we will have to get a guard dog," was her serious reply. Danny dropped it. He wasn't getting a dog. He told her they were losing interest. Teres got upset and told him that she thought their marriage was just fine. Danny began explaining bank interest and she looked at him with a smirk that said, "Gotcha." Teres was immovable, especially on the topic of adoption. Danny had broached the subject no less than ten times. Each time she shut him down cold with a firm and quick, "I don't want to talk about it."

Danny was at work when Teres took the check to the bank and cashed it. He came home from his shift at four o'clock and saw that the table was set as if they were having company, yet only for two.

"What's the big occasion?" Danny asked, hoping he hadn't pulled a bad husband move and forgotten something special.

"Well, my sweet man, I am celebrating our new life." Teres' smile dominated her face. Her eyes twinkled with barely-contained mystery. Danny didn't have a clue what she meant, but he wanted to freeze her look of complete happiness. Afraid of shattering this moment and even more afraid to ask what she was up to, he attempted a joke.

"We've been married for eight years. We made it through the seven-year itch. Is that what we're celebrating?"

"Danny! I don't know what this itch is, but today is important! Be serious!" Teres walked to the kitchen, poured two glasses of champagne and came back to the little dining room. "I would like to make a toast. But first I have a question." Danny held his breath while Teres pulled out a wad of cash from the drawer of the buffet she had found at yet another yard sale - and then had painstakingly refinished from old mahogany veneer to a crisp Federal blue. With the deftness of a geisha, she fanned out the one hundred hundred-dollar bills creating a large, curved arc of money.

"Daniel David Muldaur, will you use this money to adopt me a baby?" Danny stood there in shocked silence. Like most of the startling declarations from his wife, he was playing catch-up. He couldn't imagine what would have caused her 180-degree turnaround. He decided he didn't care what the reason was. She looked so happy. He picked her up and spun her around the room, money flying everywhere. Then he threw her over his shoulder, intent on carrying her toward their bedroom to seal the deal with more than a handshake.

"Stop! I am making special chicken. It is going to burn!" Teres hollered as they strode past the delicious smell of dinner. Without missing a beat, Danny dipped into the kitchen and backed his wife up toward the stove.

"Well, I guess you'd better shut off that oven, then. This is no time to burn down the house. We're gonna be parents!"

1992

SCITUATE, MASSACHUSETTS

DANNY SHOVED THE memory from his mind. He stopped his
furious rocking and decided it was definitely all his fault. He was the one who
had crushed Teres' dreams and he deserved the pain he was feeling. He closed
his eyes and tried to fall into an unconscious sleep.

*

Teres had awaken when Danny first left the bed. The moment her eyes
opened, the nausea began. She rolled onto her right side and curled herself into a
ball. She wished she had a saltine cracker or maybe a little package of those
oyster crackers they give you with New England clam chowder. The thought of
chowder only worsened her nausea. She wondered briefly why the tiny crackers
were called oyster crackers. She also wondered what was taking Danny so long
to come out of the bathroom. There was no sense getting up and checking on
him. She knew from yesterday morning's experience that the minute her feet hit
the floor she would have to race to the bathroom and vomit. *Oh, God.* Tears
rushed to her eyes and panic rose in her throat. *What am I going to do?* If Teres
had a dollar for every time that question had forced itself on her in the five
weeks since finding out, she would be rich. She winced at the irony of the
thought. "I am already rich," she mouthed to herself, "money is not what I
need."

The small noises coming from the master bath were not making sense.
*Jesus, Danny! Just flush the toilet, wash your hands - or don't - and slip out to
your morning nap in the sunroom!* Teres recognized the unfairness of being
irritated by her husband's slowness in the bathroom, but she couldn't help it.
These days when it came to Danny, she was stuck between fighting the urge to
lose her temper and feeling tender moments of care and concern. There was also

the larger gnawing of the guilt that chewed through her like a chainsaw. She knew she couldn't go on like this much longer. *What am I going to do?*

Finally, she heard the bathroom fan turn off. Teres shut her eyes and slackened her mouth, deftly feigning sleep as she had done so many times before. She heard Danny creep through the bathroom doorway and into the bedroom. Instead of tiptoeing past the bed and out to the sunroom, Teres felt him stop at her side of the bed. He just stood there. She could physically feel the weight of his stare and it took all her willpower not to open her eyes. The urge to ask him if he was okay was born of twenty years of worrying about her husband's well-being. It was not an impulse that was easily ignored. The minute went on for what seemed like an hour. Teres hoped Danny was unable to see the tears on her face in the darkness. She imperceptibly stiffened as she felt him bend forward and move his hand to her hair, lightly caressing the curls. Danny's hand continued to move, barely sweeping his fingers over her profile and onto her cheek. She remained as still as one of her poolside statues while his fingertips brushed across the wetness. When her husband straightened up, Teres again resisted the urge to open her eyes. In thirty seconds, he was gone. Ten seconds later, she was on her hands and knees gagging into the toilet, her tears falling freely into the water.

1992

BOSTON, MASSACHUSETTS

"TERESSA, THIS IS ridiculous. You have no choice, really. You don't even love him."

Teres whipped out of bed, pulling all the expensive bed linens with her. Her anger announced itself before one word had escaped her lips.

"This is what you think? That I don't love my husband? If you think that, then you don't know me at all! What am I doing here with you?"

Gregory saw the revulsion flash across her face as she looked at his nakedness. It was as though her passionate orgasm, just moments before, had been a figment of his imagination. He opened his mouth to say something, then he closed it again without a word. Their two previous lovemaking sessions hadn't ended well, either. He knew that speaking now would only make things worse. The pager on his nightstand vibrated violently and silently, migrating to the edge of the polished wooden surface and then falling off, onto the plush, creamy carpet. Gregory didn't dare reach over to pick it up until Teres had made her exit to the bathroom. The hospital could wait. Right now he had a pregnant, thirty-nine-year-old woman with a bad temper on his hands. Gregory realized, with a slight grin he'd immediately regret, that he was less afraid of the Medical Review Board at Beth Israel Hospital than he was of Teres.

"You think that this is funny? That this is a joke of some kind, maybe? I am so funny when I am yelling? Well, I will tell you that I can... I can... make you laugh *all day* if that is what you want!" Her fury made him want her again. Before his mind could even acknowledge that fact, Teres had stormed off to the bathroom. Gregory decided he would give her a few minutes to calm down before he checked on her. He sat up on the edge of the bed and looked down at the pager. The hospital's familiar number rolled across its flashing screen. Gregory left it, still vibrating on the floor. He reached for the phone on the nightstand and dialed the number. As he waited for the line to pick up, he felt relief flood over him. There was nothing like someone else's cardiac emergency to get his mind off his own problems. When the call was picked up, Gregory's voice became commanding and secure, despite his nakedness and the anger of the woman in the bathroom. His compartmentalized brain had already disengaged itself from the room around him.

Gregory was the first to admit that he was a bit of an egomaniac. As a heart surgeon, that trait was part of the job description. But he had perfected his superior attitude long before deciding on a career in medicine. Success hadn't really changed him; it had just made him richer. He liked money, fast European sports cars and women. Gregory was unapologetic about his lifestyle. He had earned everything he had achieved through hard work and an obdurate personality. *I am Dr. Gregory Aldo Costa, Chief of Cardiothoracic Surgery at one of the most prominent hospitals in Boston.* This turned out to be a fact he had to remind himself of at least twenty times a day; ever since that night, six months ago, when he first laid eyes on Teressa Muldaur.

Bravado aside, Dr. Costa knew that while he was busy fixing someone else's heart, the woman in the bathroom was intent on breaking his.

*

Out of necessity, Teres had become a master at crying in the shower. For the first ten years of her marriage she had cried openly in front of Danny. That eventually changed to never crying in front of him. There were two reasons why she began to hide her tears. In the early days, most of her tears were shed in shared sorrow. She was grieving *with* her husband. Even if Danny didn't physically drop a tear, his heart ached with the same sorrows as hers. Teres didn't remember exactly when that had changed, but it had. Her solitary sorrow was now best done in private. But her main reason to perfect weeping quietly in the shower was that her crying had begun to upset her husband to the point where he needed to take medication whenever it happened. Apparently, her sorrows had become too much for the both of them. *Make that the three of us,* she mused morosely, not knowing if she meant Gregory or the baby she was carrying. The renewal of her dilemma caused Teres to cry harder, but she still heard Gregory's knock on the door.

"Teressa. Are you okay?"

No. I am not okay. I am ruining everyone's life. I will go to Hell for this. "Yes. I am going to be fine," she said in a clear voice, without a hint of a sob. "You can come in." Teres had locked the door on Gregory just one time. She learned quickly that he wasn't a man to be barred from his own bathroom. Not only had she bolted the door, but she had stood in silence behind it when he had asked her if she were all right. She never figured out if he had kicked the door down or rammed into it with his shoulder. Either way, the frame had come entirely off the wall, leaving a shocked-out-of-her-tears Teres behind it. Gregory had just stood there for a moment and then calmly noted that she looked like she was okay, which he stated dispassionately was all that he had wanted to know. Teres wasn't sure if she should be scared or impressed. When she came back to his apartment the next week, the door looked as though it had never been damaged. Although the lock was still in place, Teres never used it again.

"The hospital called. They're prepping for a surgery. Is there enough room in that shower for me?"

"Should I get out?" Teres said, from behind the crackled glass enclosure of the huge stone-tiled shower room. The glass door opened and a naked Gregory, tanned, athletic and disarmingly handsome, moved in behind Teres. He wrapped his arms around her, centering his hands over the slight bulge of her belly. He bent his face down to bite at her neck and shoulder. Against her will, Teres grabbed the brass towel bar in front of her and pushed back into his hardness. Some portion of her mind acknowledged that she was letting it happen again. Her body didn't care.

1981

QUINCY, MASSACHUSETTS

THE ADOPTION PROCEDURE was a nightmare. It wasn't just the personal questions and the repetitiveness of the process, it was the home visits and reference letters. Their caseworker, Jean Broman, was a stickler. Her picayune, detail-by-detail personality manifested itself awkwardly in her looks. She was unusually short. Her hair was cut in a wedge that looked as though it were performed by machine in a barbershop rather than a hair salon. The crispness of her white shirt could be easily detected under the navy blue, cable-knit, button-up sweater which she was wearing every time they saw her. There was an exacting quality to her voice, a calculated non-dialect, that bespoke a speech therapy background, either as a patient or practitioner. Her questions, although innocent in content, appeared aimed to stump. Even if she approved of Danny and Teres, she certainly didn't show it. That disapproving persona made them both feel insecure and act weirdly. Danny, who was normally a man of few words, couldn't seem to shut up. And Teres suddenly lost all the English she had learned since coming to America nine years before. The Muldaurs were a disaster. They needed six letters of reference. Danny had easily gotten four from co-workers and doctors at the hospital. Martha Bitakis happily wrote a beautiful recommendation, a copy of which she gave to Teres. It had been strongly suggested to them by Jean that they should have at least one letter from clergy. Martha told them that Father George Mistakidis, the Greek Orthodox priest from Saint Catherine's, would be more than happy to write a referral letter. Teres, on the other hand, worried that the only man who knew everything about them might not be so willing to see them become parents.

*

She had been going to Saint Catherine's for almost two years when she had finally gotten up the nerve to go to confession. It wasn't the first time Teres wished she had been brought up Catholic instead of Orthodox. At least the Catholics had their little booths in which they could anonymously talk about their sins. In the Greek church all of the confessing was done face-to-face. Father Mistakidis was old and although Teres had never actually spoken to him, his demeanor seemed judgmental and sullen. In spite of Martha's assurances that the good priest was, in fact, a good priest, Teres dreaded making her confession. But she knew in her heart that it must happen in order for her to move even a small distance from her guilt.

*

"Holy God, Holy Mighty, Holy Immortal, have mercy on us. I have sinned, O Lord, forgive me. O God, be merciful to me, a sinner." Teres approached the seated Father Mistakidis at the iconostasis and knelt on the floor at his feet. "I, a sinner, confess to Almighty God, the Lord, One in the Holy Trinity, to the immaculate Virgin Mary the Theotokos, to all the Saints, and to you, my Spiritual Father, all my sins."

Father Mistakidis didn't say a word. Teres took a deep breath and realized that her planned speech had vacated her mind. "I faked a pregnancy so that I could get married!" There it was. She had blurted it out with no prelude lent to soften the horribleness of her deed. Teres began to cry.

"My daughter, you are not, I'm certain, the first woman to trick a man into marrying her with the specter of an impending birth. But, this, indeed, is a grave sin, an affront to the blessed Virgin Mary, who had to bear, for the sake of our Savior, Jesus Christ, a pregnancy and at the same time persuade Joseph of her purity…"

"No, no. You have it all wrong! My husband and I *both* lied about a baby in order to convince my father to let us be wed." The priest looked lost in thought. When he finally spoke, his words caused further anguish.

"And, what of your husband and the child that you later conceived to cover your lie? I have only seen you here, in this church, alone." Teres began the unintelligible blabbering of a person who has held a secret for a long time. She told him about Dr. Ruff and the bad sperm, the fact that Danny was not Orthodox, and that she was probably no longer Orthodox because of her sin. She then cried about the lies to her dear mother, who mourned a grandchild that never was, and then told the good father about the poem. She professed that they didn't deserve to be parents after what they had done. Her confession went on in an unending stream for five minutes.

Father Mistakidis remained silent, apparently drawing his own conclusions. When Teres became aware of the stark silence in the room, she realized that she must have been speaking, venting really, very loudly. At that point, Teres didn't care if all the sinners, who were waiting for their own confessions in the background corners of the sanctuary, had heard every word. She was truly here for absolution. She lifted her head and her eyes briefly met with Father Mistakidis'. She searched those eyes for a trace of compassion. What she saw may not have been empathy, pity or compassion. It was wisdom.

Teres felt Father Mistakidis place the end of his stole over her head. With the relief experienced only by the forgiven, she listened to his prayers of absolution. They were spoken in Greek with the last sentence being said in both Greek and English, "I absolve you from your sins in the name of the Father, and of the Son, and of the Holy Spirit." For her penance, she was to pray to the Virgin Mother of God with the words of the Hail Mary. Father Mistakidis suggested that Teres pray to Mary every day. He also gave her the Prayer of Repentance, the Nicene Prayer and Psalm 50, a verse used to cleanse the confessor of his sins. Just as Teres was deciding that this confession had been a good idea, Father Mistakidis dropped the bomb:

"For this to be a true confession you must tell your mother and your father about your lie." And just like that, the relief of absolution vanished. In its place was a mantle of guilt, heavier than the one she had originally worn into church that day.

So be it, Teres thought to herself somewhat defiantly, *there will be no forgiveness for me today.*

1982

QUINCY, MASSACHUSETTS

IT TURNED OUT that the Muldaurs didn't need much of Papus' money for this adoption. What they needed was stamina. Teres and Danny had been jumping through hoops for seven months, but it looked like they were finally in the home stretch. Jean Broman had turned out to be a quirky but well-meaning woman, who really did have the best interests of the prospective adoptees at the core of her reserved, judgmental behavior. Even Danny's age didn't turn out to be a factor. At forty-eight years of age, he would not have been able to adopt an infant on his own. But because the age restriction went by the age of the younger spouse, Jean Broman told them that they should have no problem putting a newborn baby into Teres' not-quite-twenty-eight-year-old arms. There was only one more hurdle left: the last home meeting with Dr. Randolph, the agency's psychiatrist.

*

Dr. Randolph's steady stream of chatter didn't seem to require a response from either Teres or Danny, so they remained quiet, politely smiling and nodding their heads in unison with the words.

The man was slight, pleasant and middle-aged. His prematurely balding hair was precisely combed from just above his left ear in a one-layer shank, over his shiny dome of a head, to a point just above his right ear. Although it looked immovable, the doctor continually patted the carefully planned hair in what appeared to be an effort to reassure himself that it was still in place. He was likable. In a profession known more for listening and less for talking, Dr. Randolph stood out as a chatty conversationalist. He hadn't stopped talking since he had entered the Muldaurs' living room, escorted by Teres who was carrying a tray of tea and her favorite cinnamon biscuits, Paximadia.

*

"This really is a lovely little house in a lovely little neighborhood," Dr. Randolph said for the third time in a row. "How long have you two lived here?" Although the information was in the folder in front of him and he had already asked the question before, his pause indicated that this again required an answer.

"Seven years," Teres answered.

"Six years," Danny said at the same time.

Seven! Get it together, Danny! We are supposed to be a team!

"Oh. Quite nice. I saw a bike in the driveway next door. Are there a lot of children on this street?" Teres took control of this question before her husband could tally up the number of children in the city of Quincy, his analytical brain always slowing down his response.

"Oh yes. Next door to us are a husband and wife who have become friends of ours. Jeff is a fisherman and his wife, Heather, works at Brewster's, the little store at the end of the street. They have two little boys…" Teres stopped talking when she saw the look of horror on Dr. Randolph's face. She turned to her side to see what he was looking at and screamed.

"Get on the phone right now, Mrs. Muldaur, and call an ambulance!"

Danny's face and body were contorted. His right shoulder had attached itself to his ear and his right arm arched awkwardly back and forth to the side and front of him. His balled-up hand was spasming in a rhythmic horizontal motion, as though he were trying to swat a fly that had landed on his belt buckle. Both of his eyes were rolled up and to the left, their irises barely visible under the lids. His stiff body began falling sideways off the couch and his legs shuddered with spasms that radiated up his body. A dark stain of urine spread across the front of Danny's tan corduroy Levi's. Teres was paralyzed. Dr. Randolph sprang into action.

"I said go! He's having a seizure! Call an ambulance!"

Teres ran to the phone on the kitchen wall. With the receiver held uselessly in her hand, she watched Dr. Randolph grab a butter knife off the little cookie tray and jam it between Danny's chattering teeth. Then he quickly laid him on his side, kicking away the coffee table in order to make room for Danny's spasming body to jerk itself around without injury. Although the fire department was located two minutes from Wallace Road, the five-minute seizure was well over before the ambulance arrived.

*

The delay in getting to the Muldaur household was not the dispatcher's fault. He didn't speak Greek. Not one word of the screaming from the woman at the other end of the phone made any sense to him at all. The more the dispatcher tried to calm her down, the louder Teres had yelled, "Come now! He is dying!" Finally, Dr. Randolph had taken the phone from Teres' clenched fist and calmly explained their emergency. Two minutes later, they heard the siren. By then Danny's body was eerily still and he was breathing on his own. But for Teres, the low, inhuman moaning emitting from her semi-conscious husband was more terrifying than the spasms had been. She was hysterical. While the paramedics attended to her husband, Dr. Randolph pulled a bottle of tranquilizers out of his bag and handed her one with a glass of water.

"Take this. It will make you feel better." Teres, never one to even take an aspirin, dutifully swallowed the pill without asking what it was.

*

The EMTs took basic information, checked Danny's vital signs and strapped him onto the stretcher. As they loaded him into the ambulance, a feeling of calm bewilderment came over Teres. She stood behind the rescue truck with her car keys, Danny's coat and her purse in her arms, not knowing

95

what to do next. She felt as if she had stepped into a dream and was no longer able to think for herself.

"Mrs. Muldaur," Dr. Randolph's voice broke into her delusional trance, "You'll want to get in the ambulance with your husband. I don't think it's a good idea for you to drive after taking a Valium. I'll lock up the house." She climbed into the back of the ambulance and sat down on the jump seat next to the paramedic, who was busy trying to find a vein in Danny's arm. As she watched the man dip the needle into the arm and move it around to strike the rolling vein beneath its surface, Teres became more detached from the situation. She knew what had happened. She knew that the man on the cot was her husband, but she could not make a judgment about what was going on in front of her. The emotional, reactionary portion of Teres' brain was on hold. She tried to ask the man if Danny was going to be all right.

"Ο σύζυγός μου θα είναι εντάξει;"

"Miss, I'm sorry. I don't speak Greek. Let me just get this line started. We're almost to the hospital."

What is he talking about? I am speaking perfect English, Teres absentmindedly noted to herself. *What a strange man.* Danny moaned. The despair in his moan made Teres cry.

*

Dwayne, the ambulance attendant, was a handsome man about Teres' age. He occasionally got a telephone number or two over the course of his work week. His feigned concern to know the outcome of the patient sometimes even led to a date. He could see that this little foreign girl was pretty and distraught. What he didn't see was the wedding ring on the hand tucked under the jacket, resting on her lap. Dwayne turned his charming attention to her. He reached over and touched her arm.

"Oh, sweetie, don't cry. Your Dad is going to be just fine. A lot of people have seizures. They come out of it as good as gold." He leaned toward her a little, *just in case she needs to fall into my arms and cry.* She didn't. Instead, she pulled her arm from his grasp.

"He is my husband," she said, in perfect English. "I am Mrs. Muldaur, not your sweetie."

Shit. The last thing he needed was somebody filing another complaint about him. He began wracking his brain for a comment to diffuse the situation, at the same time glancing toward the front of the ambulance to see if his co-worker had caught any of the conversation.

*

Teres looked up at the man and immediately saw what her mother had always referred to as 'the wolf look.' She jerked her arm from his touch and straightened her shoulders. *This man is a fool!* Before she could further chastise him for his ignorance, her husband spoke.

"I would do whatever she says, buddy," Danny's barely audible voice startled them both. "My wife is one tough cookie."

"Danny!" Teres fell onto him, crying. "Thank God! I was so scared!"

"What happened to me?"

*

Danny may have caught the word "seizure" in some of the crying and bilingual babbling. Teres sounded drunk. He tried, for the life of him, to think of the last thing that he remembered. He couldn't come up with any scenario in which this ambulance ride or his wife's drunkenness would fit. But, whatever had happened, she was okay and he was apparently going to live. He shut his eyes and decided that he would figure out what the story was later. Right now, he was as tired as he had ever been in his life. *Maybe I'm drunk, too*, was his last thought as he slipped into unconsciousness.

*

"I'm so happy that you are feeling better, Mr. Muldaur. That was quite a scare. Of course we'll have to postpone the adoption, probably six months to a year, until there's proof that there will be no more seizures or your condition will be kept under control with medications. And then there is the matter of your not being able to drive. Will you be able to resume your position at the hospital?"

Teres and Danny were back to hating Jean Broman. Every test that Quincy City's finest neurologist, Dr. Seaver, had performed had come back normal. And there had been a bunch of them, electroencephalograms, spinal tap, blood work, urine: everything perfect. As far as the doctor was concerned it was a one-seizure event. He explained to the Muldaurs (and wrote a letter to that effect to the adoption agency) that sometimes, for reasons that are not easily understood, the brain makes a decision to protect itself by seizing. He stated that it could have been brought on by Danny's medication change for his blood pressure or any number of things where the brain must make an immediate adjustment. But to the best of his highly-trained knowledge, Danny would likely never experience a seizure again. He most certainly did not have epilepsy. And although, by law, Danny would be restricted from driving for six months, he was cleared to return to work whenever he felt up to it.

It was not enough proof for the adoption agency. The Muldaurs' baby plans were put on hold, again.

*

Danny hated having Teres drive him back and forth to work. It made him feel like he was being taken care of, which made him feel like a failure as a husband, which made him behave like an ass. The confinement of the little Karmann Ghia didn't help. Somehow the passenger seat seemed to be half the size of the driver's seat. *An arrangement that works out great when it's your pretty little wife that's the passenger*, thought Danny, getting ready to blow.

"What time will you be out today?" Teres asked him, the same way that she had been asking him every morning.

"Jesus, Teres! How the hell do I know? If I get a late afternoon emergency or a bronchoscopy, I don't have a fucking clue how long it will take! I'll call you when I need you to come get me."

Teres screeched the little car to a halt on the side of the road. The 6:45 a.m. traffic whizzed by them, close enough to fluff their car with its passing wind. Danny couldn't believe that she had swung the car off the road so quickly, and so expertly. "What the hell?"

"You shut up, Daniel Muldaur! Do you think that I like this? No! I do not like this! I was trying to know if you were working until three or until seven tonight! Do you think this is my fun thing, too? It is not! I thought that I would be home with our baby and you would drive this stupid car - not this stupid car - a big car! For a carseat! Is this my plan? No! It is God's plan - a plan I *fucking* hate like I hate you right now!"

Danny had never heard the word fuck come out of his wife's mouth before. He was more shocked at that than he was that she had said she hated him. *Neither thing is a good sign.* He was speechless. And although she was done yelling, she wasn't done talking. Her next words were calm, thought out, as if she had been rehearsing them in her head.

"My parents want me to come to Greece for a month. My mother thinks I need a vacation. I told her "no," but maybe it is "yes." There is five weeks of your no driving left. Can you get someone to bring you to work?"

Well, here it is, the thing that I knew would happen, eventually. She's leaving me and I can't blame her. Danny, who had previously only been able to see this situation through his own miserable eyes, was struck with clarity. He had nothing to offer her, *nothing*, not a family, or wealth, or the optimism of a good mood. He couldn't even take his wife on a Sunday afternoon drive to the Cape. Every day had become the same. She brought him to work. She picked him up. She made his dinner. She watched him drink beer while *he* watched television. She climbed into bed beside him at the end of every day. Even while dealing with her own misery, she was a good wife. He was an asshole. But he felt powerless to change that. Danny knew that he could talk Teres out of going to Greece. All he had to do was say that he needed her. She would be happy with that. He didn't even have to apologize. He wrestled briefly with what was best for himself and what was best for her.

"It sounds like a good idea. You should go. I'll be fine."

*

Teres' body shook from head to toe. Danny couldn't care less that she would leave him and go to Greece. Of all the things they had been through together, she had never considered leaving him, even for a break. The thought of killing Danny was easier to conceive of than the idea of them being separated. She didn't want to go to Greece! But her husband had called her bluff. *Fine. I'll show you, Daniel Muldaur! You will miss me and I will have the time of my life!* Teres straightened her back, glanced into the sideview mirror and somehow pulled the little blue car back into the rush-hour traffic without getting them both killed. Although at that point, she didn't really care.

1982

ATHENS, GREECE

AS A CHILD, Teres dreamed of going to The Ancient Olympia International Festival with normal parents, who weren't working in its carnival-like atmosphere. But instead, she and her brother had been forced to hang around their parents' jewelry booth all day and help out, or at least not be a nuisance. The event was something that Teres had both looked forward to and dreaded every summer. She hadn't been to the festival in ten years; since the summer she had met Danny. A lot had changed in that time, for both the festival and for her.

It was broiling hot, even for late July in Athens. Teres had become a true Northerner over the last nine years. She swam in the icy waters of the Atlantic Ocean, shoveled snow for days after the Blizzard of '78, and, during the New England summer, she knew one day's heat could turn into the next day's frigid rain. But she had assumed that once a Greek, always a Greek and she was waiting for that theory to kick in. In the meantime, she felt drenched in sweat. Her enormous hair had soaked in the one hundred percent humidity that was common to Greece and had turned into an unmanageable life form on the top of her head. The sweet, white cotton peasant blouse that her mother had given her, beautifully adorned with turquoise embroidery, was soaked through from the sweat coming out of every pore of her body. Because of her lack of foresight in choosing the shortness of her shorts, Teres' thighs were sticking together uncomfortably as she walked. She had been delighted to find her old cut-offs, a perfectly frayed, light denim blue, in the bottom drawer of her dresser. They had fit her much better in the coolness of the house, like a fashionable pair of Daisy Dukes. Now in the sweltering sun, she felt more like a Glamour Don't.

But the heat didn't appear to be bothering her sister-in-law, Irene, one bit. She was eight months pregnant and adorable. Her perfect little ball of a stomach seemed to have no real effect on the rest of her tiny, trim body. Teres imagined Irene taking the little ball off from around her waist at the end of each day and placing it on the top of her dresser, along with her earrings and her favorite watch. Teres also imagined what it might look like to have her own little ball - or perhaps steal Irene's right off her dresser as she slept. These thoughts were not productive, or nice. She was thrilled for Nicky and Irene. And her brother was a great guy who deserved to be happy. She wondered idly why it was so easy to decide that they should have happiness, but less easy to claim her own rights to that emotion. Teres' painful bout of jealousy wasn't doing anything to diminish the excitement that she felt about becoming an Aunt. She couldn't wait.

*

"I can't believe that you're leaving before the baby comes." It wasn't the first time her brother had broached the subject of her ill-timed vacation. "We are due three weeks *after* you leave. Why don't you just stay?"

"I want to, but I have already signed up for two more classes that begin in August. And, besides, I don't think I want to leave Danny for that long." Teres didn't know if the second reason were even true anymore. Nicky's ears perked up at the sound of Danny's name. Teres had been careful to avoid any conversation concerning her husband or the failure of their adoption. She saw the look on her brother's face and knew that he was going to begin asking questions that she would not want to answer, even if she knew the answers.

"Irene! Look at the cute baby clothes over there!" Teres pointed to a booth in the distance that was filled with colorful small clothes. She grabbed Irene's arm and began walking in that direction, leaving Nicky with his words half formulated.

The clothes that this vendor had were indeed adorable. They were the expected handmade sweaters, hats and booties, but with a twist. They had all been made with yarns dyed the colors of the insides of different fruits. Each one had an embroidered emblem of that piece of fruit. Even the hat designed to look like a peeled orange had seed pearls that resembled orange seeds and strategically woven yarn which delicately sectioned off the orange sections. The company that made the clothing was called Fruity Babies, with the slogan, *Clothes so cute you could just eat them!* Both Teres and Irene were enchanted by the deliciousness of the colors.

Irene held up a tiny pair of baby socks made to look like the yellow/white of a sliced banana. "Teres! Look at these! Are they not the cutest thing that you have ever seen?" Before long the two women had a pile of clothing in front of them: the banana socks, an orange mango pair of pants, a soft green honeydew melon pullover and a pineapple hat.

"What are you doing to my son?" Nicky asked, as if he meant it.

"It could be my niece! Either way, whoever it is will look adorable in these clothes if their Auntie Tee has her way!"

A voice from behind the booth loudly chimed in on their conversation. "Ah. Don't worry, my friend. I have to admit that these juicy little baby clothes appeal more to the women than they do to the men." Nicky looked up to see who had spoken. Both men reacted with wide grins when they recognized the other. They shouted simultaneously.

"Christos!"

"Nicky!"

Teres squinted into the oncoming sun to get a better look at who the man was.

"Teressa! Don't tell me that you don't remember me?" She was still stumped. He gave her a little hint. "Pee pee boy?" Teres' laugh was loud and hard, like the short blast of a horn.

"Oh, and I see you haven't lost that horrible laugh of yours. Still spewing lemonade from your nose?"

"Christos! I can't believe it's you! What are you doing here? Didn't I hear that you went to school to be an architect? Or was it an engineer?" Teres was playing catch up on her own private walk down memory lane. Not so for Nicky.

"So how are the boys? Who has them right now?" her brother asked.

Christos' smile fell slightly. "My mother and father have them for another hour and then they're going to bring them here to me. Hopefully, Bas, Basil," he said the full name for Teres' benefit, "and Chris will be in a good mood when they get here. Yesterday they were both taking turns melting down. It was exhausting."

"Clearly the universe is paying you back for being the rotten kid that you were when *your* parents dragged you here all day." Teres had caught up quite nicely. But somehow her joke didn't go over well. Christos' smile had completely disappeared and Nicky and Irene looked uncomfortable.

"Teressa, I am definitely being paid back for something. Can I wrap up any of those clothes for you?" Christos bundled the beautiful baby clothes in tissue and took Teres' money. "Nice to see you," he said, although the look on his face said otherwise.

*

"Oh my God! I am such an ass!" Teres looked as though she were about to cry. "Why didn't you stop me?" Nicky shrugged his shoulders.

"How was I going to do that? And how would you have known? It's going to be fine, Tee. I'm sure at this point in his life there are only uncomfortable moments."

"So, what did she die of and when did it happen?" Teres wanted details, but then immediately regretted asking when she thought he might say that she had died in childbirth, as if there was a good way for a young mother to die.

"It was a freak thing," Nicky began to recount the story in his economically male fashion. "She went to take a shower and slipped on a child's toy that was in the tub. She hit her head and died."

"Wait?" Teres questioned. "Were the babies home? Was she home alone? Did she die right away?"

"What difference does it make, Teressa? She's dead. All I know is that Christos was the one who gave the boys their baths the night before and he didn't take the toy out of the tub. He holds himself responsible."

Teres was working herself up to an agitated, guilty state. "I can't believe that I made that remark about getting paid back by the universe."

Irene, normally reserved with her opinions, touched Teres' arm and said, "You probably shouldn't make this man's misery about yourself." The remark hit home in an unexpected way. Teres fell apart. Whether it was the heat, the stress, or the news of Christos' tragedy, she could no longer control her emotions. She was experiencing a true meltdown which was also upsetting Irene. Nicky scanned their surroundings for a shaded place to bring these two weeping women. He led them to a tent in an area that he and his sister had always referred to as "the old people's place" because of its proximity to the bathroom and the food area. Teres plopped onto a bench and cried harder, adding thoughts of her grandfather sitting on this same bench to her list.

"Now I miss Papus!" Her wailing had induced hiccups. Nicky ran to get them all some water. Irene looked guilty and distraught.

"I am so sorry. I didn't mean to hurt you."

"It is *not* you. It is me. I am the bad person here." Between sobs and hiccups, she told her sister-in-law about how badly things were going with Danny and that instead of staying and working things out she had run off to Greece to teach him a lesson. "And he does not even care!" She then ended this mini confession with another burst of sobbing when she said, "I have no right to be miserable! I am lucky. Poor Christos has no wife to be mad at!"

Right about this time Nicky got back with a couple of colas and some baklava. Teres took one look at the baklava and blubbered, "I hate baklava!" It was clearly Nicky's turn to play catch-up. He didn't bother trying. Instead he left the two women alone to regroup and went to the arena to grab their tickets for the play that the National Theater Company was performing that night: The Trojan Women by Euripides.

*

Oh, Christ, thought Nicky to himself, *maybe a Greek tragedy about women ravaged after the Trojan War is not such a good idea for tonight.* He was feeling as though he had his own Greek tragedy going on right about now. As he stood in line waiting for his tickets, he realized he had ordered four tickets instead of three. Their day at the festival was originally going to involve Irene, his parents and himself. When Teres unexpectedly arrived in Greece, his mother had suggested that they make the festival a "young person's day." She had also given Nicky strict orders to get to the bottom of what was going on with Teres and Danny. Although Nicky had said he would try, he had absolutely no intention of grilling his sister. If she wanted to talk, she would talk. And right now she was doing all of her talking to Irene, which was fine by him.

"Hey. Tell your sister that I'm sorry. I think I was a little rude back there." Nicky was surprised to see Christos walk up behind him.

"No. It's okay." Nicky laughed. "Actually, it's not okay. I left her under the old person's tent, crying because she upset you. My guess is that she was due for a good cry anyway."

"Looks like we're all due for a good cry. Wait, not you. You're due for a baby. How's that going?" Christos' face lit up when he asked about Nicky's looming fatherhood.

"Well, I'm sure you remember. We're excited, scared, certain we'll be the best parents, but afraid we don't have a clue. I just can't wait to get this whole thing started, actually see what it's like. I'll have to call you for advice. Where are the boys? I thought you said they were coming," Nicky and Christos shuffled along in the ticket line as they chatted.

"There was a change of plans," Christos replied, "My parents were headed here and Basil immediately fell asleep in the car. He wakes up from his naps like such a bear that they decided to spare me, and themselves. They turned around and took the boys home. My father came back to give me a break, so I thought I'd check to see if there were any tickets left for the play. I haven't seen this production since high school."

"You are in luck, my friend! I ordered four tickets, but we only need three. You should join us for the evening. You'll be doing me a favor. Your being there will put my two weeping women on their best behavior. And you know by that I only mean my sister, right? Irene is as level-headed as they come. We Giannopoulos have to marry calm people because we are such passionate disasters!" Nicky was getting a kick out of his own humor, as was Christos.

"Oh, I remember what a handful your sister was. She and your Dad went toe-to-toe on more than one occasion, with me standing there watching with my mouth hanging open. Yes. I'll take your extra ticket if you'll let me treat you to dinner afterward."

"You're on! But don't say I didn't warn you. A crying two-year-old might turn out to be a better time!"

*

Nicky turned out to be wrong. All four of them had a great time. They pronounced the play a success, concluding that you can't really overact in a story that includes post-Trojan War rape, murder and pillaging. The conversation at dinner flowed easily, with Christos being surprisingly open about what the past fourteen months had been like for himself and the boys. Even while listening to a story filled with such sorrow, Teres realized that she hadn't been this relaxed and comfortable in ages. Eating and drinking outside in the moonlight was not often done in Massachusetts. The area surrounding their table was filled with hanging lanterns, candles, children running around and music from the band playing in the distance. It was magical.

Teres also realized, with a pang of guilt, that she was having fun. The Muldaurs' lack of social interaction was one of the things that had been bothering her lately about their marriage. Yes, they had friends. But those friends seemed to be divided into two categories: his and hers. Teres' friends were from St. Catherine's and from her college classes, along with Heather and Jeffrey, who were also in their twenties and lived right down the street. Danny liked them well enough but had little in common with them. Add to that the fact that his first impression was somewhat tainted. Like many people, Heather had made the mistake of thinking that Danny was Teres' father. She had cheerfully come to the Muldaurs' front door with homemade brownies and asked Danny if his daughter was home. Although he often kidded her about it, Teres knew that those remarks stuck with him. In fact, one of their biggest fights was after Danny had referred to himself as a "dirty old man."

Danny's closest friends were all from the hospital. For reasons that Teres couldn't fathom, he seemed happy to keep his two worlds separate. As many times as Teres had suggested they invite his co-workers to come for dinner or a cookout, Danny had a reason why it wasn't going to happen.

Martha and Bemus Bertakis were the only friends who were mutually theirs. Bemus was intelligent, funny and a good friend to Danny. The two men had a lot in common because of Danny's Naval construction background. As luck would have it, they had actually frequented some of the same bars in Greece, although at different times. Martha and Bemus were close to Danny's age, which helped considerably. The problem with the Bertakises was that they were rich. As Danny often told Teres, "They don't swim in the same ocean we do." Teres thought that her husband was being insecure, but she could see his point. The Muldaurs weren't taking two vacations a year and living in a house on the water any time soon. The Bertakises had one son, also named Bemus. He was twenty-three years old and had just finished his last year at Rhode Island School of Art and Design. She and Danny had never been to a wedding as nice as the graduation party that Martha had planned for her son. Danny accepted their invitations with caution. He didn't want to be on the receiving end of anyone's goodwill or charity. It drove Teres crazy. She privately thought that her husband was simply content just being with her, and she wondered why she couldn't be just as content with only his companionship. But she wasn't.

*

"Teres, how long will you be in Greece?" Christos asked politely. Before she could answer, Nicky chimed in, again harping on the inadequacy of the length of her stay.

"Not long enough! She won't even be here when we have the baby!"

"I'll be here another two weeks. Then I have to get back to Massachusetts." She looked at Irene. "Maybe you could accommodate me by having this baby a little early?"

"Don't wish for that," Christos interjected. "We had little Christos three weeks early and he was the size of a baby bird with a touchy case of colic. Dione had her hands full keeping him from throwing up everything that went down. Nope. Let this little guy stay in the oven for as long as he wants."

"Oh! You predict a son for me!" Nicky's eyes lit up.

Christos put his fingers up to his temples. He let his eyes roll up and acted as though he were going into a trance. "I, the amazing Christos, predict a son for you..." he droned.

"We should all bet!" Nicky said, excited.

"I bet it's a boy!" Irene stated first.

"Me, too," agreed Teres.

"It's unanimous!" Nicky said, as he raised a wine glass for a toast. They all began laughing. "Let's toast to the health of my son!"

Like a flash, a little girl ran past the table and bumped into Nicky's raised arm. His wine splashed everywhere. Napkins flew off everyone's lap in a quick attempt to repair the damage.

"Oh, my goodness," exclaimed Teres. "Why did we think that hanging out with our parents for this festival week was so awful? Look at how much fun these kids are having. I would give anything to be back here, working in a booth and enjoying the festivities."

"You would?" said Christos, his eyebrows raised.

"Yes, definitely. Just watching you wrap our packages brought back a wave of memories, all good."

"Great. We have four more days and I'm short-handed. What do you think about working with me for the rest of the week?"

"What…" Teres was caught off guard. Christos saw her look and quickly recanted.

"No. I was just thinking that if you're not doing anything and you maybe want to help me out? For the past five years, four of us took care of this booth: me, Dione, my mother and my father. After Dione died, we became less than three, because we had to consider the boys and who was going to stay home with them. It sometimes seems as though my wife might have actually been two people, instead of one. But I definitely didn't mean to put you on the spot."

"I'll do it," Teres said, quickly. "It will be fun." She looked at her brother and sister-in-law. "Do you think Mama and Papa will care?"

"No. As long as you devote all of next week to them, I think they'll be happy that you're having a good time."

"Wait a minute," Christos said, "I didn't say anything about a good time." Teres burst out laughing, her slight snort causing them all to laugh. She knew full well that she was going to have a good time.

1982

QUINCY, MASSACHUSETTS

RON WATTERS POSSESSED all the traits that an emergency room doctor needed in order to withstand the rigors of a fast-paced career without facing early burnout. He was a great diagnostician, almost to the point of being a savant. Although he didn't mince words, his delivery was never offensive, making it easy for patients and staff to accept his judgment without question. Those two things alone would have made him a good doctor. But, being the last boy in a family of six sons gave him the ability to thrive on chaos, a must-have quality when it came to a busy ER. His pushy brothers also provided him with a personality that allowed everything to roll off his back. Nothing bothered Ron.

Anyone with that many natural traits would have chosen to go for the money careers in medicine: orthopedics or cardiology. But Ron had another thing going for him: his family was filthy rich with old money going back a few generations. None of the Watters boys came out of medical school owing a king's ransom to student loans. It gave them the luxury of choosing to do what they liked. And Ron liked people. He liked them enough to listen to their complaints and problems for twelve hours a day, five days a week; a job that would drive most people to drink. But for Ron, solving someone else's problems was better than thinking about his own.

For two nights in a row, he had watched Danny, a respiratory therapist who normally didn't work the evening shift, hobble around from cubicle to cubicle. Ron could never understand why his co-workers chose to suffer when an amazing talent, such as himself, was right here, just waiting to figure out what the hell was wrong with them. *Well, tonight's your lucky night, Danny Boy! I'm done watching you limp. Dr. Ron to the rescue!*

*

Danny had been ready to give up on running only a week into it, when his knee and hip began throbbing with constant pain. He had tried to soldier through it, blaming the pain on everything but the running. *Maybe it's all the extra shifts I've been picking up.* He knew that working the emergency room, with its vinyl-over-cement flooring, for sixteen hours a day wasn't doing his leg any favors. He was barely getting through his shift. *Screw this running thing. Tomorrow morning I'm sleeping in.* He was grabbing an ibuprofen from the nurse's station when one of the newer ER docs, a thirty-ish, laid-back guy named Ron Watters, tapped him on the shoulder, pointed to his leg and ushered him into an empty cubicle.

*

"What are you wearing for running shoes?" The doctor asked, probing Danny's knee and ankle.

"These," Danny said, as he looked down sheepishly at the worn sneakers on his feet.

"And you wear these all day, to walk in at work?"

"Yup."

Dr. Ron then asked him to walk barefooted across the hallway floor. Danny could feel the man's eyes focused on his back.

"You have a pretty severe pronation problem. Neutral running shoes, especially worn out ones like you're wearing now, are going to kill your knees, and eventually your hip."

"Trust me, Doc, my hip is already a casualty of this running thing. I'm fighting an uphill battle, no pun intended."

"Well, it doesn't have to be. With the right pair of running shoes, you should have no problem building up your stamina. It'll be a great way to take care of your heart and your lungs, too. Let me write down the name and address of the guy I use to fit me for my running shoes. You're going to want to get a new pair about every six months."

And that was it. The new running shoes had turned Danny into a runner. He was keeping this news to himself as a surprise for Teressa when she returned. For nine years she had been trying to get him to run with her. His wife had used threats as well as flattery, telling him often how beautiful and strong his legs looked. His reply was always the same, "I ran enough in boot camp to last a lifetime." *I wish it had been enough to last a lifetime.* At forty-eight, Danny knew that he was beginning to look like a crane. The muscles of his legs had become less obvious which made his long legs look too thin for his big body. Now that his upper body was slimming down and getting firmer from his workouts at the gym and his legs were filling back out from the running, he looked proportional. He could feel himself getting stronger by the day. Danny fantasized about how impressive his strong, new body was going to be to his wife in the bedroom. He finally understood why people became obsessed with running.

In fact, the running had saved his life. After Teres left, Danny had sunk a little deeper into the hole that he had been digging for himself. He couldn't believe how lonely and miserable he felt. He and Teres had spoken four times in the month since she had left Quincy. The bulk of those conversations was comprised of uncomfortable pleasantries about the family in Greece and his questions regarding how Teres had been spending her time. She answered all his inquiries politely and impersonally. *She didn't even ask how I was doing.* She asked him about work, about who was doing the driving and if her class schedule had come in the mail. Danny couldn't tell if his wife was truly over him or if she was just trying to torture him. Either way, he felt tortured. She sounded as far away as she was. Twice she mentioned how ridiculous it was that she was coming home before the baby arrived. *If she's waiting for me to say she should stay longer, she's got a long wait coming.* Danny had already forgotten all the selfless reasons why he had insisted that she go. He wanted her to come home. They were a couple who didn't connect well over the phone. He needed to look into her eyes so that she would know how his heart felt. He had never been good with words, and he was apparently terrible at long-distance relationships.

No. Danny did not want his wife to extend this family trip any longer. To see this new baby born would crush her, and probably destroy any chance he had of getting her back. She needed to leave Greece as planned so that they could reconnect and get back to working on the adoption, which she hadn't mentioned once since his seizure. Danny wanted to tell her all of this, but he knew that there was nothing he could say. Like most things, coming home had to be her idea.

1982

ATHENS, GREECE

"TERES. GRAB THAT carton marked "watermelon" under the table and start pricing out a few hats. I think that there's some more banana booties in there, too." It was Teres' third day and the festival was packed with people. Fruity Babies clothing was flying off the table.

"Why do I have to do all of the grunt work?" Teres asked, jokingly.

"Because, Princess, you're the only person I can boss around. Do you see any other employees?" Christos shot back at her with equal humor. Their banter over the past three days had been sharp fun for both of them. Since Teres already knew how to work a festival table, she had jumped right in as if they had been working together for years and not days. The luxury of being able to converse in her native tongue, without having to prethink every thought, had freed up her mind and let her take advantage of her naturally sassy, sarcastic wit. She was having a great time. She was also trying not to read too much into this great time. *Don't overthink it,* she kept saying in her head. *Don't compare this to home. This is not real life.*

*

On her first day, Christos had thanked Teres twice an hour for coming to his rescue. She finally told him to shut up. She also mentioned that he had rescued her, too. She told him that her parents were on the verge of tying her to a chair, focusing a bare bulb on her face and interrogating her about her marriage.

"Should I be doing that during our break?" Christos asked her with a tad more curiosity than humor.

"No. Eventually, I'm going to need to talk to somebody, and it's probably not going to be a family member. Since you appear to be my only friend in Greece these days, prepare yourself to get stuck with a lot of girl talk. Besides, we don't get any breaks. My boss is a jerk."

Christos left it at that.

After that first day of working together Christos had driven Teres back to her parents' house in Nea Makri. It took over an hour to get there and another two hours to get back to *his* parents' house, in Mandra, on the opposite coastline. They both decided that that wasn't going to work and agreed that she should stay at his mother and father's house for the next two nights.

Mr. and Mrs. Tsakalos lived in a modest three-bedroom villa. During the festival they had decided to keep their grandsons at their house for the week, rather than take the long drive to Christos' apartment in Rafina. The Tsakalos' household was completely set up for the two boys. Predictably, most of their favorite toys had ended up there, as well as the necessary clothing, toddler seats, and other items essential to raising a couple of rambunctious boys. Tom Tsakalos had even built his grandsons a swing set in the small area behind the house, formerly his wife's vegetable garden. When Teres and Christos arrived there for Teres' first night as a guest, the boys were already in bed and Christos' mother looked exhausted. Christos immediately joined his father in picking up the toys, books and sippy cups that were strewn all over the parlor. Teres took his lead. She tossed her overnight bag in the doorway and went straight into the kitchen to clean up the dinner dishes.

"No, no! You are a guest in our house! Please stop this, Teressa!" Nina Tsakalos looked appalled.

"Let me do this for you. It is wonderful that you've opened up your home to me. Besides, I love doing dishes."

Nina yelled into the living room, "Your friend is a big liar, Christos!"

"I know, Ma," was the response from the other room. Teres grinned. So did Nina.

"This is the second night in a row - make that the third night, that I have seen my son happy." Teres didn't know what would be an appropriate reply. Christos came through the doorway of the kitchen with his hands full of children's dishes and tea cups.

"Ma. You're letting them eat in the living room?"

"Shut up, Christos! I'm letting them eat wherever they want!"

Teres could see where Christos had gotten his feisty comeback training. His mother was a firecracker. Christos put the dishes down on the counter next to the hot, soapy water-filled sink. He grinned at Teres.

"You look right at home."

"Your mother doesn't believe me, but I love doing dishes. There is something about the hot, sudsy water and monotony of the task that relaxes me. Danny thinks I'm…" And there it was. Teres had casually said her husband's name and didn't know where to go with it from there.

"Crazy?" Christos' mother interjected quickly. "All husbands think that their wives are crazy!"

Tom Tsakalos rounded the corner and in a quiet, conspiratorial voice he said, "And all husbands are right." Teres felt thankful that Tom and Nina had helped her uncomfortable moment pass. She sensed that Christos' parents were people who didn't need to know all the answers. They were just content to see their son happy again, no matter what the reason. She smiled gratefully at the older couple as she thought to herself, *Where the hell are you going with all of this, Teressa Giannopoulos Muldaur?* Then she cleared her mind and let the task at hand, with all its magical calming powers, take over the direction of her thoughts.

*

It was the last day of the festival. Christos appeared amped up, unable to stop talking. He had babbled all the way to Athens. His chatter was making the dread that Teres was feeling a little worse.

"The best part about these past few days is the way that you understand what teamwork looks like. It's one of the things I like about you. You make working together fun, but you're also a good slave," Christos chided. Teres noticed that he waited to make certain that she was at least partially offended by his statement before he spoke again. "You're a girl who really knows how to take orders. That's important in a boss-employee relationship." Teres still didn't take the bait. Christos being offensive and Teres feigning anger had become a joke between them.

"You're not going to get a rise out of me today, Boss Man." She was already feeling depressed by the thought of the last few days becoming a memory. This had been a nice break from reality, and so much fun. Christos' boys were as adorable and different from each other as two little guys could be. Teres was already in love with them both.

*

That first morning, they had awoken expecting to find their father in the guest bedroom and instead had found Teres. Little Chris, who had just turned four, began yelling. It wasn't with fear; it was with excitement. "I found a lady! Yia Yia! Papus! Come here! I found a lady instead of Papa, and she is really, really pretty!" Christos had come running in from the sofa, pulling his pants on as he ran. He hadn't thought about the fact that his boys might be traumatized by waking up to a strange woman in his bed. He was still tripping over one leg of his trousers when he swung into the room. Basil, mostly non-verbal at two and a half, was standing beside his brother in silence, both of his hands were hanging by his sides and a confused look covered his small, dark face. Christos, on the other hand, was at the head of the bed, still pointing at Teres as though he had discovered a dinosaur. "Look, Papa! She is so pretty, like Mama."

She is beautiful. And yes, how could I have missed that she resembles Dione? was the thought that ran through Christos' mind, as he took in Teres' wild halo of hair, beautiful lips and darkly framed eyes. But what he said to his boys was, "Wow, you guys are right. She is really pretty. Where do you think she came from?" They both turned and looked to their father for an answer to the mystery. Then the mysterious woman spoke.

"Hi guys. You must be Basil and Chris. I'm Teres. You can call me Tee if that's easier. I work with your Papa." And as suddenly as it started, the mystery was over. "Are you guys hungry? I am starving!" Teres shooed them away so that she could throw on some clothes. "Get the boys some juice and I will get up and make us some tiganites for breakfast."

*

Breakfast had been delicious. The delicate little pancakes were cooked to perfection, then buttered and drizzled with honey. Teres had cut up two pears into thin slices and sprinkled them with cinnamon and sugar. Since she had become accustomed to somewhat weaker American coffee, cooking the fine grains of the beans in the briki was definitely a little hit or miss. She opted to err on the stronger side and then cut the coffee by half with sugar. Christos thought it was delicious and Nina and Tom were just thrilled to sleep in for a few extra minutes and then have breakfast waiting for them.

"What a treat!" Nina proclaimed, as she sopped up the juices created from the marinated pears with what was left of her tiganites. "You are an amazing cook, Teres! Did your mother teach you to cook like this?"

"I think that it might have skipped a generation. My mother does not love the kitchen. I learned everything from my Yaya. She still does all of the cooking at my parents' home."

"Well, she did a good job," Nina said and then turned her enthusiasm to her grandchildren. "You see that, boys? You have a lot to learn from me! You need to listen to your Yia Yia!" The boys ignored her as though she hadn't spoken, which didn't seem to bother their grandmother at all.

*

"Teres. I don't want to make you mad on our last day together. I don't know what I want. But I do know that I can't go back to having nothing to look forward to when I get up in the morning."

Teres felt her stomach do a little flip. She didn't know if it was from fear, or excitement; the second emotion being one that she had no right to feel. She continued to pack up the boxes of leftover clothes, organizing slowly and meticulously, as though she could make this last day of theirs go on a little longer. "Christos, I don't know what to say…"

"I'm not asking you to decide anything. I'm just saying that a little bit of hope, an opening in the dark doorway of possibilities, would give me a reason to wake up happy. I know that you're feeling what I'm feeling, or at least some of it. It's just that ever since my wife died…"

"My husband is not dead. Danny is not dead. I am still married," Her three times of telling the same fact was twice said for her own benefit.

"I know that, Teres. But I don't know anything else. You promised that…"

"I promised nothing," she interjected.

"But you had said that at some point you would probably talk to me about what was going on in your marriage," Christos sounded deflated, like a man who knew where this conversation was heading.

"Yes. I wanted to talk to you about Danny, about everything. But that was when I thought we would be talking as friends. When I realized how I was beginning to feel, and saw how you felt that way, too, it seemed... not a good idea to add more to it, or to betray my husband with an intimate discussion with a man… who I have... inappropriate feelings for." She turned away and reached for another box.

*

Christos put his hand on her arm and turned her back to face him. Teres didn't stop him. *She has feelings for me.* That's all he needed to hear.

"Just tell me one thing. Why did you run back to Greece without your husband?"

"I couldn't be there with him, because I could not make him be happy."

"You make me happy." Christos moved closer. "You make my boys happy. My parents adore you. We could have so much together. We could have another ba…"

"Don't!" she snapped back at him. "Stop talking right now! Do not tell me how happy we will be and how I will get to have a baby and be a mother. Life does not work that way, Christos. And you know that I am right! Sometimes life does not let you pick and choose from a list of things that you think will make you happy. Not all of life's options are on every person's list! For you, having your wife alive, it was not on your list. For me, having a baby was not something that I could pick like an apple from a tree."

"Teressa. I'm not saying that you fit on my list! I'm saying that we have feelings for each other that could develop into a deep love and a wonderful life." He knew that he was losing the battle.

"There is a man at home that I have a deep love for. Is it easy? No. But I have no right working on a love with you when I haven't done everything I can for my love with my husband."

How can I argue with that? And the cloud of depression drifted back into his life.

*

The ride to the Giannopoulos property was starkly different from that morning's commute. Christos couldn't think of one thing to say that would fill

121

the void. Their conversations, which had been so comfortable for him during the past week, had now become painfully impossible. He had anticipated a much different ending for this day. His plan had been to take Teres to dinner, talk about their relationship - *maybe even kiss her* - and begin to put his life back together. Christos realized, feeling somewhat foolish, that he had made up a future that didn't exist. The silence between them was killing him. *But not as much as tomorrow's emptiness will.*

*

For Teres, there was a certain satisfaction in their inability to communicate. Knowing how quickly things changed in their relationship had given her hope for a turnaround in her marriage. She realized, in the darkness of Christos' car, that she was actually smiling. The dark doorway of possibilities, for herself and Danny, had just opened a little wider.

As they pulled into the Giannopoulos yard, Teres readied herself for an awkward goodbye. Before either one of them could open their mouths, the passenger door flung open. In the stark light of the overhead bulb she saw her father. He looked frantic.

"Teressa! Thank God you are home! Danny is in the hospital!"

In the blink of an eye, Teressa's life was changing again.

1982

HOUGHS NECK, MASSACHUSETTS

THE ROAD MOVED easily under Danny's feet. He wasn't even winded at this point, three miles. He couldn't wipe the grin of accomplishment off his face. *I'm going to run a road race!*

Ron had told him about the race two weeks ago. Danny had thought he was joking when he brought it up.

"I've never run a race in my life. I'd be a disaster," Danny sputtered, taken off guard.

"Are you kidding, dude? You're gonna be in the perfect position, like a sandbagger or a ringer!" Danny wasn't getting it. The doctor made things clearer. "Danny, the races are broken down by age categories. You're forty-five?"

Flattered, Danny said, "Forty-eight, and a half."

"Woo hoo!" Ron whooped. "You're in the forty and over category. You could actually win this race, even as a novice. Of course it would be cooler if you were fifty already."

"Says you," laughed Danny, cautiously excited about the possibility of running, let alone winning, a race. "Where do I sign up?"

*

Today was Danny's last practice run before the race. Ron had made up a training schedule that he had followed to the letter. It consisted of two days of short runs, followed by a long run day (usually the length of the target race, which in this case was a 6.6-mile quarter marathon) then a day off. The schedule ended with today's short run. Danny had chosen a 3.9-mile route that he liked because there was plenty to look at. It was in Houghs Neck or *the scene of the crime*, as he referred to it in his mind.

Teres had been less than a fan of that area of town since the submerged car incident. It was crazy how smart and yet illogical his wife was. With Teres, you were as good as your last miracle. It wasn't as if she was unforgiving of people. It was more in the nature of, "I do not want to go to that restaurant, that is where I lost my favorite earring." She remembered every time that something didn't go well and then hung on to the details for dear life. At first he felt slighted because Teres' grudge against Houghs Neck was centered around it being "that place that drowned the little blue car," and not because it was the location of his heart attack. Then he realized how often she avoided any discussion of his collapse that day. Danny had been to The Neck a number of times since then, mostly just to sit in the car, drink a cup of coffee and enjoy the ocean view. But this month he decided that it was his favorite place to run; off the main roads, but with plenty of route choices.

Today's run was going well. The weather was warm with low humidity for July. The layout had hilly ups and downs that were challenging, but not too frustrating. *I'm almost finished and feeling great!*

Tomorrow, race day, he was meeting Ron at the Squantum Point Park at eight in the morning for their nine o'clock start time. The race route was called the Squantum Loop. Danny had already run the whole thing once and made a horrible straggler's kind of time, not even breaking eleven minutes per mile. Even out of shape, the length of his legs should have gotten him to a ten-minute mile. Ron had laughed when Danny told him about the bad performance. Then he assured him that once his adrenaline kicked in on race day, he could plan to shave off a minute per mile from his best time. *I sincerely doubt that.*

Like most races, this one benefited a charity, Cystic Fibrosis. Ron reminded Danny to keep the spirit of the event in the forefront of his mind, ending his sermon with the joke that he, himself, was going for the gold! Danny didn't see a gold medal in his own future, but he *was* excited. He even purchased a disposable camera for the big day. The only thing missing was Teres.

He wished that he had told her about the running thing. She would have been so proud. She might have even cut her trip short so she could be home in time for his race, or maybe not. That was the thing with his wife, you never knew which direction her mind was going to travel. She might be thrilled that he had started to run, or she might be bullshit that it had taken her leaving in anger for him to do what she had been telling him to do all along. *I still wish she was here*, was Danny's last thought as he ran down to the end of Winthrop Street, planning to round the curve onto Sea Street, where his car was parked.

*

Jimmy Bassanelli hated his job. It was supposed to be temporary work that he was going to take until his luck changed; that was four years ago. Driving a sanitation truck for the city of Quincy was the kind of job where you were lucky to be on the city payroll, but you weren't lucky, because it was garbage. He knew the only thing worse than being a garbage man was being a garbage man in the hot summer with a route like Houghs Neck. He hated The Neck because the roads were tiny, and the people obnoxious. *There's always some asshole parked illegally on the side of the street, like it isn't hard enough to get this fucking truck down these ridiculous roads!* Half his time was spent backing up and figuring out plan B. This morning was no exception.

Jimmy had just left the Atherton Hough Elementary School. It was the only pickup stop he didn't hate. This was for two reasons: the dumpster was around back with plenty of turnaround room and it was his last stop of the day. The school was mostly closed during the summer months, but the dumpster was always full. Jimmy had his suspicions that all those rich summer people were using it to dump their trash on their way out of town, rather than pay the pick-up fees. He didn't give two shits about who put their trash in the container. But he was pretty sure that all the beer cans and wine bottles weren't from the second graders at the school. *Ha! Maybe it's the teachers.* He laughed to himself at his amazing wit. He could feel his mood lightening up with this last stop. Now, off to the landfill to *dump out all this shit*. That part was a nightmare, acres of foul-smelling trash. He had to remember to buy himself another jar of Vicks VapoRub. He wondered why he still had any sense of smell left at all, between the burning odor of the trash and four years of shoving camphor up his schnoz.

Jimmy reached down to grab what was left of his Vicks on the shelf below the dash. *It must have rolled over to the corner*, he thought, as he ducked his head down to look. He didn't see the BMW parked at the intersection of Darrow Street and Sea Street, just twenty feet from where Winthrop meets Sea.

*

The trash-loaded, twelve-ton truck hit the brand new silver-colored sedan with a force that propelled it into the crosswalk of Winthrop and Sea just as Danny was running around the hairpin curve toward the little elementary school, where his refurbished, bright blue Karmann Ghia and another bottle of water were waiting for him. He had borrowed Ron's Walkman which he quickly silenced when he heard the doctor's bad music choices. But he kept the headphones on rather than carry them. His eyes were down. Danny was consumed with watching his step and admiring his new running shoes. He never saw the slammed car coming; it turned out to be a blessing.

1982

NEA MAKRI, GREECE

IT WAS TWENTY-ONE kilometers from Nea Makri to the airport in Athens, roughly a thirty-minute drive. That was plenty of time for Teres' father to get personal with his questions about her marriage. He seemed to know plenty of the facts. Obviously Irene had talked to Nicky, who then relayed everything to their mother, who then told Papa. *It's just as well. I can't avoid this conversation forever.* She answered his questions with as much honesty as she could muster.

"Yes, I love him. But it is not always about love!" Teres explained and complained at the same time.

"Yes. It is, Teressa," was her father's emotional response. "You can let a million things become the issues, but in the end it is most definitely about love."

"Papa! I have never stopped loving my husband. But we are so different. Things are not easy, and sometimes not bearable. I wonder why we fell in love in the first place."

"Love is not a why thing. It does not need a reason to happen," he countered. "But you need to know that loving someone doesn't mean that you must be with them."

Teres was confused. *Was he advocating a divorce?* First her father said that it was all about love and now he was saying that she didn't have to stay with her husband. "Papa, I don't really see what...."

*

What exactly do I mean? Nick was torn. Had Danny been his first choice as a husband for his only daughter? No. He was twice her age and from a country so far away. But he loved her. It was obvious in all the ways that counted. And the Giannopoulos family had grown to love him.

Like any man who has taken a wedding vow, Nick knew that marriage was hard. There were storms to be weathered and something to be said for those who could weather a storm. He and Katharine had weathered a few. But this was his Teressa and he couldn't bear to see her in pain.

"Listen to me, Teressa. Only you know what you can handle in this life. If being a mother is not possible and it is the only thing of your heart, I cannot say that you must be with Danny. But let me say this: Danny cannot have what you want, either. If he could give you a child, you would already be a mother."

"I know, Papa. Please don't worry about us. I just want to get home, make sure that he is all right and get our lives back on track. I love my husband."

The exhaustion in her voice signaled the end of the conversation better than any words could. He would say no more.

"I know you do, Γλυκό μου κορίτσι, my sweet girl."

1982

QUINCY, MASSACHUSETTS

TERES WAS AFRAID to go into the room. What she could see through the doorway was enough to make her look around for a basin to handle the vomit that threatened to rise past her throat. Danny's face looked black, not purple. His head was bandaged, his right eye puffed out with sutures above and below. Stitches ran down the left side of his bottom lip and across his chin. One leg was casted and hanging in traction. The other leg was also casted, but only from the knee down, its protruding toes still crusted with dry blood. He was either asleep or unconscious. There was something draped over his IV pole that looked like a new T-shirt with a race number stapled to it. Teres was confused. *Maybe this isn't Danny* was the briefest of a dozen thoughts running rapid-fire, like bullets from a machine gun. She could see that his left arm, which was strapped to an intravenous board, looked to be okay. But she couldn't see Danny's right arm. For a fleeting moment she wondered if the arm was gone. Then he slowly lifted the missing arm, putting his hand up to his forehead and emitting a painful moan. Teres rushed into the room.

"Oh Daniello! Oh my God, oh my God, oh my God." All this was said in a hoarse whisper, as though she were trying not to wake him. "What have you done? Please tell me that you are going to be okay." Teres needed to hold him but she couldn't figure out what part of her husband was safe to touch. She held the hand hanging off the end of the IV board. His wedding ring, which she had logged hours of time twirling while holding this hand, was gone. Teres couldn't make the connection as to why his hand felt different. She was crying uncontrollably by this point. Danny squeezed her hand. It was enough to slow her sobs.

"Hey," he said, with his lips barely parted and his eyes still closed.

"Hey," she said back to him, feeling calmer now that she knew his brain was functioning. He opened his good eye. Teres leaned forward and kissed the small unbandaged space above it.

Danny lifted his right arm, his elbow bent at a ninety-degree angle. "Feel my muscle."

Teres couldn't understand him. She thought he had said "feel my muscle."

"Baby, what did you say?" Teres asked him softly.

"Feel my muscle," he said again, more intelligibly. He flexed his right arm. The muscle bulged. Teres hesitantly felt it, confused that this was what he wanted. A grin appeared on the half of Danny's mouth that he could move. The movement of his face caused another groan of pain and water sprang to his swollen right eye. But he wasn't done impressing his wife yet. In a low voice, with the effort of forced articulation, Danny stated, "You were right. I feel much better when I'm working out." And then he passed out cold from the pain.

*

It was twenty minutes later when Dr. Ron Watters stopped by the ICU to check up on Danny. What he found was Teres slumped over the side of Danny's hospital bed, her square, wooden visitor's chair barely underneath her. Danny was asleep. At first he thought she might also be asleep. But then he heard the rhythmic words of prayer coming from beneath the pile of dark hair that covered her face and was partially flung over her husband. As an emergency room doctor, Ron could recognize the sound of prayers in any language. Although he didn't want to interrupt her, he decided that he should. Danny's wife might be more worried than she needed to be. Ron lightly tapped Teres on the shoulder. "Um, Mrs. Muldaur?"

His touch caused Teres to jerk upright, which made her chair slide out from under her startled body. He wasn't quick enough to catch her and Danny's wife fell to the floor in a heap. She stayed there, taking the opportunity to totally fall apart. She went from praying to being unable to catch her breath.

"I can't breathe!" She gasped, holding onto her chest. Ron sprang to action. He grabbed the oxygen mask and cannula from behind Danny's bed and pulled it over Teressa's face, ripping some of her hair out in the process with the tight, unforgiving rubber head strap.

Way to go, idiot!

"Oh, Jesus! I'm sorry! Teressa, right? Try to take slow, deep breaths. You're having an anxiety attack. *Which I'm pretty sure I just helped cause.* I'm Danny's friend, Ron."

Ron and Teres were both on the floor. The chair had scooted halfway into the corridor. One of the nurse's aides heard the commotion and stuck her head into the room. She then ran out and called a code blue.

The overhead announcement of, "Code blue in ICU, room 228, Code blue in ICU, room 228" not only sent everyone working the intensive care unit scrambling, it also woke up the patient, whose twenty-five plus years of code blue instinct, coupled with hearing his own room number, caused a rise in his heart rate and respirations. Ron, on the other hand, had no idea what room he was in. He just knew that it was the one near the satellite pharmacy station, which was manned by a pharmacist named Bruce, the most hilarious guy in the hospital. He wondered briefly if he should get off the floor and help out with the code. It came as a complete surprise to him when the crash cart came slamming around the corner. It got as far as the doorway, the chair and the two people on the floor preventing it from coming all the way into the room.

*

Danny was suddenly more awake than he had been since the accident and he sure as hell wasn't going to let anyone start pounding on his chest. He was fine. *But what the hell is going on beside me on the floor?* Before he could

131

painfully formulate the question, he saw Ron pulling his wife up onto a chair which he was dragging under her using his foot. With his left eye, Danny saw that his wife's eyes were closed and there was an O2 mask on her face. His heart rate began to go through the roof.

"What are you doing to my wife?" Danny spat the words through his damaged lips.

*

Ron looked up from his task of riling up and then calming down Mrs. Muldaur, and grinned at Danny.

"Hey there! Good to see that you've joined the living!" Teres opened her eyes. Ron turned to look at her. "And look! You didn't end up passing out! This is all working out great! Hallelujah!" He then addressed the bewildered staff, who were piling up in the doorway, ready to save a life. "Sorry, guys. It looks like everyone in this room is going to live. The code was a false alarm."

*

The coffee tasted great, even for cafeteria coffee. Teres couldn't believe how American she felt by admitting that she preferred the taste of drip coffee that was made in a thirty-cup urn to an individually boiled brew. Sipping hot coffee was helping her to keep it together while Ron painted the dire picture of the events of the last few days.

"Everyone knew that you were in Greece, but nobody knew where to find you. We didn't even know your maiden name. They brought Danny into Quincy City by rescue because it was faster than going uptown. Thank God - or not really - that I was on duty in the ER. He had no ID on him and he was a mess. Everything looked fixable, but he had suffered a substantial head injury which we were watching for excessive swelling or a subdural hematoma - a brain bleed that might need fixing." Dr. Watters paused, took a sip of his coffee and then continued. "Anyway, yeah. A couple of hours into this your husband's blood pressure spikes and his brain shows signs of stress. Another CT picked up a subarachnoid hemorrhage. So rather than go in, we took a wait-and-see approach with increased Beta blockers and Mannitol. It paid off. That doesn't mean that somewhere down the road we might not have to go in and put in a clip or a clamp, but for now the prognosis is looking good."

"So how did all of this happen? Was it because of that blue car?" Teres had been pressuring Danny to get a safer car for the past year. Danny had told her that he would get one the minute they were approved for an adoption, which had made her furious, as if having a wife weren't reason enough to stay safe.

"Mrs. Muldaur, can I call you Teres?"

"Of course."

"Teres, Danny wasn't in a car. He was just finishing up his run. A trash truck hit a parked car that slammed into him. He's lucky to be alive. He's lucky he didn't lose a leg."

"I don't understand? Why was my husband running?" Teres began to feel like she had been plopped down on another planet. *What am I missing here?* This doctor, Ron, looked confused as well.

"He was training for the race? This was his last practice run before the quarter marathon," Ron said to her, slowly, as though she were the one with the brain injury.

"My husband does not run. He is not a runner." *What is this man talking about?*

"Mrs. Muldaur, Danny has been training for the last four weeks. He must have told you. You're a runner, right? Danny told me that running was easy for you because you started out running the mountain roads in Greece." Dr. Ron laughed and added, "But he didn't tell me that the real reason it was easy was because you were half his age. That old dog! I can't wait to give him crap about this!"

The room began to swirl. Teres put her head down and more tears fell. She felt like he was talking about a man that she had never met. This doctor knew everything about her and she had never even heard Danny mention his name. What else was Danny keeping from her? Teres' thoughts went immediately to the worst-case scenario. Maybe leaving him for so long had made him move on. Maybe he didn't even love her anymore. *Oh Danny! I have ruined everything!*

Teres' crying became something that Dr. Watters could no longer ignore. He got up from the table and came around to the other side to sit beside her. He awkwardly put his arm around her. She lifted her head up. "Are you my husband's best friend?" Teres recognized the oddness of her question. But, in light of everything that had happened to Danny and the vastness of the number of unanswered questions, this was what she needed to know. *Does my husband have a best friend that I do not know about?*

Ron Watters hesitated, and then answered simply, "Yes, I am your husband's best friend. Do you need a real hug?" Teres nodded her head. Dr. Ron pulled her up from her seat and hugged her tightly while she cried on his shoulder. Teres suddenly felt better, even hopeful. Seeing that this man truly cared had taken some of the burden of worrying about Danny, a burden she had carried alone for nine years, off her shoulders. It was enough to pull her out of her helpless mode and into action.

"Okay," she said. "We will be partners in getting him better, yes?" Dr. Ron nodded his head and then they shook on it.

"You betcha. It's probably gonna be a lot easier than teaching him to run." Teres decided that she liked Danny's new best friend.

*

Danny's recovery was slow. It had been fifteen days since the accident and his doctors were getting ready to move him to a rehabilitation facility not far from the hospital. Teres was scared for Danny to be away from the constant care of the Quincy City staff. Although her guess was that her husband might get more rest once he was removed from his place of employment. After Danny had gotten out of the intensive care unit and was put on another floor, his room had become like a revolving door. Teres had no idea that her husband was so popular. She was clearly flabbergasted by how many of the nurses who came in to see Danny had similar reactions when meeting her.

"So this is the wife that you've been hiding? We thought you just made her up to get all the girls around here to leave you alone!"

Teres slammed a smile onto her face, although she was getting kind of sick of this.

"Yes, I am real!" She said brightly to Danny's latest female visitor. Danny looked over at his wife, as though he could read her mind. Teres doubted that. After a few polite words and a hug and kiss on the cheek for Danny, the nurse cleared out of the room.

"Daniello, really? Why didn't you tell me that you were the Casanova of this hospital, and why don't I know all of these women? You could have introduced me…"

"Tee. Stop it," Danny wasn't seeing the humor, or her point. "It's a big hospital and you know that I'm kind of a private guy."

"Yes. Private from me. I am, apparently, the only one who does not know everything about your life." Teres wanted to slap herself for her ridiculous insecurities. But she was unable to stop this line of thought, even while knowing that it was the last thing that her husband needed to deal with.

"Teressa, they are just co-workers. I don't even know half their last names. Shit, I don't know some of their first names. Can you please cut me some slack?"

Before Teres had a chance to apologize, Ron marched into the room. He enthusiastically clapped his hands together and practically shouted, "Okay, team! Are we ready for the big move?" Teres noticed that Danny's face had brightened the minute Ron walked in.

"I'm sure as hell ready. My wife has some reservations."

"Teres! This is progress! Danny's gonna get those legs moving. Don't you worry. We're sending over a ton of painkillers to go with him. He'll do just fine."

"I am not worried about his pain," Teres replied.

"Jesus, I am," muttered Danny.

"I am worried about that thing breaking in his head - the thing that you should have put a clip on. You know, Danny had a seizure six months ago..."

"I know," said Ron. "I was here for that performance, too. Teres, one thing has nothing to do with the other. Danny's last CT scan came out great and he's ready to roll. You need to stop worrying so much."

Teres looked over at Danny. His face was less bruised. His stitches had been removed, and his right eye was completely open, its fractured socket healing nicely. He was doing good. But with Danny, you just never knew. Teres inhaled deeply. She decided that it was time to stop anticipating disaster and join Dr. Ron's cheerleading team. She clapped her hands together. "Okay! He looks good! Let's do this thing!" Danny laughed out loud at his wife's turnaround.

"Wow, babe." And to Ron he said, "You might have to come live with us for a while when they discharge me for good."

"No way," Ron said with a wide grin. "While it's true that what I know about marriage can be written on the head of a pin with a magic marker, my guess is that you two are a mess!"

"Yes, they are a mess," said a familiar voice. In came Martha Bertakis, her husband trailing behind her.

"Martha!"

Teres hadn't seen them since she had run off to Greece. Martha greeted her with a warm hug.

"How are things going, my sweet friend? Your troublemaker of a husband looks better. And how are *you* doing, Dr. Ron?"

Teres again felt left out. *How does everybody know everybody and I don't know this?* "You two know each other?"

"Oh, I never got to that part of the story," Ron said, then launched into telling it. "We couldn't find you. We didn't know where you were in Greece. So, I was telling Tony - Danny, you know him, kind of a seedy guy that works in maintenance - well, I was telling him that I was gonna break into your house and figure out where you went. So, here I am talking to this guy and instead of him giving me hints on how to break in he says, 'Why don't you just call the police and have them get in touch with the airport, or you could go to the Greek Church. Maybe they know who Danny's wife is." Ron laughs. "That's what I get for judging people!" Martha Bertakis picked up the story where Ron left off. She jerked her thumb at Ron.

"This man comes into St. Catherine's and starts asking questions about you. I don't know him, so I refuse to tell him anything. Right after he left I decided that maybe I should figure out why he was here." Then Ron jumped back into his version of the story.

"So, I'm getting into my car and she comes running out, yelling, 'What do you want with Teres?' Which of course meant that she knew you, since she didn't say Teressa," Ron continued. "So after I convinced her that I wasn't there to bring you back to your homeland, Martha got in touch with the church in Nea Makri…"

"Greek Orthodox Church of Saint Nicholas," Martha interjects, again.

"Right. And they knew your family, and gave us your father's phone number. So, anyway, that's how I found you. It wasn't easy. Sounds like nothing's easy with you two."

"You're telling me," Danny muttered from the background, somewhat ignored.

The good doctor looked pleased with himself. "It still would have been fun to break into your house. Okay. I gotta go back down to the ER. That ambulance should be here any minute to bring you to rehab and I'll come by tomorrow to check on you."

Danny looked irritated. "Can't they just put me in a wheelchair and drag me over there? It's across the parking lot for Chrissake! I could practically walk there."

"If you could walk there you wouldn't need to go there," Bemus Bertakis finally put in his two cents. "But, seriously Danny, I think you should just trade that ugly matchbox car of yours in for an ambulance. I've never met a guy who had to be rushed to the hospital as much as you. Ya know, I've never even see the inside of a rescue truck, let alone gotten a ride." Martha punched her husband's arm.

"Don't tempt fate."

Teres had been silent through most of this conversation. For the first time since her marriage to Danny, she felt like they were part of something that included other people. Maybe her worry about their marital isolation had been all in her mind. These were their people. They cared about her and Danny. And more importantly, Danny had let them in. The unstoppable, inevitable tears began to roll down her cheeks. Martha noticed them first.

"Teres! Honey, what's the matter?"

"I love you all. Thank you for being our friends."

PART II

1962

SORRENTO, ITALY

GREGORY WAS THE pride of his Italian family. His parents, Joseph
and Louise, were born in Italy and had lived on the Amalfi Coast in the beautiful
seaside village of Sorrento until just before their only son turned fifteen.
Gregory's twin sisters were nine years old when they came to America in the
summer of 1964. They didn't remember much about their lives in Italy, but
Gregory did. He remembered every detail about his early years in Sorrento. He
remembered the lemon groves and the colorful doorways of the village houses.
He remembered how much time he spent watching the wind whip through the
second-story lines of laundry that hung from one building to the next. He
remembered the sense of belonging that came along with the knowledge that his
great-grandparents had grown up in the same neighborhood. He loved those
streets and alleys. For years after the move, Gregory could shut his eyes and
easily conjure up the sights and smells of the local marketplace and the
surrounding trattorias: delicious, narrow-roomed restaurants which his father's
wealth had allowed them to frequent on a regular basis.

Gregory's parents had enjoyed a life of luxury and leisure in those
days. His mother never worked and wasn't heavily involved in charity. The only
extra thing that Gregory remembered her doing was her weekly devotion as a
member of the Prelature of the Holy Cross and Opus Dei. The Roman Catholic
organization was shrouded in secrecy and although Gregory had heard rumors
that deprivation and mortification of the flesh were commonly practiced in order
to achieve closeness to God, he couldn't remember his mother ever denying
herself a thing, let alone imitating Jesus' suffering through flagellation.
Belonging was just part of a family tradition. Both of her parents had been
members.

While his mother oversaw the family home and kept a tight rein on her children, Gregory's father worked as a private contractor for the government. His weekly trips to Rome appeared to be more in the nature of dinner meetings than conferences and most weeks included an overnight stay, to which he sometimes brought his wife. During the rest of the week, Joseph checked in at his local office in Sorrento and was home for dinner by five o'clock, despite following the tradition of taking a two-hour siesta each afternoon.

The Costa children had much less free time than their parents. They were expected to fulfill their parent's expectations by studying hard in school and staying out of trouble. Joseph Costa spent many hours lecturing his children on the importance of one's reputation and the significance of being a Costa from Sorrento. The respect of his peers and community were of utmost importance to Gregory's father and he wasn't going to let a scandal by one of his children ruin it.

On Sundays, Gregory assisted services as an altar boy at Sorrento Cathedral. He hated it. But because he performed to perfection, it was Gregory who was asked to do all of the special services, funerals and baptisms by Monsignor Pozzi. Being an altar boy had taught him that hard work, even if it was work that he hated, brought respect and admiration from others. But the minute the service was over, Gregory would practically run back down the aisle and quickly extinguish the rest of the candles before rushing into the sacristy behind the altar to change out of his alb. Then, while his parents stood on the church steps with their adorable twin daughters and greeted every living person in the city of Sorrento, Gregory would impatiently wait for them to pile into the car for their weekly Sunday drive. He loved those family car rides. It was always a thrill to sit in the back seat of their 1962 Lancia Flaminia Berlina while his father flew down the hilly coastal roads, which were so narrow and steep that Gregory dared not look over their edges. Joseph Costa drove with such reckless confidence that every Sunday ended in a fight between Joseph and his wife. But that car was the envy of all Gregory's friends. It was a shiny dark blue with whitewall tires. Its front and rear side doors opened toward each other, creating the need for Gregory to wait until his mother totally exited the front seat before opening his own door in order to avoid collision. This was especially true when Mrs. Costa was running from the car, angry, crying, or both, with the twins, Maria and Maura trailing behind her.

Because of Gregory's position as the oldest son, he was the only child his father would take for a sail in the family's prized wooden sailboat. It was a Gozzo Sorrentino, an easily maneuvered boat with a small triangular sail. Joseph had built it with his own father when he was just a boy. Gregory handled the boat with as much ease as his father. On calm days they meandered along the coastline, looking for gusts of wind to push them faster. But Gregory didn't need the thrill of strong winds. He was content with less speed because the slower the boat traveled, the more his father talked. With just the two of them in the boat, Joseph Costa's stories were anything but childlike. He told his son all the mythical stories of his youth. But he also spoke of God, and sex and marriage. Gregory felt like he was living in a man's world every time he and his father were alone in the little vessel, skimming over the unique shade of the blue water that existed between the Sorrento coast and the Isle of Capri.

It had been like a drug to Gregory: the boat, the water and the male camaraderie. Even now, as an adult, he could instantly conjure up the iridescent glow of the Blue Grotto cave as the sunlight transformed it into an unnaturally-illuminated azure. Each time he and his father had taken their little *Il Mio Destino* into those caves, he imagined the stories of the beautiful Sorrento sirens, mermaids whose intoxicating voices had led many an unwary sailor to his death. At the tender age of fourteen, Gregory had known that he and his family were living in a paradise. And he would never manage to completely forgive his father for taking them all away.

1963

SORRENTO, ITALY

"IT WILL BLOW over." Louise Costa's voice was quiet and hopeful. She was ready to launch into a convincing case as to why her husband was wrong. Louise wasn't ready for Joseph's angry reply.

"Jesus, woman! Are you out of your mind? This type of shit doesn't blow over. This shit floats downstream and right now that's where I'm sitting! Downstream!"

"But, Joe, I don't understand? It happened thirteen years ago. No one is going to hold you to something that happened so long ago. Maybe…"

"Shut up, Louise! Don't you think that I've exhausted all of my options and every connection trying to avoid this? I've known about it since last summer! Do you think that I would come to you with this if I had any way of figuring it out? No. It's over. We have to leave the country. I've arranged for…"

"What are you talking about? We are *not* leaving Sorrento!"

The platter of fish that Louise had spent half of Christmas Eve smoking and then simmering with tomatoes and herbs, fell to the tile floor of the Costas' beautiful kitchen.

*

The crash was not nearly as loud as their voices had been, but was certainly a more justifiable reason for Gregory to enter the kitchen. His parents stared silently at him as he came through the door.

"Ma? Pa? What's going on? The girls are out there crying and Nonno and Nonna are putting their coats on to leave." At fourteen, Gregory's appearance and voice had already changed to that of a man, although at that moment his legs were trembling like those of a child.

"Everything is fine, Gregorio. Go tell the girls that dinner will be ready in a few minutes." his mother said, trying to end the confrontation.

"Stay," his father commanded. He went to the cupboard and took out two water glasses. From another cupboard Joseph grabbed the bottle of Sambuca, a drink he reserved for holidays and special occasions. "You may as well hear it from me," he said as he filled a glass with liquor.

"Joseph, no! There is no reason to involve our children..."

"Gregory is not a child!" Joseph sounded ready to roar again, but then softly added, "Go and tell the girls that they can open one of their presents." Louise hesitated for a moment and then walked out of the kitchen, slamming the door behind her. Gregory watched a small, but not quite amused smile play briefly across his father's face. "Make sure that you marry a woman as fiery as your mother, especially if you're going to put her through as much shit as I have."

Gregory was already confused. His father had given his mother a wonderful life, everything that she could possibly have wanted. *What is he talking about?* Gregory hoped, in his naive, but adolescently sex-focused way, that this was only about another woman. He had heard of men who had mistresses and their families did just fine. His father poured another glass of Sambuca and handed it to him. Gregory took a sip.

"Have you ever heard of the Marshall Plan?" Gregory shook his head no. "The ERP? No? Jesus, what do they teach you in that school of yours?" Gregory remained silent. His father continued.

"After the Second World War ended, Italy was a mess. The bombing had taken its toll in Turin, most of Rome, Naples, Palermo, Foggia, all over the country there was devastation. The factories and roads were bombed, schools and - well - you know that part. It was only twenty years ago, not even."

"Yes," Gregory nodded, not having a clue where this was headed. "I studied the bombings in history and I have seen where there are still places ruined from the war." His father's face became red with anger.

"Not many ruins left!" Joseph shouted at his son. "You should have seen it before it was rebuilt!" Gregory nervously sipped more Sambuca. His father's irrational behavior was scaring him.

"There was a program, put forth by the Allies, called the Marshall Plan. It was money, given to the countries that were destroyed by the war. Lots of countries got money, United Kingdom, France, West Germany, Greece, Italy - and more countries. Millions of dollars to rebuild and get the economies back in shape. The E-R-P, European Recovery Program."

Joseph slammed down the rest of his glass of liquor. Then he poured himself another full glass, saving an inch at the bottom of the bottle which he used to top off his son's glass. Gregory wanted to gulp down every last drop. He was pretty sure his father wouldn't even notice in the state he was in. *This is like waiting for a bomb to drop*, thought Gregory, adding a tiny smile to the irony of his thought.

"Do you think that this is funny? Maybe they don't teach you this in school because it's an embarrassment to take money from your enemies. But maybe when you're liberated from Communism, your enemies are your friends. Sometimes it is difficult to tell your friends from your enemies. Let us raise a glass to the Allies who bombed us into oblivion!" Joseph raised his glass. So did Gregory, the nervous smile wiped off his scared face. "Salute!" Gregory's father again drank most of the clear, white, licorice brew, then slammed the glass onto the marble countertop. His mother tentatively opened the kitchen door and peeked her head in.

"Get out!" The door shut with a thud.

"Please, Pa. Just tell me what's wrong. Maybe I can help."

Joseph smiled at his son. Gregory was comforted by the glimpse of his father's normal personality. "Okay. I will continue. It was 1950. I had a friend in the government. He chose my construction company to do some of the rebuilding of part of the harbor area in Palermo. It was bombed late in the war, after the bombing of Sicily. The entire harbor had been destroyed along with the warehouse buildings for commerce and the boat marinas. The government wanted to get the merchant trade business going again for the sake of the economy. So they stopped concentrating on museums and artifacts and decided to put what was left of the ERP money into only things that would help Italy's economy. It was a good job for my company. If I hadn't had a friend in the government, I would never have received the job."

"That sounds right," Gregory said with as much positive inflection as he could muster.

"Yes," his father said. "It would have been a good job, a great job, except that my government friend was a crook. I was giving him receipts for all of the work and he was billing two times that amount to the Ministry of Economy and Finance, and then keeping half for himself. When I discovered this, I threatened to turn him in. He said that he would take me down with him, that he had created proof that it was me who doubled the bill. He offered me a deal to keep my mouth shut." Joseph dropped his head as though he was done with his story. There was a long silence. Gregory thought he heard his father begin to snore, but it was a snort, a laugh of sorts. He lifted his head and spoke quietly.

"Go ahead. Ask me if I took it. Ask me if I took my friend's deal and pocketed enough money to double the size of my company and buy this beautiful house that we are drinking in." Gregory remained silent. Joseph exploded. "Ask me!"

"Pa, did you…"

Joseph immediately calmed down, as if relieved by the question. His face brightened into a conspiratorial smile. It was the smile that he always reserved for his favorite child on one of their big adventures. "Yes, my good, beautiful boy. It's true. Your father is a hypocrite, a liar and a thief. Now go and open one of your Christmas gifts."

1964

DORCHESTER, MASSACHUSETTS

THE COSTA FAMILY was gone from Sorrento by the middle of July. Since not one word of Joseph's part in the scheme to defraud money from the Marshall Plan had yet come to light, their community was astounded by their sudden departure. Louise had tried in vain for seven months to convince her husband that they should stay. She was confident they would get through it. And even if Joseph *was* implicated, Louise felt that the punishment wasn't going to be as bad as her husband feared it would be. But Joseph knew the truth. He had been in communication with a solicitor in Rome for the past eleven months.

The attorney, Ramon Xuereb, was originally from Malta, but licensed to practice in Italy. He had permanently moved his practice to Rome after successfully representing a client from the Italian Ministry whose case was similar to Joseph's. Ramon could see the writing on the wall. With his newly acquired reputation and the amount of government graft that had been taken in Italy during the previous two decades, Ramon suspected he would soon be as busy as a one-armed paper hanger. After briefly looking into the case, his advice to his new client, Joseph Costa, had been expensive and clear: "Sell your house and take your family to America before all of your assets are frozen. I will represent you from here."

*

Living in America had taken some getting used to. For Gregory, it wasn't about making friends and feeling a sense of community. He knew that part of his life was lost forever. It was more about the logistics of living in an area where no one knew just how important you were. The Costa family had become nobodies overnight. They were only acknowledged in the same way that most newcomers were acknowledged: with suspicion. Ramon Xuereb had made all the living arrangements prior to their arrival. He had told Joseph that buying a house was out of the question, because even if he used cash for the purchase it would be easily traceable. So, instead, they were living on both floors of a two-family home which Xuereb had rented for them in an Italian section of Dorchester, Massachusetts.

Seventy-seven Willow Court didn't sound so bad to Gregory – from a distance. Because his imagination could stretch only as far as his previous experiences, he envisioned the old courtyards of Italy: ancient stone buildings with arches that towered well above his five foot, ten inch frame. They were beautiful places, surrounded by trees, flowers and fountains. By contrast, what he found when they finally arrived at Willow Court was a tiny driveway of a road comprised of eight residential buildings, four of which had backyards that abutted the commercial properties along Massachusetts Avenue. The house itself was a run-down, boxlike structure with a peeling brown front door surrounded by equally-dilapidated red painted clapboards. The two windows that could be seen from the street were covered in filth and road dust and had heavy shades which completely shut out even a hint of the room's interior. Gregory wondered in that first moment of seeing their future home if his father had the guts it would take to even put the key into the lock and open the door. He envisioned Joseph turning to them, laughing, with a new plan on his lips, spoken in his favorite sailing jargon, "Coming about!" And then he'd take his little family and steer them into the wind. Their sails would slap about as the boom tried to make up its mind which way the wind was going to push it. There would be a moment of indecision. But then the wind would cause the sails to billow out, swinging the boom over to the other side, and the Costa family would head in a new direction, *far, far away from this ugly house.*

But, this was July in Dorchester. It was five o'clock in the afternoon (eleven o'clock at night, back home) and still sweltering hot without the slightest breeze to propel them in a different direction. The air didn't smell like there was a body of water anywhere in sight. But there was an unfamiliar smell that Gregory would later identify as coming from the huge laundry on Mass Ave, behind their house. And the dust on their windows would turn out to be terminal because of the sand and gravel pit located at the end of Willow Court. Gregory looked at his exhausted family. His father had no choice but to open the door and usher them in. Gregory was mostly worried about how his mother would react if the inside of this house was as bad as the outside. She had stopped talking somewhere over the Atlantic and looked as though she could fall to the cement pavement at any moment. Her perfect mask was gone. All that Gregory could see on his beautiful mother's face was fear.

*

Their travel day from their homeland had begun eighteen hours earlier, at five o'clock in the morning. The car ride from Sorrento to Rome had been achieved with awkward enthusiasm. Gregory could see that his mother was trying to make the trip an exciting adventure, their first plane ride, for the sake of her children. Leaving their home in the dark of night had been difficult. But having to suppress their words and emotions for the three-hour drive to the airport, because their attorney was doubling as their chauffeur, had been nearly impossible. As Mr. Xuereb walked them to the gate, he supplied Gregory's father with more documents, envelopes and last words of advice. Gregory couldn't make out what they were saying. But as he watched their faces, he was worried that they would never see Italy again. He also had the feeling, since Mr. Xuereb wouldn't shut up about how much he loved their car, that they would never see their beautiful Lancia Flaminia Berlina again, either.

"Gregory, bring your sisters to the bathroom before we get on the plane." Joseph's everyday authoritative voice showed no hint of trepidation for this unwanted excursion.

"Pa, I can't go into the ladies' room!"

"Just wait outside the door and holler into the bathroom if they take too long." And to his daughters he cautioned, "Hurry up, piccoli gattini, we don't want to miss our plane."

Gregory smiled at his father's use of the endearment, *little kittens*. His sisters had indeed been little kittens. Maria and Maura, two months premature, hadn't even weighed four thousand grams combined when they were born. Gregory had been watching over their health and well-being since the day they came home from the hospital. He had been only three and a half when his baby brother had died, just twelve days after coming into the world. Gregory had never gotten to see the tiny infant. His father had explained to him that baby Louie was in Heaven with the angels and that Ma was coming home without him. Gregory's young mind had registered the loss in a manner much older than his age. He stood alone in his room, upset but unable to define his emotions. He had wanted a baby brother so much and knew instinctively that a brother was a precious thing to lose. Gregory decided in that moment that he didn't like the feeling of losing anything.

Well, I'm losing a lot right now, he thought to himself as he ushered the girls to the bathroom. *I'm losing everything.* Then Gregory looked down at his two little sisters in their summer travel dresses. They were excited and adorable. He suddenly realized that what the Costas were taking with them was much more valuable than what they were leaving behind. Gregory forced his head up and his shoulders back. He knew that he would protect these little girls with his life. "Come on, gattini. You heard Pa. Hurry up so we can get on the plane. We're going to America!"

1992

MYSTIC, CONNECTICUT

GREGORY COSTA WAS in love with his car. It was an arrest-me-red 1990 Ferrari F40. Ever since *Car and Drive*r magazine had reviewed the "not made for your average consumer" vehicle in February of 1991, and had proclaimed it a "mix of sheer terror and raw excitement," getting one of his own was all that Gregory could think about. He had managed to snag this one four months ago for the bargain price of a half million dollars. His Ferrari could go from zero to 100 mph in just over eight seconds. Gregory had heard (but not yet proven) that it only took the F40's midship-mounted, twin-turbocharged 2.9-liter V-8 engine 23.6 seconds to get up to 170 mph. Right now, Dr. Costa was only doing sixty-five and his passenger, Teressa Muldaur, was already terrified.

With unrelenting persistence, Gregory had convinced her to come with him to a conference in Mystic, Connecticut. The event focused on emergency response to cardiac arrest. It made complete sense for a heart doctor to attend. And it made an equal amount of sense for Teres, as the owner of an ambulance company, to be there. The fact that they were traveling together to this conference would only have seemed odd to those who knew them.

*

"Did you make that appointment to see Dr. Aarons?" Gregory's voice was casual, as if designed to make Teres feel like he wasn't harping on the issue, which he was.

"Yes, Gregorio. I have an appointment." Teres didn't turn her head to look at him when she spoke. She knew that if she gave him an inch he would take a mile in this, or any, conversation.

"Teressa, did you tell them that you are an elderly primigravida?"

So much for non-engagement. In just one sentence Gregory's customary intensity had resurfaced in his voice. She wasn't up for a battle. Two questions sped through her mind: *What can I say to end this quickly?* And *Is this how Danny feels when I'm winding up for the pitch?* Teres decided to try humor, knowing full well that it never worked with her.

"Gregory, I gave the receptionist my date of birth and told her that I am ten weeks pregnant with my first baby. From those two pieces of information she would know that I am an elderly primigravida - an old woman having her first child."

"This isn't funny, Teressa. Women need a lot of care during pregnancy, but after thirty-five, there are certain tests and considera..."

"I know!" Teres' battle to end the conversation and hold her temper were both lost. "Stop badgering me. I am seeing the OB next week. We will talk about all of those things and I will tell him what I am willing to undergo for testing!"

"Willing to undergo?" Gregory's voice boomed above both the engine and the stereo of his toy. "That's it! I'm coming with you to the appointment. It's my baby, too. I won't have you denying any of the necessary tests..."

"Pull this ridiculous car over! We are done for the day! You will not tell me what you will have me do! Pull over, now!" Teres reached for the door handle, as though she would actually open it. Gregory ground the car to a halt on the side of the highway. He shut off the engine without saying a word. Even with her eyes closed, Teres could feel him staring at her as she exhaled slowly through her nose, her hand like a death grip on the door handle. She opened her eyes and looked at him. "Thank you for stopping the car. It is small and it, you, make me feel claustrophobic. Can we talk about this - solve what we can, now, and then not bring it up again for today?"

"Yes," Gregory replied with complete control. "You tell me what you're thinking and then I'll tell you what I'm thinking. Good?" He looked

151

earnest and sounded willing to hear her. Teres nodded her head and shut her eyes, formulating where to begin.

"I am terrified, I mean *really* terrified, Gregorio. I am living two lives, neither of which I can give up. You think that you know me because we are intimate. You only know the parts that I show you. My body... has never been this happy, aside from throwing up every day." Teres smiled ruefully at her own joke.

"I'm sorry about that, *bella madre*," he whispered sincerely.

"I know that it will end soon. But, even nauseous, my body is hungry for yours. That does not make us a couple, or soulmates, or able to be together. I have been married to Danny for almost twenty years. We have had a life that you could not possibly understand. The things we have been through make my love for him unbreakable."

Gregory interrupted, "Teressa. I'm not saying that you have to stop loving Danny. I'm saying that you need to put that part of your life behind you and acknowledge your love for me, and for our baby."

Teres held back the tears and continued, unwilling to be sidelined. "Stop and listen to the rest of what I have to say. Even though my love for Danny is unbreakable, Danny is not. If he finds out what I have done, loved another man, it will kill him. And Gregory, I know that I sound dramatic when I say that, but it is true. This will kill my husband. And, yet, I am not willing to make this pregnancy disappear."

Gregory looked panicked by Teres' reference to an abortion. But he remained silent, as she had asked.

"I know that it is my last, my only, chance to have a baby. And, yes, I have feelings for you that are quite possibly love, when I'm not busy hating you for ruining my life. Every day I have a new plan. I will leave Danny and be with you. I will stay with Danny and tell him that I was artificially inseminated. I will tell him everything and beg for his forgiveness. I will run away from both of you and raise my baby myself." Teres could see Gregory's expression becoming dark and dangerous as she spoke. She gave him credit for not blowing apart at her words.

"None of these plans work for Danny. I have made my bed, so to speak. I am not looking to make a decision that makes me happier than I have ever been. I will go to Hell for this lie to my husband. So, every day I decide to do nothing, except take care of my body and protect this baby that I am carrying. To that end, Gregory, I will do whatever Dr. Aarons tells me that I should. There is no reason for you to come to my appointment. It would only make things more uncomfortable and I promise you that I will tell you everything that the doctor says. Is that good, Gregorio? Can we just keep this little baby of ours safe for now and not make plans about our future? Will you live with that for a while longer?"

*

Teres' speech had taken only minutes. But for Gregory many lifetimes had passed. The portrait of each lifetime changed with every option that Teres had pondered. There was a version of life with them as a family, another where he would somehow agree willingly to allow another man to bring up his baby, and then there was the scenario where he never got to know his own child at all: an idea that was appallingly unacceptable. *Will I live with this a while longer?* What choice did he have? It was a lot to ask of him. He had been patient for six months already, well before there had been something as immense as a child at stake. Gregory knew that he was not revered for his patience. *What choice do I have?*

"Teressa, I appreciate your honesty. I'm sure that there have been other women in my life who've been honest with me, but I wasn't interested in their true feelings. I'm a man who could never be bothered figuring out the needs of a woman. Sex, yes, but not love. It's too much work - no payoff. This is different. I love you. I care about what you think. And don't forget, this messes up my life, too. I'm a doctor who had an affair with his patient's wife. But I want this baby, and I want you. And you're wrong about Danny. He's stronger than you think. I know because I did the work on his heart and it's perfect."

Teres' temper flared. "If you think that you know my husband better than I do, you are mistaken!"

"I'm telling you that Danny is in good shape. *I* performed three perfect coronary artery bypass grafts on his heart. I am the best cardiothoracic surgeon in Boston. Danny was lucky to have me. If nothing else goes wrong for him - cancer, a stroke - he could live to see his nineties." Gregory saw the look on Teressa's face, a mixture of guilt and sadness, overshadowed by anger. None of this was what he had wanted to say. He had resorted to his fallback dialogue: *Go to the clinical when things get emotional.* Gregory used this maneuver all the time when talking to families about their loved ones. Whether things were going well or poorly, the minute they became emotional, he would stop thinking of his patient as a person and begin to think of them as a living cadaver. It was a technique he had learned early in his career. But "go to the clinical" clearly wasn't working in this situation.

"Teressa, what if we put a time limit on making a decision? I promise I won't pressure you, but this baby will. You're already looking different. Your breasts are fuller, your face softer." *There I go again, heading to the clinical,* "It'll only be another month or so before the pregnancy's noticeable to everyone. What if we decide at the end of next month? You'll be starting your second trimester."

Gregory reached into the small area behind the passenger seat and grabbed his black leather backpack, which traveled with him always. He pulled out the small brown leather pocket calendar with the gold embossed lettering of his name, *Gregory A. Costa, M.D., FACA.* It had been this year's Christmas gift to his patients and hospital staff. He remembered how Danny had grabbed a couple of them with the glib excuse of, "I think I earned these, Doc." Gregory flipped to the month of February.

"February 29th is a leap day - Sadie Hawkins Day." Teres looked confused. "You've never heard of Sadie Hawkins Day? It's the day when a girl can ask a guy out, or ask him to marry her. In Italy we called it St. Bridget's Complaint, which is really Irish. It supposedly started when St. Bridget complained to St. Patrick that a woman had to wait until a man asked her to marry him. So on this one day, every four years, it's acceptable for the woman to be the one who asks the man to marry her. What do you think?"

*

Teres watched Gregory's face become hopeful and somehow younger than his forty-two years as he talked about his leap day plan. *Of course this would be a leap year. The great doctor Gregory had willed it so.* But his boyish enthusiasm always made her heart soften for this arrogant, life-changing man. She was a pushover for this side of him, when his guard was down and he wasn't being an important, somewhat pompous ass.

Although it had been Gregory's strength that had first attracted Teres to him, it turned out to be his unexpected gentleness that had made her feelings for him grow. Teres knew that Gregory had an angry side when he felt threatened. And yet, somehow, she was not afraid to anger him. It was more the nuisance of getting through his anger and to the bottom of his real feelings that made her sometimes tread cautiously. The two of them appeared destined to be on the opposite side of every issue. Well, at least they were on the same page when it came to this pregnancy. They both wanted the baby enough to risk ruining their lives.

"Okay. I will make a decision by February 29th. But don't plan on me getting down on one knee." Gregory looked relieved.

"It's a deal. But let's get one more thing out of the way before I fire up this rocket ship. I got the invitation to Danny's 60th birthday party. Are you serious, Teressa? I can't go."

"Then you should not have told him at his last appointment that you would be honored to attend his big day. He will be so disappointed if you don't come," Teres said in all seriousness. "You can stay for a while and then use work as your excuse to leave. Danny loves you."

"I know," Dr. Costa muttered, ironically. "I only wish that his wife loved me as much as he did."

"Maybe you will have to do some more work on her heart. I have heard that you are the best." Teres didn't crack a smile because her words were not a joke.

*

Gregory tossed his backpack behind Teres' seat and then started the engine. Cautiously, because of the F40's rear and side blind spots, he pulled into the southbound traffic on Route 95. He felt a sense of pure optimism, which in turn created a foreign feeling of emotional lightness. Although she hadn't yet given him an answer, the wellbeing of the woman in the seat beside him took on a greater meaning than it had just moments before. Her safety was now everything to him. Uncharacteristically, he remained in the slow lane, silently calculating the resale value on his ridiculous red car. According to *Car and Driver*, the Ferrari's worth would double by spring. Gregory's smile broadened. *Everything is going to be perfect. She'll come around. What choice does she have?* Feeling the sense of accomplishment that comes with any successfully performed surgery, Gregory mentally patted himself on the back and then focused on the traffic and the night ahead.

1982

QUINCY, MASSACHUSETTS

"I AM NOT badgering you," said Teres insistently. "I am just saying that it looks like this might end up being a lot of money. Martha said that cases like these could end up in the millions."

Danny tried to think of a way to put off having this conversation with Teres. He knew that whatever he said wouldn't make her idea disappear for good. But maybe it would give him some reprieve while he finished his *grueling walk of death*, as he referred to the latest get-Danny-back-in-shape workout plan concocted by his wife and Ron.

Before he had even been discharged from the rehab hospital, the wheels of torture had been set in motion. Every fun thing that he owned had been taken out of the spare room and moved into the basement of their house. Somehow Ron had maneuvered his personal Proform 330X treadmill up the front stairs, through all the small doorways, and into the tiny spare room of the Muldaurs' modest Wallace Street home. It took up the better portion of the floor, leaving just enough room for the stereo system and a small weight bench. Danny had a hunch that keeping the music and all his favorite albums around had been Ron's idea. Teres was willing to paint the room gray and blacken the windows if she thought it would help him concentrate on getting better. *My wife is back in drill instructor mode.*

Another matter that had been set in motion was the lawsuit. Over the course of Danny's hospital stay, a number of ambulance chasing attorneys had come by to talk to him or just leave a card. Most of the time he had pretended to be asleep, a tactic which had served him well in the past. For Danny, figuring out this legal crap smacked of the kind of long-term pain in the ass that would make the adoption thing look like a cakewalk. It was Bemus Bertakis who finally convinced Danny to begin the process. Bemus had an Irish friend who practiced personal injury law in Boston. His name was James Flannigan. When Danny met him for the first time, he was struck by Flannigan's smiling good nature. It made up for the fact that Danny failed to understand most of what the attorney had to say, with his thickly accented legal jargon. "It's all paperwork, Daniel. You'll not have to say nary a word. Your medical records will speak for themselves."

This was an idea that appealed to him, letting the wheels of justice roll along without too much input on his part. He already had his hands full with things like getting out of bed in the morning and negotiating the ten steps from his bedroom to the bathroom, as well as keeping his wife from purchasing a bullwhip to encourage his progress. Danny retained him and then didn't give the event another thought. He wasn't even interested in getting updates from Flannigan. This left Teres doing most of the talking, which was something Danny realized a little too late wasn't a good idea.

Martha, Bemus, Ron and Teres had all been brainstorming about what to do with the money that Danny's broken body would procure. Even though Danny had been in a painkiller-induced fog, he remembered the moment when the lightbulb went off over Teres' head and the idea was born. It was that stupid remark that Bemus had made in the hospital as a joke: Danny should buy his own ambulance. The notion had latched itself onto his wife, apparently with the help of his friends. He couldn't think of anything that he wanted less than an ambulance company. As far as he was concerned, it was a ridiculous idea.

*

Teres had done her research.

The city of Boston had one major ambulance company, Anderson Ambulance. Anderson had been around since the 1940s and had the market for patient transport pretty well sewn up. Yes, there had been other companies that had sprung up here and there throughout the years. But none of them had had the clout or reputation needed to take away very many of the contracts that Anderson had established with every major hospital, rehabilitation facility and nursing home from Plymouth to North Adams.

Call Anderson! It was not only the company slogan; it was also the first thing that was visible on their half-page ads in the yellow pages of every telephone book in the greater Boston area. To make matters worse, Anderson Ambulance wasn't doing anything wrong. Their staff was highly trained in emergency medical procedures, successfully making the transition from transport services to life-saving techniques throughout the years. As many would-be competitors had come to find out the hard way, Anderson Ambulance was a hard act to follow. But Teressa Muldaur, and her new friend, Dr. Ron Watters, thought that maybe it was time to give them a run for their money. And as Teres had predicted, her husband was one hundred percent against the idea.

*

"Teres, have you heard the saying, 'Don't count your chickens before the eggs are hatched?' We don't have the money yet. It could take years before we see anything from this. You know how the court system works…"

"Seamus said…"

"It's Seamus now? Is that what we're calling our attorney?" Danny pulled the red emergency shutoff plug out of the treadmill's dashboard. The treadmill quickly went from its painfully slow pace of 2.0 down to zero. Danny stood there, still holding on to the railings. "Teres, you're going to have to cut me some slack on this. I can barely deal with what I've got going on now without the nightmare of starting up a business that's certain to fail."

"Just listen to my plan. If you do, I promise I won't badger at you." Danny knew his wife sincerely thought of herself as a person who could rein in her harping. He knew better than to hope, but he also needed a break from the treadmill. He didn't think he had what it took to finish this afternoon's two-mile, uphill walk. If he played his cards right, she would let him off the hook.

"Fine. Hand me my cane and grab me a soda, then I'll listen. But just because I'm gonna listen doesn't mean we're gonna do it. It's a bad idea." Teres handed her husband the cane, then ran to the kitchen to get a cold Fresca before he changed his mind. By the time she came back, Danny was resting in his favorite chair in the living room.

"Wow. You move much faster getting away from the treadmill than you do going to it." She wasn't joking with him. "Okay, so here is the whole plan. We all think it is something that can work..."

*

Two Frescas and forty-five minutes later Teres was finished speaking. Danny had to admit that he was more than impressed. They still weren't going to do it as far as he was concerned, but it was a darned good proposal. His wife and her accomplices were ready to get the ball rolling while Danny was recuperating. They would work on getting the Massachusetts licensing requirements figured out, and then see what was involved in becoming providers for the three major insurance companies, Blue Cross, Aetna and Medicare. After that was accomplished, they planned to purchase one used ambulance, maybe a 1970 Chevy Conversion Van or less preferable, a 1970's Cadillac Ambulance, using the money that Papus had left Teres. Ron would be the medical director, which, by state law, required a licensed physician, and they would hire four part-time EMTs to start. Bemus and Martha wanted in on it financially, as did Ron. But Teres insisted that at the start she was only willing to risk her money and Danny's money. Her friends could decide later if investing in the company was a good idea.

They had even come up with a name for the company, Accelerated Ambulance, which put them in front of Anderson in the phone book. Ron felt quite certain they could pick up some small contracts and then grow from there. No one would leave their day job. Martha said she would be happy to get Teres started doing the paperwork and help out in any way she could. Seamus (James) said he would do pro bono legal work to set up the company, then build it into, or out of, any settlement that should come their way. Danny felt compelled to tell his wife that pro bono means "free" not "later." Other than that, Danny couldn't find a thing wrong with the plan, except the obvious, "What if I don't get a settlement for my accident?"

"Danny, that is what I started to tell you when you were on the treadmill, which you should get back on. Seamus said that it is not *if*, it is *when* - the case will not be going to trial. The insurance company for the trash business wants to settle out of court. Seamus said six months at the most."

Danny shut his eyes, as if closing them would give him some privacy from Teres' pleading look. It was always strange to have the final say on something that he had no part in planning, which was the story with most things in the nine years that he had been married to Teres. It didn't look as if he were going to have a large part in running this big adventure either, which was fine with him. The truth of it was that not only was this a good plan, it was Teres' money, her dream money from Papus. *What about the adoption? Is she trading one dream for another?* And like the witch that he knew his wife to be, Teres answered his question as though she were reading his mind.

"I know that you are worried about the adoption." Danny watched his wife's eyes gently take in the battered mess that he still was. Wearing just his workout shorts, the scars were glaringly apparent under the brace on his left leg. His right ankle wore a lace-up support that he would probably don for the rest of his life. But overall he thought he looked pretty good. Dressed in long pants you would hardly be able to tell that he had been in a terrible accident just eleven weeks prior, unless, of course, the light hit the scarring on his face and revealed the shadow formed by the dent in the zygomatic process of the frontal bone of his right eye. Teres told him the scars gave his face character, but her sympathy-filled eyes implied otherwise.

"Danny, it is eight months since your seizure. We could call that horrible lady and see where we stand. But my guess is that she would worry that maybe we have our hands too full to put a baby in them."

Danny almost said that it was now or never. But he couldn't do that to her. He stopped himself from reminding her how old he was: fifty, soon enough. It seemed ancient. This accident had taken away all the youthful power he had gained from running and working out while Teres was in Greece. *What a waste!* He hadn't even had the opportunity to give his wife one night's carnal bliss to showcase his newfound abs and strong legs. Danny wondered if he would ever be able to get back into that kind of shape again. *Probably not.* Well, he had to give her something. Instead of a child or a young husband with a hot body he would give his wife the go-ahead on a project that would probably go belly up in a year, taking with it any chance of an easy retirement. *Here goes nothing.* Danny forced an enthusiastic expression onto his face.

"I'm in. It's your dream money and if this is your dream, I'm in." Danny barely got the words out of his mouth when Teres flung herself over to his chair and wrapped her arms around him.

"Oh Daniello! Thank you! This will be so good for us and I promise that you will not regret it!" Danny sincerely doubted that would be the case.

1966

DORCHESTER, MASSACHUSETTS

LIFE IN AMERICA didn't turn out to be that terrible for Gregory and his family. For the first two years that the little Costa family lived on Willow Court, they worked at making the best of their situation, determined to act as though the legal proceedings in Italy were of no concern. Joseph had immediately gotten a job as the manager of a group of Italian stoneworkers. Since nothing had become public about the embezzlement in Italy, it had been easy for Joseph to use his contacts and credentials to obtain the position. The company's current, prestigious project was doing all the concrete, brick and tile work of the newly designed, and somewhat Euro-contemporary, Boston City Hall. Much of both the interior and exterior of the building was either brick, quarry tile, or concrete, taking its architectural cue from the town halls and public spaces of the Italian Renaissance. This was a method of construction with which Joseph was quite at home. The owner of the commercial construction company, Al Marino, couldn't believe his luck in finding a project manager of such intelligence and expertise.

Joseph Costa's English was coming along quite nicely, as well. The fact that he made himself easily understood was one of the deciding considerations in his hire. For six months before moving to America, Joseph had forced his family into nightly English lessons. He began by using basic cassette tapes with beginner lessons and a testing pamphlet. He had also purchased a children's English picture dictionary which Gregory, Maria and Maura had mastered in no time. But their mother wasn't able to remember a thing despite her obvious intelligence.

Although she had never attended university, Louise had held an important position as the first assistant to the chairperson of the election committee for the Italian Republic Parliament. Joseph met his wife on April 18, 1948, on the day of the first general election after the war. He was immediately drawn to both her beauty and efficiency. They courted and were married within a year, giving birth to Gregory in January of 1950, shortly before Joseph's ill-fated governmental contract offer. Louise had, in every respect, been the perfect wife and mother. There had been nothing she wouldn't do to please her husband, which was why her inability to learn English drove Joseph crazy.

*

"Louise! Per l'amor di Dio! La parola è "cat!" Although Joseph knew that yelling at his wife would only make her less able to think, he couldn't stop himself. The deadline for the move to America was coming up quickly and his family wasn't ready. Quietly, in Italian, he said to her, "I know that this is difficult, but I'm pushing you for your own sake. If something should happen to me, and I'm not there to speak for you, you will need to be able to communicate in English."

"If something happens to you and you leave me alone in America, I will kill myself!" Louise fled to her bedroom, leaving Joseph and their three scared children sitting silently at the long dining room table. Joseph looked at his oldest child.

"Gregory, your mother is going to need a lot of help. This has been hard on her. I want you to promise me that if something happens, and I have to come back to Italy without you all, that you will do your best to take care of everybody. She'll be all right once we get there and get settled." *Con l'aiuto di Dio, with God's help and a lot of luck.*

*

"Of course, Pa," Gregory promised. His mind flew to a series of questions about what taking care of a family entailed. It was a task that seemed both simple and complicated at the same time. *Keeping the family safe and alive*

164

is the entire thing, Gregory decided, hoping that if the time ever came his father would try to be more specific.

*

Gregory had lost the ability to feel at ease. The strange thing was that before coming to America, he hadn't realized that the feeling of ease was a thing you could lose. His body and his mind were on guard all the time. As an outsider it was important to walk the narrow line between being inconspicuous and overachieving. To be granted a good grade as a foreign student was an unusual occurrence in the Boston Public Schools. If your English wasn't good, you were considered stupid. Nobody looked for ways to help the process of immigration along. It was sink or swim, and Gregory wasn't a sinker.

As his bad luck would have it, speech class had just been made a new requirement for every ninth grader in Boston. Having to perform his speeches in English made it impossible for Gregory to sound like he even knew what he was talking about. *Sembro un idiota!* The minute he stood in front of the other students, he lost all his newly-found American words. His speech teacher, Mr. Donohoe, had to reprimand and silence the class more than once during Gregory's first attempt.

At the end of the class, Mr. Donohoe had pulled him aside and told him that any time he experienced a problem with confidence during public speaking, he should envision the audience without pants. Mr. Donohoe assured him that no matter how important or judgmental the audience was, Gregory would have an advantage over them because at least *he* was wearing pants. It was all about perception. The pants trick worked. But Mr. Donohoe's lesson also taught him the value of creating a perspective, real or not, which would allow him to make his point, achieve his goal, or just get his way in life. Since he was determined to be heard, Gregory worked tirelessly to learn English and rid himself of his Italian accent.

When Gregory relayed to his father how helpful Mr. Donohoe had been, Joseph went right down to the school to ask the speech teacher if he would consider privately tutoring the entire Costa family. After agreeing on a payment of a new stone wall and brick walkway for Donohoe's family home, the two men exchanged telephone numbers and shook hands.

*

"My father is a tief," Gregory said in response to Mr. Donohoe's question.

"*Thief*, Gregory. *Tha, tha.* I know that using the combined "t-h" isn't done in Italy, but it's the only way to say it in America." Although Gregory appreciated the constant correction, Mr. Donohoe seemed to have overlooked the fact that Gregory had just told him that his father had been extradited to Italy because he was a thief.

"My father is a criminal," Gregory reiterated, taking the easy way out phonetically on a most difficult conversation. "Years ago he took money from the Italian government. He is now facing charges and will most certainly go to prison." The look on Donohoe's face told Gregory that this conversation had ceased to be a language lesson.

"Gregory! I'm so sorry. Does your family have what it needs? Will you be staying in Dorchester?" Mr. Donohoe had made a beeline right to the questions that Gregory had yet to answer for himself.

*

The Costa family had come to mean a lot to Mike Donohoe in the past year and a half. At thirty-one, Donohoe was conveniently split in age between Gregory and his father, and had come to consider them both friends. Joseph and his son logged an entire spring and half the summer of working after dinner and into the darkness on Mike's stone wall and walkway, letting him work as their assistant. It quickly became one continuous language lesson, with Mike learning as much Italian as the Costas learned English. Linda Donohoe, Mike's wife of four years, fell in love with the little immigrant family the moment she finally met all of them at a cookout she hosted to celebrate the new look of the Donohoe yard. She turned out to be the friend and mentor that Louise so badly needed. They shopped and cooked together, Louise showing Linda how to make homemade gnocchi and a true Italian gravy. Linda, in turn, gave her new friend her secret, open-up-cans version of American Chop Suey. They were a great fit. Louise could knit. Linda could sew. Together they made modern, psychedelic floral drapes for the twin's bedroom and heavy gold drapes for Louise's drab street-front parlor.

Joseph had told Mike on more than one occasion how grateful he was for the smile Linda had brought back onto his wife's face. Both he and Joseph were thrilled with their family's newfound friendship.

And now they're in trouble.

*

When Gregory hadn't shown up to school for over a week and Louise didn't pick up Linda's phone calls, Mike decided it was time to go over to the Costa house to make sure nothing was wrong. What he found there was a house so fully closed down that he thought the Costas had moved. The gold drapes, which Louise always insisted on having open for as long as there was a hint of daylight, were closed tightly with no sound of life behind them. After repeatedly banging on the door and ringing the bell, Mike Donohoe got on his knees and opened the small mail slot, trying to look inside. The angle of the opening allowed him no visual access. He was getting ready to give up when heard a little voice, almost a whisper.

"Mr. D. Is that you?"

"Maria! Maura!" Donohoe could never tell the girls apart, by either voice or appearance. "Yes, it's Mr. D," he shouted into the little rectangular slot. "Can you open the door?"

"Ma said that we can't open the door to anyone." Mike began his non-threatening campaign with the eleven-year-old twin just as the door opened.

"Hello, Mr. D. Please come inside." Gregory's quiet, but commanding, voice spoke from above Mike's head as he awkwardly got up from his knees.

*

As luck would have it, Joseph's good fortune in getting such a great foreman's job working on Boston City Hall had proved to be his undoing. Like many government projects, there had been some discreet give-and-take of monies in the handing out of contracts to various vendors. They turned out to be small amounts and fell into the category of relatively harmless, *cost-of-doing-business* type of transactions. But some whistle-blowing from a disgruntled contractor who failed to win the bid had prompted an early audit of the entire project. While no one was indicted on any charges, the microscope under which the management and contractors found themselves uncovered the newly-pending embezzlement charge waiting for Joseph in Rome. The Massachusetts State Auditing Commissioner felt compelled to do the right thing and alert the Italian government as to Joseph Costa's whereabouts. They arrested him at work with several of his employees looking on, one of whom would later tell reporters he always knew Joseph was hiding something.

Mike Donohoe had missed the tiny three-sentence paragraph in the middle of the article about the state audit in the Boston newspaper. Although he knew his good friend Joseph worked on the project, Mike hated the design of the building and thought the City Hall committee had been fools to choose it. That, along with his general lack of interest for any debate, gossip or speculation concerning the running of the City of Boston and politics in general (including school committee politics), had made him skim over the article without actually reading it. Gregory, on the other hand, had read it several times.

*

When Joseph didn't come home from work at his usual time of 5:45 that evening, Louise feared the worst. Because almost two years had passed without even a hint of bad news from their attorney, *the worst* for Louise meant a construction accident. At first she decided that her husband had probably just missed his bus. Then, when the second bus arrived at the corner of Boston and Mass Ave. and Joseph wasn't on it, Louise began to worry in earnest. She was certain her husband had been hurt, or worse, killed. The cranes used to hoist the large slabs of marble and concrete were always a problem in Italy. Because of their constant use, they were rarely taken out of service for maintenance. It was nothing to hear about a worker or two, or ten, being killed on the job when a cable snapped while carrying a fifteen-ton slab of concrete. *My husband is dead.* Louise just knew it. By the time she sent Gregory to the job site it was after nine o'clock and she was nearly paralyzed with fear.

*

The construction site was dimly lit and empty. Gregory wandered around for a few minutes, trying to decide what he should do next. He noticed a portable building with a sliver of yellow light streaming under its door. Maybe his father...

"Hey, Kid! The place is closed. What are you doing here?" Gregory couldn't tell if the man was a police officer or a security guard. But he was wearing navy blue and holding a stick.

"I'm looking for my father. He works here, Joseph Costa. He didn't come home from work tonight."

*

Allen Moore had been a police officer for the City of Boston for twenty-five years. As far as he was concerned, being a cop had turned into a boatload of shit. Between dirty hippies protesting the Vietnam War, blacks causing trouble wanting things they couldn't have and lawyers screwing it up for everyone, Allen couldn't wait to be done serving as one of Boston's finest. *Five more years*. Then his youngest, Colleen, would be out of college. With a sizable government pension, he could work part-time once he retired; maybe tend bar at the local pub or work a few shifts as a bank security guard. He just needed to stay alive for a few more years. Each day on duty Allen had, like his father before him, whispered a prayer to Saint Michael, the Archangel and patron saint of police officers, before putting on his uniform:

Saint Michael the Archangel, defend us in battle. Be our protection against the wickedness and snares of the devil. May God rebuke him, we humbly pray, and do thou, O Prince of the Heavenly Hosts, by the power of God, cast into Hell Satan, and all the evil spirits, who prowl about the world seeking the ruin of souls. Amen.

At this point in his career, Allen truly believed he needed protection from his enemies. That included this Dago kid, hanging around corners in the dark of the night, where he didn't belong.

"I don't give one shit about your Wop daddy. You need to get your greasy ass off this property before I haul you in." Allen walked toward Gregory with his billy club slapping into the palm of his left hand. Gregory didn't move. "Did you hear me? Are you deaf, or just stupid? I said get moving!"

Gregory began to speak and Officer Moore began to swing. It didn't last long. One hit to the head and Gregory was knocked unconscious.

"Jesus Christ! You stupid little shit!" Allen Moore said to the motionless body. "You are gonna fuck this up for me, aren't ya?" Moore reached down to check the boy's pulse. He was still alive. In the shadow of the darkness he dragged Gregory's lifeless body across the brick entrance and around to the back of the half-built City Hall. Then he left him for dead on the grassy embankment of Congress Street and never gave the boy another thought.

*

It was the morning sun and the smell of diesel fuel that woke Gregory from his unconsciousness that next morning. His hair was matted with blood and his tongue could feel the jagged edge of a broken tooth. He tried to piece together the events of the night before and was only successful when his mind registered the navy blue uniform of a police officer walking toward him. Gregory panicked.

"I'm leaving! I'm leaving!" He sputtered these words as he tried to get up and run. The officer caught him as he fell.

"Son! What happened? Did you get hit by a car? Are you okay?"

Yes, that's right. I was hit by a car when I came to find my father. Gregory's mind quickly adapted to this lie. "Yes. My father works here and he didn't come home." He pointed to the construction site which was filling up with workers. "My mother sent me out to find him last night and I got hit by a truck…"

The officer wanted to call an ambulance to take Gregory to the hospital. Gregory insisted he needed to find his father. After a little convincing, the officer put Gregory into his cruiser and drove him to the other side of the building. He then told him to wait inside the vehicle while he ran out and spoke to the site manager.

After what had happened the previous night, Gregory was not about to stay in this policeman's car. He tried to open the door and began to sweat when he saw that there were no window or door handles on the inside of the back seat.

He was running through his escape options when the officer returned with
Joseph's boss, Al Marino, in tow.

*

Al Marino had spent the last ten hours feeling guilty for his part in the
deportation of Joseph Costa. Costa had turned out to be his best hiring decision.
Marino had truly come to like the man. He was even-tempered and hard-
working. And unlike many of his foremen, Joseph responded to most requests
with an easy smile and a can-do attitude. Over the past fourteen months Costa
had bailed Marino's ass out on more than one occasion, the largest of which was
his handling of the wrong shipment of concrete; a compound that Marino knew
little about when compared to an Italian contractor like Joseph Costa.

To say the Romans invented the Mother Lode equivalent for cement
mixtures would be an understatement. They were the masters. The presence of
volcanic ash, forming reactive aluminosilicate compounds in Italian concrete,
dates back to 400 B.C. Pozzolanic activity (the pace and ability for concrete to
harden in wet conditions) is calculated differently in every cement mixture,
changing both the permeability and the compressive strength of support
structures such as the columns that were being constructed on the facade of
Boston City Hall. The wrong cement compound for this project would have
resulted in devastating consequences. Joseph Costa had picked up on Al
Marino's bad choice and then allowed them both the delusion that the cement
had been ordered correctly and then shipped incorrectly. It was a mistake that
Costa could have held over Marino's head in the form of a bribe or special
favor, but didn't. In return, he hadn't even had the guts to tip Joseph off about
the pending deportation. The man might have run or he might have stayed.
Marino realized that the question of whether he could have helped Costa's
situation was one that was going to stay with him for a long time.

And now Joseph's kid was sitting in a cruiser wondering about his father, and hit by a truck, to boot. Jesus Christ.

The officer opened the cruiser door.

"Thank you, Stan," Marino said to the officer, and to Gregory he said, "Young man, are you able to walk?" Gregory nodded his head and stepped out of the back seat of the police car. With Marino's help, Gregory walked the short distance to the portable trailer which Marino referred to as "the office." Once Gregory was seated, Marino assured the police officer that he could take it from there and the officer left. Al and Gregory sat in silence, neither sure where to begin.

"Is my father dead?"

The kid's as direct as his father, Marino thought with another pang of guilt. "No. Your father's alive. He was arrested by the Italian police yesterday…"

"Is he gone?" Gregory's wide eyes were the only thing that betrayed his fear.

"I don't know, they…"

"Please take me home. I have to tell my mother."

"I really think that I should take you to the hospital, I'll call your mother and let her…"

Again, Marino was unable to complete his sentence before the boy said firmly, with a presence much older than his years, "Take me home, now."

*

Between the sudden efficiency of the Italian government and the State of Massachusetts' need to justify a costly city audit, the normally sluggish wheels of extradition had rolled along with the quickness of a jackrabbit. His father was already handcuffed and on a plane back to Rome by the time Gregory painfully stepped out of Marino's Ford F100 on the morning after the arrest. In

Gregory's hand was a paper with Marino's name and telephone number. Gregory had promised he would call if there was anything the Costa family needed. As the truck drove away, Gregory crumpled the paper into a ball and threw it in the weeds. Then he stumbled up the stoop, unlocked the door and slipped inside.

When Gregory's eyes adjusted to the darkness, the first thing he saw were his sisters' tear-streaked faces. "Where's Ma?"

"She's in the bathroom and I think she's dead," Maria sobbed.

Gregory hit the staircase at a run, oblivious to his own pain. He got to the bathroom at the top of the stairs and began banging on the door. "Ma! Ma! Are you okay? Answer me! Are you okay?" The girls had come up the stairs and stood fearfully behind their brother. He turned around and shouted at them, "Go back downstairs and sit on the sofa in the front parlor! Don't move until I come get you!" They scurried off, hysterical. Gregory backed up on the landing as far as he could without falling down the stairs. Then, with all of his might, he rammed his shoulder into the bathroom door. It splintered open.

The mid-morning sun streamed in from the tall window above the heavy claw-foot tub, momentarily blinding Gregory. He expected to see his mother either drowned in a deeply filled tub or lying in a pool of blood from her slashed wrists. He saw neither. Louise Costa was sitting on the toilet, wearing the same dress she had been wearing the night before. Her shoulders were slumped forward and her head hung down between them. Louise's feet were planted wide apart and set flat on the linoleum floor and her hands were hanging loosely to either side of her thighs. She should have fallen over. Yet she was balanced with the precision of a Barnum & Bailey Circus act. Gregory looked at her closed eyes and assumed she was dead from an overdose. Then she moved.

"Gregorio."

Gregory flung into a rage. He yanked his mother up by her shoulders and shook her like a rag doll. "If you ever do that to the girls again you had better be dead!" His mother's head flung wordlessly back and forth with his thrusts, her eyes still closed, face expressionless. He picked her up and put her into the tub, turning on both the cold and hot water to full blast. Louise started screaming. Gregory held her down, not letting her escape from the force of the single spigot.

"He's not dead! They deported him back to Italy to stand trial."

Louise stopped screaming. A moment later Gregory turned off the water. He reached up to the shelf above the toilet and took down a towel, which he threw on the floor by the tub. Gregory turned his back to his mother, as though ready to walk through the shattered door, and then said with authority, "Dry off and get dressed. Then come downstairs and make the girls some breakfast. We'll talk after I walk them to school. We have a lot to figure out."

As he walked down the staircase, Gregory attempted to make up his mind about which problem he should handle first: his father's arrest or his dislocated shoulder. He decided, based on the pain, that his father could wait. *There's probably nothing I can do about that situation anyway.*

*

Attorney Xuereb was not taking his mother's calls. Every time she called, his secretary said he would get right back to her. That was eight days ago. Gregory was tempted to go outside and scrounge through the overgrowth by the front door for Marino's telephone number. He thought better of it. This wasn't a phone call type of conversation and he would be better served by saving that favor for when he really needed one. Just as Gregory decided that his only option was to go to Mike Donohoe for help, he heard Maura at the door, saying Donohoe's name.

"C'è un Dio," Gregory praised aloud, a phrase acquired from his father. Although at this very moment he, himself, was not convinced of a greater power's existence.

One hour later Gregory had Mike Donohoe up to speed on the Costa family drama, excluding, for the sake of her reputation, his mother's breakdown. Although Mike had been outraged when he heard about the beating that Gregory had taken courtesy of the City of Boston, both of them agreed that a visit to the BPD was futile and would probably worsen the family's situation rather than help it. As for the story of Joseph's embezzlement, Mike's comment was filled with philosophical sympathy, "God, I hope no one ever judges me by my worst day or my worst deed," he had said. "It sounds like your father had no choice but to go along."

By the end of another hour, the two men had outlined a plan: first, find out how and where Joseph was, and second, investigate the Costas' reserve of available funds. A close third on that list involved figuring out where the family stood when it came to their own deportation. Although they were in America legally and using their own names, anything could happen now that Joseph had been deported. Gregory's mother was ready to go to the police with her hands up, turn herself in and get a one-way ticket back to Italy. Both he and Mike assured her that the Italian government had no interest in the rest of the Costa family and would certainly not finance a plane trip home. Gregory remembered his father saying that the yearly immigration quota for Italian immigrants was low. Had it not been for Joseph's money and Attorney Xuereb's clout, Gregory and his family would still be on the waiting list to come to America. *Maybe being poor wouldn't have been so bad, after all.*

The Italian Consulate was located on Atlantic Avenue, in convenient proximity to both the North End, where the highest concentration of Italians lived, and the construction site of Boston City Hall. Mike proposed that the two of them take a field trip there the next morning, assuring Gregory that he had plenty of sick time on the books and a day off from teaching wasn't going to hurt anyone. Maybe the consulate would be able to tell them something about the status of Joseph's criminal charges, since his lawyer had been no help at all.

With a plan in place, Gregory walked Mr. D. to the door, thanking him for everything.

"It's Mike now, Gregory. I'm glad to help. But just because you've been put in this position doesn't mean that you're going to drop out of school. Your education will get you farther than any help from me will. I'll do what that I can for you and your family, if you promise me that you'll stay in school."

"It's a deal - Mike. I'll see you in the morning." The two men shook hands and Mike left.

Gregory's shoulders relaxed momentarily with the relief of having a plan and a friend in Mike Donohoe. They immediately tightened up again when he thought about his next task: *how to get my mother to be of any help whatsoever?*

*

Since the night her husband left, Louise had been close to catatonic. Gregory had only gotten her to make the daily calls to Xuereb by dialing the number himself and then handing her the telephone. Her expression didn't change each time the attorney refused to come to the phone. By physical rote, she cooked meals with the food that he brought home, but she hadn't made a bed, showered or spoken more than a one-word answer for over a week. Gregory wasn't worried about her. He was pissed.

*

Out of habit, Gregory knocked on his parents' bedroom door before he entered. He needn't have bothered. He found Louise in the same position that she had returned to after cooking breakfast for the twins that morning. She was sitting on her unmade bed, staring at nothing. He walked around the bed to the window and pulled up the shades. The glare of the sunlight didn't cause his mother to blink. It was as though all the sensory mechanisms between the world and her brain had been turned off. Gregory had planned to interrogate Louise with the intensity of the Spanish Inquisition, but changed his mind when he saw the depth of her stupor. Instead, he decided to go through every drawer in his parents' bureau and look for clues as to their finances and stability. Louise didn't even flinch when Gregory emptied the first drawer onto the bed beside her.

After rifling through his mother's brassieres and undergarments, Gregory found a small, white satin purse that he remembered seeing in his parents' wedding pictures. In it were all their passports and birth certificates. Tucked inside his father's passport was his most recent paycheck and an envelope filled with seven hundred dollars. *How long does seven hundred dollars last for a family of four?* Gregory mentally calculated how much he had spent this week in groceries and lunch money for the girls. They were going to have to start bringing their lunches to school.

There was nothing notable in the next two drawers, just clothing and some packets of family photos. Wanting to make certain there wasn't anything important wedged between the pictures, Gregory dumped the packets onto the bed and fanned through them, spreading them out evenly across the bed sheets. Something caught his eye. It was a small black-and-white photograph of a tiny baby in a hospital incubator. The baby looked to be peacefully sleeping and perfect, wrapped tightly in a white blanket with pastel stripes. Without needing to, he turned the photo over to look at the date on the back: July, 1953.

Suddenly the loss of baby Louie was too much to bear. Clutching the picture to his chest, Gregory quietly melted down the side of the bed and onto the worn black-and-white vinyl tiles of his parents' bedroom floor. He curled into a ball on his undamaged left side. When the torrent of sobs began, Gregory jammed his fist into his mouth so that his sisters, dutifully doing their homework at the kitchen table below him, would not hear. He decided that now was as good a time as any to mourn the absence of a brother who he had never even met.

1985

QUINCY, MASSACHUSETTS

DANNY HAD BEEN one hundred percent right and one hundred percent wrong about the ambulance business. On the minus side, it had been every bit the hassle that he knew it was going to be. Getting contracts, wading through insurance claims, hiring staff, firing staff; dealing with the state regulations and government bureaucracy had all gone exactly as he had anticipated. It was like a well-choreographed disaster movie where the world somehow survives. He hadn't been on the front line during most of the start-up mayhem and he had still felt the stress and pressure of listening to all of it secondhand from his wife and the man who had now become her best friend, Dr. Ron Watters. *They're like the dynamic duo*. Both of them were obsessed with challenges. "Bring it on!" had become their favorite saying.

On the plus side, the business became relatively successful overnight. It appeared that most of the health care facilities in the area were getting tired of dealing with Anderson Ambulance due to the regime change when the younger Anderson took over the company. The arrogant, new owner made no secret of his self-important notion that Anderson Ambulance was the only game in town. The timing for Accelerated Ambulance couldn't have been better. By the time that Danny's nine hundred thousand dollar settlement came in (which turned into seven hundred thousand after paying Seamus and the medical experts), the little business was one year old and chugging along with all of its permits in place. As president of the company, Danny was the one to officially decide how much of that insurance money was going into the business. The slow-growth model, which Ron and Teres had originally presented, was thrown out the window and replaced with a "seize the day" version that gave Danny a constant sense of anxiety. After speaking to a financial consultant, Martha and Bemus Bertakis' to be exact, Danny opted to put together an investment portfolio of two hundred thousand dollars, leaving half a million for the business. For a man who had come from generations of people working paycheck to paycheck, having this much money to deal with was terrifying. His wife, on the other hand, seemed to know exactly what to do with the money. With the business now underway, Teres began to nag her husband into building a house.

It wasn't that Danny wanted to live in the little three-bedroom Wallace Street home for the rest of his life, *or maybe I do*. It was that from his perspective the Muldaurs already had a pretty full plate. Six months after the "trash truck incident," as Teres now referred to it, Danny had returned to work at Quincy City Hospital. He had refused to leave his job, even once the business of rescuing and transporting people was fully underway. Danny promised his wife that he would help out as much as he could, but he was clearly happy to stay out of the day-to-day running of the company. It was a busy life. Some weeks he and Teres couldn't find the time to share a meal together, both of them going in opposite directions. Adding architects, building permits and searching for a lot of land to their already burdened lives seemed stupid in Danny's opinion. They had just gone through that with the new location for the business.

A new house could wait.

*

"You thought that opening an ambulance company was stupid, too!" Teres had again twisted Danny's words. "And look what we have now, Daniello, a thriving business, money in the bank." Danny had wanted to remind his wife that it was his broken body that put A.A. (as he referred to their business because it was going to drive them to drink) on the map and gave them money in a bank account. He didn't think that it was wise to use more of that money for a down payment on land. *I'm fifty-two for God's sake! So much for the idea of early retirement.* But there was no stopping his wife. Before he had time to make a better case against it, she had found a secluded two-acre lot of land in the seaside town of Scituate.

*

Everything about the town of Scituate appealed to Teres. She had discovered it by accident on one of her "contract" days. Every Tuesday, no matter what, Teres went on a carefully planned excursion in search of new contracts for A.A. This had become such a successful system that she didn't dare stop once the company was up and running to optimal capacity. She just modified her weekly trips to include checking up on the accounts that were already in place. Everyone at Accelerated knew that Mrs. Muldaur was on the road on Tuesdays and although it was Danny's designated day in the office, most of the staff's questions waited until "Mrs. M" was around. It didn't take anybody long to realize that Danny generally deferred to his wife.

One warm Tuesday in May, Teres' route took her south, from a small rehab facility in Quincy to Jordan Hospital in Plymouth. She had made an appointment with the director of Jordan's Outpatient Services for four o'clock in the afternoon. It was a beautiful day. After she snagged the business at the little rehabilitation facility (which primarily consisted of half-mile patient transports between Quincy City Hospital and the rehab), she still had three hours to kill, so she decided to drive along the water from Quincy to Plymouth.

Driving for the fun of it was Danny's thing, not hers. Teres actually had to concentrate on not getting on the major highway. Instead, she followed Route 3A into Hingham and searched for the coast, taking a left toward the water at every opportunity. Eventually, she found herself on Atlantic Avenue in Cohasset, which led right to the parking lot of Little Harbor. The scene before her was like something from a postcard. She jumped out of her car, overwhelmed by the quaintness and beauty of the area. For a woman who had grown up on one of the most gorgeous coasts in the world, Teres felt as though she were seeing the water through different eyes. *I could live in a place like this.*

This was the first time since her marriage to Danny that she truly wanted much more than what she had. Her desire to own an ambulance company had been born of her need to have a fulfilling project, with all of its obstacles and challenges. It was not a move designed to give her a more pampered existence. But looking at the waterfront homes surrounding the harbor made her jealous. Somebody lived in these homes. Somebody was having a life where they walked out their door, across their expansive, manicured backyard and down to the dock where their twenty-five-foot O'Day sailboat was tied up, just waiting to give them an afternoon of blissful leisure. She and Danny could have this if they wanted to. But Teres knew, without even talking to Danny, that of the two of them, only she would want a life such as this. *A house with a dock?* Danny would shoot himself over the cost, the insurance, liability and maintenance. He would never go for a house on the water. He would insist that their home was fine, they could put in a pool.

But the Wallace Street house wasn't just small, it was in serious need of updating: a new kitchen, landscaping, they both wanted a garage. Since the place needed so much work and Danny dreaded living though renovations, maybe she could get him excited about building a new house. They could find a neighborhood that was close to the water and away from the city. If she found the perfect piece of land, maybe Danny would fall in love with it enough to live through a little more upheaval.

Teres jumped back into her car, excited about her plan. She continued to follow the coastline, darting in and out of areas that looked interesting. When she hit the town of Scituate, things became quieter, more off-season. The streets were a little narrower. Surfside Road turned into Ocean Drive which became Rebecca Road. Teres could see a lighthouse in the distance. Most of the stilted houses along the water were just beginning to show signs of opening for the summer. All of a sudden she realized she was in some kind of Irish community. Every home had a quarterboard sign on the front with either the owner's name or a quirky title for the house. *They are all Irish!* There was Murphy, O'Malley,

O'Shea and Connolly along with Sweeney, Morgan and O'Leary. *Danny would love this place!*

Sometimes her husband was a bit more Irish than at other times. Danny had told her that he occasionally elevated his Irish in self-defense to counteract her intense Greekness, and although he envied the Giannopoulos family's rich sense of history, it made him feel like an orphan. One time he made scones for Teres from a recipe he told her was part of a family tradition. She later found the recipe earmarked from a Good Housekeeping magazine she had bought at the store a couple of months earlier. It was obvious to Teres that Danny was desperate for family ties. But with his height, reddish brown hair, now gone mostly gray, and ruddy complexion, he was never going to pass for a Giannopoulos. She was married to an Irishman. *What if I could get my Irishman to join a clan like this one?*

Teres wound around the bend and pulled into the parking lot in front of the Scituate Lighthouse. She exited the car, nearly getting caught in the door when the wind whipped it shut. She wished she had been dressed for exploring. The jetty to the right of the lighthouse looked like an inviting place to walk had she not been wearing heels. Teres chose to stick to the crushed seashell pathway leading to the lighthouse. On her way, she stopped to read the plaque describing the lighthouse's history:

"1636   1976
OLD SCITUATE LIGHTHOUSE
DURING THE YEAR 1810 THE U.S.
CONGRESS VOTED 4000 TO BUILD A
LIGHTHOUSE AT SCITUATE HARBOR.
DURING THE WAR OF 1812 ABIGAIL AND
REBECCA BATES YOUNG DAUGHTERS OF
THE LIGHTHOUSE KEEPER PREVENTED
A BRITISH NAVAL FORCE FROM SACKING
THE TOWN BY PLAYING A FIFE AND

BEATING A DRUM. THEY HAVE GONE
DOWN IN HISTORY AS "THE ARMY OF
TWO" AND THEIR COURAGEOUS ACT
HAS BEEN RECORDED IN MANY
TEXTBOOKS AND STORY BOOKS.

SCITUATE HISTORICAL SOCIETY"

What a great story: two women fend off the entire British invasion by playing music that makes the enemy think the militia is coming! The story reminded Teres of the ancient Greek tale of Hydna of Scione, who swam ten miles through stormy seas to cut the anchors of the Persian naval fleet, causing them to float adrift and smash into each other rather than attack Greece.

After exploring the area around the lighthouse, Teres returned to her car to check out the rest of the town. She kept to the coast, following Lighthouse Road into what appeared to be a more village-like center of Scituate along the harbor - which was serene and beautiful. Deciding that she was starved, Teres parked along the main street in search of a bite to eat. Just past the ramp going down to the boat slips, she found a sandwich shop with outdoor benches facing the water. She ducked inside.

The woman behind the counter chatted amicably while preparing her tuna sandwich. She told Teres about all the little businesses in the area and the differences between newcomers, longtime summer residents and year-rounders.

"Do you know if there are any buildable lots around here?" Teres asked the woman.

"Yup. There are still lots of neighborhoods on the outskirts where you could build a house, not much here by the water. Unless you want to buy an old place, tear it down and then spend the next two years, and a wheelbarrow full of money, dealing with the historical society to get your permits - or the hysterical society, as my husband calls them."

"Which direction would you go to look from here?" Teres' interest hadn't waned at all in spite of the woman's insinuation that the Scituate Historical Society was a force to be reckoned with. *I have cut my teeth on the Massachusetts State Licensing Board! You cannot scare me.*

"Keep following Front Street and you'll run into First Parish. Go left or right from there," said the woman, as she packed up the sandwich and the four orange cranberry scones that Teres would later use to sweeten the conversation with Danny. She was too worked up about the prospect of a new house to sit by the water and enjoy the day. She'd eat in the car. Teres grabbed a handful of napkins. She'd need them if she planned on being presentable for her meeting at Jordan Hospital, between eating and driving and looking down side streets. She practically trotted to the car, anxious to begin her search.

*

The sandwich was good. Somehow that added another checkmark to the plus column for living in Scituate. For the middle of a Tuesday there was no traffic. But this was the beginning of May and Teres knew the traffic would change dramatically after Memorial Day. That fact triggered a deadline, *and I love deadlines.* She needed to get Danny to see the area before it became a madhouse. She was used to her husband's first response to her ideas as being one of total reluctance, if not downright refusal. If she wanted this to happen, she had to present it as a totally hassle-free possibility. Teres felt like a defense attorney any time she came to Danny with a plan. She had to have her case completely researched with her facts verified or he shredded her vision. She could understand her husband's reluctance, but she was only thirty-two years old and not done with the prospect of exciting decisions and changes. Maybe Danny was ready to start planning for retirement, but not her. *I'll present this as our retirement home!* Teres' mind was busy building her case when she hit the crossroads of Front, First Parish and Kent Street. She halted at the stop sign, looked up and saw the first of two amazing things:

Directly in front of her, on the grassy area across the street, was a statue of the Virgin Mary carrying Baby Jesus. It wasn't a typical rendition of the Madonna. Its gloriousness was in its straightforwardness. Mary stood tall and solemn on a cube of granite that surrounded an embedded brass plaque depicting the names of the statue's donors. Her eyes were downcast and a simple robe covered her head and shoulders. An expression of pure maternal rapture was frozen in time upon her perfectly chiseled face. But the Infant Jesus was another story. He was so vividly real. He was balanced in his mother's arms precariously, suggesting he might at any moment struggle from them in order to get down and play. His fat little hand was reaching up to his mother's barely visible hair as though he wanted to yank on it, the way any child would. Teres had seen a million statues of *Theotokos*, the bearer of God. There was something that moved her differently about this one. She sat at the stop sign, staring at Mary and her child, who were permanent front-lawn residents of a simple stone and white church.

The church was called Saint Mary of the Nativity, a Catholic church. "Yes, Catholic," Teres acknowledged out loud, "with such an Irish population." She turned the steering wheel to take a right onto First Parish Road and saw the second amazing thing, a small sign:

Lot for Sale by Owner

Two Acres

The sign was low to the ground on a wooden stick, placed just to the right of the church. Teres pulled into the parking area and wrote down the telephone number listed at the bottom of the sign. There was nothing to give a clue as to the property's location. Surely it wasn't the church. The sign was homemade with black, stick-on letters evenly spaced on a piece of white-painted plywood. She looked around to see if she could find anything else to indicate where this land might be. There was nothing. She decided that instead of waiting until she returned to the office to call, she'd go inside the church and see if anyone had information about the land.

*

Jerome Reid was busy cleaning the woodwork of the church pews with Old English furniture polish. Because the wood was a medium stained oak and he liked the richness of a slightly deeper finish, Mr. Reid would have preferred to use the darker version of Old English. He also liked the smell better. But Memorial Day was approaching and the parishioners would soon be wearing white. There was no point in tempting fate with the possibility of an oily stain ending up on the back of one of those manly blazers with the big shoulder pads that women were so fond of wearing these days. *Plain ugly style, if you ask me. Women should look like women.*

Jerome loved this church. There was always something to clean. For a simple structure, it was filled with interesting nooks and crannies that collected their fair share of dust and debris. Kids were known for putting anything from cracker crumbs to boogers inside the hymnbooks and missalette holders. All of it had to be dug out and readied for the next batch of little monsters, whose parents would give them whatever they wanted if it kept them quiet during Mass. He was a caretaker crew of one and he didn't punch a time clock. This meant he could come and go any time that he pleased, which also meant that he could escape to this sanctuary when things got too confusing at home, which was often.

Jerome knew his wife had all she could handle with the care of their daughter, Nancy. She had been born to them rather late in their marriage. The doctor had taken one look at her and announced that although it was a shame, at least their baby girl was always going to be their baby girl. They had made a life out of taking care of this less-than-perfect gift from God, but sometimes it got to be too much for Jerome. He hated to add to his wife's burden with his own ill temper. So whenever he felt his anger and dissatisfaction with life coming on, he'd walk the short distance between their house and the church and do a little cleaning until he felt like he could go back home and do justice to his blessings from God. The church was always spotless. Reid didn't get paid much, but he didn't care. His family had owned most of the property on Kent Street behind the church. Every time he felt the financial pinch, he would call his engineer and have him slice off another conforming ANR lot. These were the best in his mind because Approval Not Required meant no fighting with the town board or asking for favors. The last one had kept him for quite a while, maybe ten years. But, it was time to sell off another lot. Jerome thanked the Lord that his father had been a miser when it came to holding onto property.

The engineering firm he used had formulated a plan to maximize the property. Most of the parcels were created using a pork chop design, which called for the bulk of the lot to be set deep into the property to provide privacy, thereby making it more appealing and worth more money. Then a long twenty-foot-wide strip connected the inner piece to the road, making the lot buildable and not land-locked. Jerome always thought the layout looked more like flags than pork chops. *I don't care what they call them, as long as they sell when I need them to.* Just yesterday, Jerome had pulled the sign from last decade's sale out of the church cellar and plunked it into the ground. Now this woman was here asking about it. *Praise God, for his timely answer to some of my prayers.*

*

"Hello?" Because of her eyes' reluctant adjustment to the darkness, Teres wasn't certain that she had actually seen a person perched between those first two rows of the church. The man stood up, dust rag and oil in hand.

"Yes? What can I help you with? Father Monroe is at the rectory, if that's who you're looking for." The man pointed his hand toward his right.

"Well, no. I am wondering if you know anything about the land that is for sale, outside." Teres felt ridiculous having added the word "outside." *Where else would land be?* The man stared at her, as though he either didn't know what she was talking about or he was sizing her up. It made her uncomfortable. She turned to leave. "It's okay. I will call the number on the sign. I am sorry to bother you."

"Wait." The man moved to the aisle, where he turned and genuflected before the altar.

Well, that must get tiresome. Teres mentally estimated the number of times this man must have bowed while polishing the wooden benches.

"It's my land," the man said. "Are you looking to buy it?"

Teres felt flustered by the oddness of this man. She discarded the long conversation that she had been planning about relocating to an area like Scituate and simply said, "Yes." He looked at her for a moment longer and then nodded his head.

"Good. Do you want to see it now?"

*

Teres was glad she kept her rubber boots and raincoat in the trunk of her car. Her full, lightweight floral skirt would have been shredded in these woods. As it was, her classic London Fog raincoat was taking a beating.

Jerome Reid had explained the price and particulars to her when he handed her a copy of the plot plan. He had assured her that it was a good, fair price and not open for negotiation, adding that land in Scituate goes fast. With a brief, "Let's go," Mr. Reid began walking south on Kent Street and quickly darted into the woods, negotiating an access through a small overgrown trail. Teres had followed obediently behind the man, acutely aware that she was going into a densely wooded area to a lot that the owner had described as "secluded and private." *What am I thinking? Danny would kill me if he knew.*

"This land has been in my family for three generations," The man said, without turning around to look at her. "You'd have to pay the fee to have it perked, but nothing in this area ever fails a perk test." Teres wondered what a perk test was as she tried to disengage herself from a vicious strand of briars without destroying a brand new pair of nude pantyhose. They hiked for about ten minutes, weaving in and out of strands of trees and bushes, then came to a stone wall outlining an opening. As they walked through it, everything changed. No longer were they in a thicket of indistinguishable vegetation. They were standing in a patch of ground made up of worn, semi-degraded pine needles and leaves. The clearing was surrounded by tall oak and pine trees, along with gigantic rhododendron bushes, just beginning to bloom. It was like stumbling upon a magical forest.

"We used to camp out here as kids. Out of habit, I've kept this part of it cleared out," Jerome Reid stated, without a hint of nostalgia in his voice. "My father built the stone wall. He always talked about building a house here, but never got around to it."

"It's beautiful!" Teres couldn't contain her excitement. Since the price was not to be dickered with, keeping a poker face seemed unnecessary.

"There's more to walk. We can come out again this weekend when your husband's off work. It's a lot of money, he'll need the details."

The man's assumption that Teres was unable to absorb information, being all dressed up and looking for ways to spend her hard-working husband's money, annoyed her; especially since she had never mentioned a husband to this man. Lately there had been a number of situations where Teres had been the one to ask the question, and the man (or woman) looked above her head and answered Danny. It was infuriating. She was tired of fighting her way through to the point where she was taken seriously. Danny never had this problem. He just had to be tall and male in order for people to assume he knew what he was doing.

"My husband will love anything that I love." *Well, that just made it worse. Now he thinks that I am so pampered that my husband will give me anything I want.* "What I mean to say is that I do not need my husband's permission to purchase a piece of land. He trusts my judgment." *Shut up, Teressa Muldaur! Of course you need Danny's permission to buy a piece of land!*

"Okay, Ma'am. But I would be happy to show him the property, just the same. I know that if my wife..."

"Mr. Reid," Teres interrupted with authority, "After I research this parcel and make certain that it is right for our needs, I will purchase it - with cash."

"Alrighty then, Mrs...."

"Muldaur, Teressa Muldaur." And then they shook on it.

*

"Jesus Christ! Are you outta your mind!" Danny wasn't even attempting to tone down either his anger or the volume of that anger, in spite of the fact that they were having this discussion in the office, beside an open bay of ambulances and staff. Teres walked around the desk and shut the door.

"Really Danny? This is your response to my news? To make us look like asses in front of Doug and Roger? Nobody else needs to hear how mad you are at me for making your life better." Teres' voice was dangerously controlled.

Danny wanted to just throw his hands up in the air and say, "Fine. You win. Do whatever you want with our lives, our money, our time. Just tell me where and when to show up to sign the latest round of paperwork." But he didn't say those words. Instead he tried to reason with her from the perspective of being pathetically in need of quality time with her, which was true.

"Teres, honey, we are just beginning to get the business to run a bit on its own. We should take a breath, enjoy our success a little before we begin the next big venture. Building a house is not easy. There are decisions, and..."

"I can make all of the decisions. I like planning things and seeing them come out to be my vision."

"I know. But what about the time we were planning to spend together? Why don't you plan that? It's been three years since we saw the family in Greece and weren't we gonna take that cruise to Bermuda at the end of the summer? How're we gonna do all that while we build a house?" These tactics never worked, but Danny had to try something. "I feel like we never have time alone anymore. Or when we do, we're both too tired to do anything."

"Danny, it is just this last thing. Once the house is built we will live in it for the rest of our lives. If you only saw the land and the harbor and the no traffic." Teres may have been speaking calmly, but Danny knew she was getting all wound up because her accent was getting thicker. If the past was any indication, he guessed that she would blow any minute. So he decided to give up on this tactic and say what he really thought.

"You're killing me. And I mean really killing me. I just need some fucking rest, Teres. I'm fifty-two years old and we've been through a lot. When is this gonna get easier? I don't wanna be in my fucking grave by the time I get a little peace." Danny may as well have hand-picked all the worst words and catchphrases. He knew before she started yelling that he had just started a war.

"I am killing you? This is what you say to me? I have spent every minute since the day I met you worrying about you, and your health, and your happiness! My dream of a beautiful place to live, for you to retire someday, out of the city, away from the neighborhood full of kids and noise that you say you hate? This is how I am killing you? Fuck you, Daniel Muldaur. Fuck you and the horse you rode in on!"

Jesus, he hated her sometimes, with her passion and her logic and the foul language that she used so sparingly that when she did, he knew she meant

193

it. And why, for the love of God, did her anger always trump his. When Teres went crazy, it never made him angrier. Instead, it made him feel bad, probably because he knew what it took to get her to that state. She really did want a nice life for them. Hell, she had already given him more happy moments than he had ever felt the right to hope for. *Why am I such an asshole? I say no to every good thing my wife wants to do for us.* She was going to win anyway, so he might as well make it worth his while.

"It was a Karmann Ghia," Danny said, with a hint of amusement that could have gone either way.

"Huh?" Teres said. She looked confused, like she didn't know what had just come out of her angry mouth.

"It was a Karmann Ghia that I used to ride into your life, not a horse."

"Sorry, Danny. I am a bitch."

"I know. Let's both take the day off tomorrow and spend it checking out Scituate. I know a great little place on the water to have steamers and a drink," Danny suggested, happily dispelling the notion that his wife knew everything about him. The puzzled look on her face told him that he had hit his mark.

"When was the last time you were in Scituate?"

"None of your business, Teres," he replied with fake seriousness. "You think that you know where I'm at every minute of the day? Well, I've got a life, too." Danny grabbed his wife and pulled her down onto his lap so that she could feel the telltale sign of how easily he was giving in. This wouldn't be the first time they had used the office for a little romance. He decided that he better wait until the guys left the building, since make-up sex was usually louder than everyday sex. And this was not only going to be make-up sex, it was going to be *I'm-giving-you-everything-you-want* sex. Just thinking about it put a smile on Danny's face.

His grin deepened when he thought of how mad she would be to find out that his secret Scituate trips were just his weekly golf outings with Ron to the Scituate Country Club, a beautiful nine-hole course on the water located just four minutes away from Saint Mary of the Nativity Church and what would apparently be the Muldaurs' future address. Danny busied himself with the taste of his wife's deliciously foul mouth. *It looks like we're in it together again.*

1992

SCITUATE, MASSACHUSETTS

TERES HAD BEEN gone for twenty minutes. The likelihood of her returning for something she had forgotten was pretty low at this point. Danny had told his wife that he wasn't feeling great and that he was going to hang around the house for a little while to see if his stomach settled down before heading into the office. She had kissed him on the top of the head and told him that he should probably just take the day off. She wasn't planning a full Tuesday on the road, only a short run to Mass General and then she'd be in the office all day. Danny knew that her concern for him was genuine. She had given him a list of things that he could eat to settle his stomach and then left the jar of lemon Brioschi on the counter.

Brioschi was his wife's favorite antacid. It was produced in Italy and meant to be taken mixed with water. But, before you mixed it, it looked like little pieces of lemony styrofoam. And just like the Italians, Teres used it for everything: indigestion, upset stomachs, canker sores. She even added some to her pasta sauces in order to reduce the acid. He had been shocked the first time he saw her mix it into the tomato paste and olive oil in the bottom of her large stock pan. But now he used it for everything, too.

Looking over at the jar, Danny wished that he had come out to the kitchen in search of the Brioschi last night, instead of going through the baskets in the bathroom closet. He decided he had better take his wife's advice and have a big dose of Italian antacid before beginning the distasteful job of snooping around her stuff.

Danny wasn't the kind of guy to get to the bottom of anything. Most of the dilemmas in his life hadn't required that kind of due diligence. They normally smoothed themselves out using his time-proven method of neglect and disregard. Any problem that really required action was usually left up to his wife to investigate. He found if he ignored the problem it would not only go away,

196

but would sometimes improve dramatically under his wife's handling. That wasn't going to happen this time. He was going to search the house and get answers to this pregnancy test thing. *If I had any guts, I would just ask her.* Danny knew that it wasn't lack of courage that had kept him from just confronting Teres this morning. It was the possibility of pushing her into saying something she wasn't ready to say, something that might signal the end of their life together. That didn't take guts. It took resignation.

*

He had methodically torn the house apart and found nothing. Everything was so perfectly normal that Danny could almost convince himself that he hadn't found a box of pregnancy tests in his bathroom closet, except for the fact that he had inspected the box twice when he searched the whole bathroom for clues.

There were a variety of stories he had been telling himself for the last eight hours. Maybe the test belonged to one of the girls at work. Why then would Teres have it here at the house? Maybe his sister-in-law, Irene, had taken a pregnancy test when she, Nicky and the girls had come to visit last summer. Although their girls were already nine and ten, Nicky continually joked about trying again for a boy. Even that plausible explanation didn't ring true for Danny.

Teres had been acting strangely. She was moody and quiet. And for a woman who normally leapt out of bed at the crack of dawn to go running or get the day started, she had been sleeping in a lot and waking up tired. But the biggest tell-tale sign was that she had stopped drinking wine.

Every Christmas, Teres' father loaded up their small wine cellar with cases of wine from his favorite vineyard. For the past month or so, Teres hadn't opened even one bottle of her favorite Xinomavro Wedding Wine. She said she was giving up wine for a while because it was making her gain weight. Danny may have bought that as an excuse for Teres not drinking at home, but she also declined the champagne toast at Martha's annual New Year's Eve bash. Even Danny, on all his alcohol-forbidding medication, had toasted the New Year (and then snuck a couple of bottles of Heineken into his evening). He wasn't stupid. His wife was pregnant. By whom and how far along were the questions.

Danny sat on the edge of their king-sized bed. He put his face into his palms and tried to decide what his next move should be. He had nothing. There was no next move for him, only for her. This was her situation, not theirs; hers and whoever the hell she was fooling around with. *Oh God! My wife doesn't fool around,* and he meant that in every sense of the word. *My wife is serious, intense, religious for Chrissake! Teressa Giannopoulos Muldaur doesn't fool around. I can barely get her to crack a smile sometimes, let alone fool around.* Danny's mind fought against the thought of his wife being with another man. But the evidence was pointing otherwise. He looked up from his hands. Right in front of him, on his wife's dresser, was her creamy white, mother-of-pearl jewelry box. Everything important to her in this world was in that box. He knew it was locked with the little 18-carat gold key that she wore on a chain around her neck.

Danny picked up the box and checked the lock. It was simple. He could break it open in a minute's time. He already felt like a dirty criminal with all this subterfuge. But breaking open Teres' perfect shell box, a gift from her father on the day of their wedding, would put the emotions Danny was feeling into a new category of disgusting. He decided whatever was in there could remain a mystery. Thinking about violating her jewelry box made Danny reach a decision about what he would do from here: he would wait and do nothing. Pregnancy is a dilemma that won't take forever to resolve. In the meantime, Danny would pretend that everything was fine. He would do this because no one in his life, not his parents nor his friends, had ever been as good to him or shown him the kind of love that Teres had.

Danny stared at the box full of all the memories that his wife held sacred, and promised himself that he would treat her with the love and respect that she deserved. He owed her that much. He suspected that keeping that promise would most likely require a full case of Brioschi.

1992

BOSTON, MASSACHUSETTS

DR. ABEL AARON'S office was sterile-looking, sophisticated and modern, with chairs that were not particularly comfortable; exactly the type of decor that Teres hated. The receptionist had given her a stack of medical history forms to fill out before seeing the doctor. She was struggling through it. Every question that was directed toward the baby's father caused Teres, out of habit, to begin writing answers that pertained to Danny: *Have you ever had a miscarriage? If so, how many? Have you ever experienced infertility? If so, has your husband had a sperm analysis in the past two years?* The family history portion of the questionnaire was easier since she didn't know much about either man's family's health history. *Oh, dear God. What a mess I'm in!* How do you write down emergency contact information when you are having a baby by a man who is not your husband? She decided to put Martha Bertakis' name and number on that line.

A dozen times Teres had picked up the phone to call Martha, but then didn't dial the number. If Martha knew about the baby it would make it real, as if being at the most prestigious OB-GYN office in Boston weren't making it real enough. Besides, Martha had her hands full planning her daughter-in-law's baby shower. At thirty-five years of age, Bemus Jr. was finally making his mother a grandmother. Teres' announcement would certainly upstage that joyous news. She could never do that to her best friend. The shower will be one more event that Teres would have to get through with a lie on the tip of her tongue. The thought of it brought her mind to Danny's birthday party. Instead of causing her to cringe, Teres reflexively began to go through the celebration details in her head, making certain she had everything covered: *Guestlist? Check. Food? Check. Pregnant adulterous wife? Check.*

"Ms. Giannopoulos?" The nurse's voice breaking into Teres' thoughts was a mixed blessing. She jumped at the sound of her maiden name. Hearing it said out loud made her feel like an imposter. Teres got up and followed the nurse into a small room. After taking her blood pressure and getting her weight, she handed Teres a hospital gown and began walking down the hallway, expecting Teres to follow. "I'm going to go over some of this paperwork while you get changed. It opens in the front and there are hangers on the back of the door for your clothes."

The nurse opened the examining room door to let Teres enter and there sat Gregory, in a chair beside the exam table. He stood as she entered. His smile made Teres want to slap him. She politely waited for the nurse to close the door behind them before she raged at him.

"What are you doing here? I told you that I wanted to do this alone! You have no right to disobey my wishes!" Teres began to cry. "Why are you doing this to me, Gregory? I thought that we made a deal, that you would not push at me. *This* is pushing."

Gregory's look wasn't apologetic. "I had a break in my schedule. I knew you'd be here and there'd be medical questions you wouldn't know the answers to." The logic of his words were both killing and satisfying Teres. "I don't have to stay for the whole appointment, just the history... and maybe hear the baby's heartbeat?"

"That *is* the entire appointment! Fine. I don't want you here when they do the internal exam. And leave the room while I change into this johnny."

"Seriously?"

Teres' look told him not to press his luck. He opened the door and stepped out to stand in the hall. While she was changing, she heard Gregory speaking in the corridor. It appeared that he was talking to the doctor. Teres couldn't hear Dr. Aarons, but she could make out every word that Gregory said:

"Abe! Good to see you. And thanks for seeing Teressa, I know you're not taking on new patients. Yeah, I don't know why I'm waiting out here either. She kicked me out. You know how women are. She's probably ready..."

201

The knock on the door made Teres scramble to finish putting on the robe. She was going to kill Gregory. The reasons for his death were mounting up quickly.

"Ms. Giannopoulos, I'm Abel Aarons." Teres reached out to shake the doctor's hand, exposing a breast in the process. Dr. Aarons appeared not to see. "How are you doing today?"

"I am... nervous and good," Teres replied without one glance toward Gregory.

"All right, then. Gregory tells me that you are almost twelve weeks along with your first baby. Congratulations." Gregory's face lit up behind Dr. Aarons' head. Teres couldn't help smiling.

"Yes. It is my first baby and I am excited... and a little scared," Teres admitted. She couldn't decide at this point if having Gregory in the room was comforting or annoying until Gregory piped in:

"It's my first baby, too!"

Teres went with annoying.

"Great. Let's examine you and make certain you're on track with your dates and that everything looks normal," Dr. Aarons said, pushing a button on the counter to alert the nurse to come in.

The next thing she knew, she was having an internal examination with Gregory standing over her asking questions. To give him his due, his questions weren't about the process being performed in front of him. They were break-the-ice kind of questions, like "How are things going in the new office?" and "Have you been down to that golf course in New Seabury?" All asked while Dr. Aarons fished around inside of her with his eyes closed like he was trying to create a Braille map in his mind.

"Everything looks good."

How would you know, you had your eyes closed the whole time, Teres thought, but said, "Thank goodness. Do you think that I am eleven and a half weeks along?"

"You might be a little farther than that, more like twelve or thirteen weeks along, judging by the size of your uterus."

"Or maybe we're having twins." Gregory said, excitedly. "My sisters are twins."

Gregory has twin sisters? How could she not know this basic fact about a man she had been seeing for months, a man who was going to be the father of this baby (or babies) that she was carrying. Suddenly, the room got small. Everyone was standing too close to the table that she was lying on in her barely-dressed state. Teres could feel the panic rising in her chest. She had to sit up. She pulled her feet out of the stirrups with just one thought in her head, *Why isn't Danny here?*

*

When she began to hyperventilate, the doctor had insisted that everyone clear the room. That included Gregory, who was clearly furious, but left without arguing.

"Ms. Giannopoulos, are you okay?" Dr. Aarons asked, concern showing in his voice.

"No," said Teres through gasps and sobs. "I am not okay. I am not Ms. Giannopoulos. I am Mrs. Muldaur and my husband is not the father of this baby." Dr. Aarons didn't look surprised, he looked sympathetic. Teres wondered if Gregory had already told him the truth.

"Do you take something for your anxiety?" he asked.

Anxiety isn't my problem. "No. I have never had these attacks until this baby, this affair," She realized how stupid that sounded, as though she had given birth to many babies and had multiple affairs.

"Do you feel threatened?"

Teres pondered the question for a moment. *No.* She didn't think she felt threatened, harassed maybe, pressured for sure, but not threatened. "No."

"Do you want to terminate your pregnancy? You don't need Dr. Costa's permission to do so," Dr. Aarons said gently.

"I have wanted a baby, always. My husband is unable to father a child and years ago we dismissed the idea of a sperm donor... I want this baby."

Dr. Aarons reached into a drawer and pulled out a business card. He took a pen from his front pocket and wrote a telephone number on the card. "This is a support group for women. The number I wrote on the back is my home telephone number. Your safety and health are my first concern. If you feel threatened in any way, by either your husband or this relationship, you can call this number. My wife, Marion, works for this organization and will get you help. Are you living with your husband?"

"Yes, but Danny would never hurt me," Teres knew she sounded like every woman who proclaimed that her husband would never hit her. But in this case it was true. Danny would kill himself before he struck her. More tears filled her eyes at the thought. She took a slow, deep breath to stop their fall. "Truly, I am fine."

"Are you ready to let them in so we can get a good listen to the baby's heartbeat?"

Teres nodded her head "yes" and Dr. Aarons pushed the magic button again, letting everyone know that it was safe to enter. *The hysterical woman is going to be fine*, Teres thought, unsure if this were true.

*

The baby's heartbeat was strong, steady and reassuringly singular. After going over all their medical history, Dr. Aarons suggested that mutual bloodwork might be the way to go if they wanted to better cover their bases. There were two genetic diseases that were carried by both Greeks and Italians, but Dr. Aarons was only concerned with one of them: Thalassemia, or Mediterranean Anemia. He worried, based on what Gregory recalled about his brother, that this disorder might have been the cause behind the infant's death (another sibling of which Teres had been unaware). A simple blood test would show conclusively if Teres and Gregory were carriers for the genetic anomaly that causes Thalassemia.

"Are you sure you won't have an amniocentesis?" Gregory asked Teres for the third time in ten minutes. Abel Aarons responded for her.

"Greg, she said no. And I already told you, the maternal serum alpha-fetoprotein test will give us a clear enough indication of whether or not your child has Down's syndrome. If the numbers look suspicious, we do further testing. But the AFP has to be done around seventeen weeks, so we should get an ultrasound as soon as we can to determine exactly how far along Mrs. … Teressa is."

"How soon?" Gregory asked, in his typically persistent manner. Teres felt no such urgency for the testing. Having heard the baby's heartbeat and knowing she now had an advocate in Dr. Aarons, she felt calmer, more relaxed. She could almost view Gregory's annoying traits as those of a worried father-to-be.

"Will you tell your secretary to call Gregory with the appointment?" Teres quipped. "I am certain his uterus will work just fine as a stand-in." Abel laughed. Gregory didn't.

"Teressa, let me see if they can get you in for an ultrasound today if you have time."

"Yes, I have time." She looked at Gregory "Do you have time?"

"I cleared my entire afternoon," he said. Teres wanted to slap him. Gregory wasn't even trying to hide the fact that his plan all along had been to be here for her appointment and then take her back to his apartment. He must have called Aaron's office to find out the date and time the minute she told him that she had made an appointment. And just like that, she was back to hating him for being the controlling ass that he was.

*

Teres and Gregory's affair had been missing a few pieces vital to most love affairs. One of them was pillow talk. Since Gregory had never been a fan of post-sex conversation (he correctly suspected that verbal intimacy furthered relationships in a manner that was not in his best interest), he wasn't good at it. Teres, on the other hand, always felt so guilty after having sex with Gregory that she inevitably picked a fight over the first thing that popped into her head. Her fight topics had included: her having to leave and him wanting more sex, him having to leave when she had told Danny a lie in order to have more time together, the presidential race between Clinton and Bush, and the dissolution of the Soviet Union. Having enough issues to fight about was not a problem for Teres and Gregory. Having something other than sex to unite them as a couple *was* a problem, right up until the moment they saw their baby on the grainy black-and- white ultrasound screen. Suddenly they were a team; a team who couldn't wait to get back to Gregory's apartment, make passionate love and then lie in bed and talk about their baby.

*

"Gregorio, why did you never tell me about your younger sisters and your baby brother? You said that you had no family."

Gregory thought about the answer to that question. He wanted to say something funny about how it was easier to get a woman into bed if she thought that you were a lonely orphan. But instead, he opted to tell her something he had rarely told anyone, the truth. It was a part of him that few people knew. And of those people, most only knew it in bits and pieces. Gregory decided that if he was ever going to have a chance at a future with this woman and their child, it was time to put away all the ghosts of his past. It was time to tell Teressa his story.

1968

DORCHESTER, MASSACHUSETTS

IT HAD BEEN two years since Gregory had seen his father. In the span of that time his feelings toward Joseph had gone through an emotional metamorphosis which could only be described as a combination of the five stages of grief and the angst of teenage hormones. The final emotion that Gregory's psyche settled on was an acceptance of the thinly veiled hate that he felt toward his father for the lies and hypocrisy, as well as for the hell his family had subsequently endured.

*

Three weeks after Gregory and Mike had filled out paperwork asking the Italian Consulate for an inquiry into Joseph Costa's case, Gregory received a letter in the mail stating all the details that he already knew to be true: Joseph was on trial for embezzlement of money from the Italian government, the Costa family's status in the United States was legal, and the consulate had no jurisdiction over the case or any ability to pass on information to the family. The judgment had concluded with the suggestion that he hire a private attorney. Gregory had crumpled up the letter and thrown it into the trash without showing it to his mother, who was quickly going from bad to worse.

Louise's inability to rally through this situation was making Gregory's decisions more difficult. At first he thought that maybe he or his mother should take what was left of the money and fly to Italy to confront Xuereb about the case and the state of Joseph's finances. But Gregory knew that it would be useless to send Louise in her current condition. And he couldn't go and leave the girls alone with her for the same reason. He decided to call his grandfather in Sorrento and see what he knew about his father's situation.

Twenty-five minutes later, Gregory wished he hadn't made the call. Nonno was worse off than they were. He told Gregory that shortly after Joseph's arrest, the Italian government confiscated any Costa family holding that had ever been supported by or purchased in Joseph's name. This included the villa that his grandparents had lived in for sixty years. Apparently the older Costa had put the villa into his son's name over twenty years ago, but had accepted the title back six months before Joseph left for America. The small stone house, which had been in the family for generations, was being seized by the government. Gregory's grandparents had one week left to remove their belongs and find a place to live. They were moving in with Joseph's sister, Elena, her husband, Baldo, and their four sons.

His aunt Elena was furious with her brother and refused to take Nonno to visit him in prison. Nonno had cried through most of the telling. He left Gregory with Elena and Baldo's telephone number and whispered, "Essere bene, il mio coraggioso ragazzo," before hanging up the phone.

Gregory needed a plan. If he could get his mother to drag herself out of her misery and either take better care of the twins so he could go to work after school, or get herself a job while the girls were in school (or preferably both), they would be able to stay right where they were. Contrary to Louise's desire, they had nothing to go back to in Italy. Gregory had already spoken to their landlord Walter, who told him his father had paid the year's rent in advance, leaving them with three months before they had to pay for anything except oil, electricity and food. *At least he did something right.* Summer break was one month away. Maybe Gregory could get a job working for Mr. Marino, his father's old boss. *I guess it's time to take the man up on that offer to help.*

*

Waiting for Al Marino in the office trailer was causing Gregory anxiety. Suddenly, this didn't seem like a good idea. Who knew how the guys who worked for his father really felt about him. Gregory had only seen the good side of his father's behavior. Maybe he had been an asshole as a boss. *Maybe I'm headed into a situation where I'm going to get the shit kicked out of me again in the same exact place as the first shit-kicking. Maybe...*

The door opened and Marino walked in with his hand extended. "Gregory, it's good to see you. You look like you've healed up well after that terrible accident. How are you doing?"

Gregory stood. "I'm fine, sir. We're all fine," he lied. "I'm here to ask for a job. I need a job for the summer. I have a lot of skill in stonework and I'm a hard worker. I can work as many hours as you have available..." He knew that he was rambling, but he couldn't stop himself.

Al Marino stepped in and stopped Gregory's ill rehearsed speech with one word: "Yes." Gregory felt flooded with relief as Marino continued talking. "I'll hire you. And if you're anything like the worker that your father was, I'll be glad that I did. When are you done with school?"

"Three weeks, sir. I can start in three weeks," Gregory said, realizing that this only gave him three more weeks to either find someone to look after his sisters or get his mother that electric shock therapy that he had read about in psychology class. At this point, he didn't care which one of those options presented itself first.

*

The next two years flew by in a rush of work, sleep, school and study. Al Marino had been a good boss, making allowances for Gregory any time he couldn't be at the job because of his family. The minute Gregory turned eighteen, Marino pulled some strings and got him into the stoneworker's union, which meant an immediate increase in both pay and benefits. His mother had managed to regroup enough to get a part-time job working at the commercial laundry on Mass Ave. behind their apartment. It was hot, tedious work that didn't pay well, but it gave her a reason to get herself cleaned up and dressed every morning. Gregory wasn't expecting, or getting, much more than that from her.

But the girls were another story. Their brother's expectations for them never wavered. Like his father, Gregory believed in pushing Maria and Maura with hard work and the admonishment to keep themselves out of trouble. He held a tight rein on his little family. Their lives had trotted steadily forward because of Gregory's strict adherence to schedules and rules. The girls were thirteen now and subject to the temptations and flirtations of all teenaged girls. To make matters worse for their brother, they were true beauties. The twins were identical in looks, with huge eyes, curly black hair and prematurely woman-like bodies. But they were opposites in personality. Maura was serious and thoughtful, like her brother. But Maria was a combination of adventurer like their father and crazy like their mother. She was a handful.

*

"You're not wearing that. Go change," Gregory said to Maria after looking at the length of her skirt. He was almost bored with the argument before it began, having had it so many times in the past few months.

"It's not even short! Everyone wears skirts like this!" Maria's pout had zero effect on her brother.

"Not you. You're not wearing it, so I guess not *everyone* is wearing it." Gregory had a difficult time keeping the sarcasm out of his voice. He wanted to be a good parent to Maria, but he was always torn between that and being a rotten older brother. This morning he chose rotten brother. "Seriously, Maria, go change right now. Why don't you wear that stupid long, flowered thing you had to have so badly? If you make us late for school, I promise I'll kill you with my bare hands." She stomped angrily up the stairs, which brought attention to the height of her heels and made him yell, "And change outta those ridiculous shoes! You're going to school, not a fashion show!"

Gregory had two important things going on that morning and he didn't want to be late for either one. At eight o'clock in the high school gymnasium, he was scheduled for the retake session of the SAT exams. The first session, given in the fall, had been held on one of the Saturdays that Gregory had committed to work. Because of the limitations of his school schedule, working weekends and after school were his only options for bringing in enough money to support the family. This second testing session was primarily going to be filled with students who had done poorly on their first effort, whose parents had pushed them into trying to improve their scores with a retake. Many were already waitlisted at colleges where the admissions officers were waiting to see if they could improve their scores before giving the go-ahead for acceptance. Not so, Gregory. He knew that in spite of his 3.9 GPA he was going to work full-time for Marino Construction after graduation.

The second (but personally more important) thing that Gregory had planned was asking Valerie to the prom.

Valerie Lyons was the landlord's daughter. Her family owned half the houses on Willow Court. She represented the exact middle of the nine children born to Walter and Valentina Lyons. They lived right across the street from the Costas.

Gregory had once been invited to take a tour of the Lyons' home when he went over to drop off the rent envelope. He had been awestruck. Walter had converted the building from a three-family tenement to one spacious home. The lower floor consisted of an industrial-sized kitchen, huge dining room and a front parlor with a half bath. The second and third floors each had three bedrooms, a bathroom and a front parlor. To say that Walter Lyons was wealthy may have been an understatement. Gregory knew that most of his properties were inherited and *all* his rents were collected in cash.

Valerie had been the object of Gregory's affection from the day he first laid eyes on her. She was strictly the Irish-looking side of her Irish-Italian parents. She had straight, fine, light brown hair, light eyes and freckles. What made her stand out even further was the fact that her siblings were all dark-haired and dark-eyed like their mother. Perhaps it was her Irish looks that made her Walter's favorite child, a fact he never tried to hide from his other children.

Valerie Lyons was smart. She was one year younger than Gregory, but they were in most of the same classes due to her advancement and their mutual love of science. For the past year they had shared homework answers, jokes, notes and a microscope. In Gregory's early Sorrento life, the Costas and the Lyons would have been on the same social standing. But here in the United States, Gregory knew he didn't stand a chance with her. Since the situation was hopeless, he had forced himself to ignore the butterflies that floated through his stomach every time Valerie spoke to him.

Going to his senior prom hadn't even crossed Gregory's mind until the week before when Mike and Linda Donohoe had invited the Costa family over for dinner.

*

"Are you and Valerie going to the prom?" Linda Donohoe asked Gregory.

"What? Why would I go to the prom with Valerie?" Gregory's face immediately reddened. *Just because I think about her all the time?*

"Mike told me that you two were an item." Now it was her husband's turn to look embarrassed. Linda persisted, in the same way every woman who sees love in the air persists. "You should ask her. She's not going with anyone. A pretty girl like that with no date to the prom? She must be waiting for someone special to ask her."

"Maybe she's waiting for it to be her own senior prom. She's just a junior," Gregory said, trying for a tone that indicated he couldn't care less.

"Just saying," said Linda, with a smile, as she got up to get dessert. The seed had been planted.

*

The testing went well. He had no problems with the exam once he made the effort to put the girl and the prom out of his mind. As he knew he would be, Gregory was the first student finished. Even after rechecking his answers, he was still the only one with his head raised from the task. The proctor, Mrs. Johnson, gave him a look that clearly said "You've rushed through this and you'll be sorry" as Gregory handed her his test answer packet. He just gave her one of his award-winning smiles and headed out to the hallway in search of Valerie's class so that he could be right by her door when the bell rang.

There she is! Gregory's heart gave a little flutter. Valerie walked out of the classroom and started hollering to him before she got within normal hearing range.

"I can't believe you missed Biology! Mr. Tatano..."

"Will you go to the prom with me?" Gregory blurted out loudly while walking toward her, three people still between them.

"Yes, I will," Valerie answered, without hesitation.

"Good. I'll pick you up at six, on the day of the prom," Gregory said, as if there were another day he had in mind.

"Fine," she replied. They walked past each other without stopping and continued in opposite directions toward their next classes. By lunchtime, half the school was talking about the adorable way that Gregory Costa had asked Valerie Lyons to the prom.

*

Although the Costa family had no use or money for an automobile, Gregory had gotten his license the minute he was able in order to drive Marino Construction's 1958 Ford F100 pickup truck. As the only extra vehicle on the jobsite, it was used by everyone for everything from picking up a worker, to hauling cinderblock from the local Grossman's. The truck was fun to drive because it couldn't be killed. The first gear had stopped functioning five years before Gregory got behind the wheel, which had made learning to drive in it nearly impossible. Going from stop to move was more like jump starting a car than driving one. Inside and out, the car was covered in debris: sheetrock dust, mortar and scraps of everything from roofing material to Italian submarine sandwiches.

This truck would be a cool vehicle to take to the senior prom if I was rich and doing it as a lark thought Gregory. But it's another story when everyone knows that you don't have a better car sitting in your driveway at home. Nope. It wasn't going to happen. And he couldn't just walk across the street, knock on Valerie's door and say, "Here is your corsage and bus pass." Just when Gregory was getting ready to use a big chunk of his preciously saved emergency fund to hire a limousine, Mike Donohoe came to the rescue. He offered to drive them in his brand new 1968 Oldsmobile Delta 88. It was a sporty looking four-door version with all the bells and whistles: aquamarine exterior and white leather interior. Mike told him he had volunteered to chaperone the big event, so he was heading in that direction anyway.

Since Gregory had no idea how Walter Lyons felt about his daughter going out with a poor Italian kid with a vanished father, he decided that having Mike as their chauffeur could only help his case. *What father wouldn't want his daughter chauffeured to her high school prom by one of the most well-respected teachers in the school?*

Linda Donohoe had made it her job to get the tux. She told Gregory she wasn't going to let a young man, who she viewed as a son, go to his prom in anything ridiculous. It had to be a classically cut black tux, complete with cummerbund and the right footwear. She took Gregory's measurements and ordered the tux while he was at work. On the day of the prom, she picked it up along with a wrist corsage for Valerie, having mysteriously found out her dress color in advance. The Donohoes were making it easy for Gregory to have a memorable night. *If only my family would do the same*, thought Gregory, when his mother stayed home from work sick on the day of the prom. And then there was Maria.

*

For reasons unknown to Gregory, Maria was being a bitch. They had already had three major fights by the time Gregory was getting into his tux and splashing on the men's cologne he had picked up the day before at Woolworth's. He was ready to strangle her.

"What's your problem? It's one night! I want you to stay here with Ma while I'm gone. She's sick."

"She's not sick," Maria slammed back at him, "She's lazy, she's mental and she's crazy! It's just a movie for Chrissake! Maura will be home, I'm going."

Something snapped inside of Gregory. It had been such a long time since he had done anything age appropriate, like go to a movie or hang out with friends. He had given up his entire youth so his sisters could enjoy theirs. And here she stood, in his face and whining about giving up this one night, a night Gregory hadn't even known how badly he wanted, until Maria stood ready to ruin it. He was hanging on to his temper by a thread.

"Sometimes, I wish Ma was dead." Maria hadn't said it loudly, or even in anger. She had said it with the simplicity of a self-centered thirteen-year-old girl who was railing against the obstacle standing in the way of *this* moment's immediate want. A tiny thought of agreement flashed through Gregory's mind. The acknowledgment of that brief desire to be rid of the woman who had given birth to them all made Gregory lose his carefully garnered control. He slapped Maria across the face with a force that landed her onto the bed behind her.

Maria didn't cry out. Instead, she stared at her brother with such a look of hatred and disbelief that Gregory immediately regretted his action. "Maria. I'm sorry! I didn't mean to…"

His sister got up from where she had fallen and rushed past him, her disgust for him made more obvious by the way she carefully avoided brushing against his tux in her passing. She flew down the stairs. Gregory stood there unmoving as he heard the front door slam hard enough to wake the dead.

He wanted to rage against her, make this all her fault. But instead, his self-loathing and shame caused a pain to form in the pit of his stomach. He just stood there, staring into the mirror above the dresser. Suddenly, Gregory saw his father's face reflecting back at him. How could he not have noticed before how much he resembled Joseph? The thought shook him. *Am I a bad person like my father? Or maybe I'm worse, having struck my child?* Gregory unconsciously corrected his internal question from "child" to "sister". For a moment, he debated going after her. He realized with alarm that he would have no idea where Maria would run to if she were in pain. Gregory had been so busy supporting them and laying down rules, that he didn't even know who his sister's best friend was. None of the Costa children had ever brought a friend to their home because of their embarrassment of Louise. Gregory had heard both of his sisters mention various names, but he couldn't conjure up one. He looked at the watch on his wrist, a black leather-banded, Swiss-made Diantus, left behind by his father. Mike was going to be there to pick him up in five minutes. It was too late to do anything about his sister. Gregory conceded that his family was just going to have to work out this night's problems without him.

*

The twenty-minute ride from Willow Court to Lombardo's in Randolph had begun with awkward formality. Mike Donohoe had parked his Delta 88 in front of the Costa doorway, gotten out, walked up the stoop and rang the doorbell, just as any good chauffeur would. Maura answered the door, hugged Mr. Donohoe and then yelled for her brother. After the men shook hands, Mike grabbed his camera and took a picture of Gregory and his sister.

"What's the matter? Maria can't be seen with you because your handsomeness outshines hers today?" Mike kidded Gregory. "And, where is Louise? Linda gave me a list of the pictures I needed to take. She even pulled out our old prom pictures."

"Sorry about that, Mike. This beauty will have to do." Gregory pulled the ever-compliant Maura in closer for another photo. Then he kissed her on the head, telling her to check on their mother occasionally. As Gregory began walking across the street to Valerie's house, Mike grabbed him by the arm.

"Oh, no you don't! We're doing this the right way!" Mike trotted to the car and opened the back door for his passenger. "Get in. We're going around the block and then pulling up to the Lyons' front door, just to make it official." Gregory jumped in, laughing and thankful for his friend's determination to make this night perfect, ridiculous as it was. After Mike closed Gregory's door he ran over and handed Maura his camera, instructing her on its use and when to take the pictures. Then he stood at attention in front of the car while Maura took aim, making the "limo" and driver her first picture.

"You're really taking this chauffeur thing seriously," Gregory kidded as Donohoe maneuvered the turn-around at the dead end of Willow Court with a more-than-three-point turn. "What if Val's looking out the window and she thinks I've stood her up?"

"This is serious stuff, Gregory. My first date with Linda was the prom, only I was the junior and she was the senior. You never know how important a night might be until something comes out of it. Plus, this is how Linda said I needed to do it. She was hopping mad that she couldn't come."

Less than a minute later, the car had pulled up to the front of the Lyons' house and Gregory got out, corsage in hand. When he rang the bell, Walter Lyons came to the door and looked at him as though he had never seen him before and had no idea why he was standing there.

"Hello. Can I help you?" Lyons said. Gregory was confused until he saw the grin on Maura's face behind the camera and heard Mike laughing behind him. *Apparently everyone is in on this joke but me.*

"Yes. I'm Gregory Costa and I'm here to pick up Valerie Lyons," he said, formally playing along.

"Won't you come in," Valerie's father said with equal formality. Then he broke character and said to Maura and Mike, "Why don't youse all come in? Tina wants to take pictures and she made punch and hors d'oeuvres. It'll only take a couple minutes."

*

Gregory's eyes were blinded by the flashbulbs. The entire Lyons family had assembled in the huge dining room for the prom picture-taking extravaganza. Valerie looked beautiful. Her dress was blue, cinched at the waist with a full skirt and a style straight out of Coco Chanel. Her fine brown hair had been teased into a high French twist. Gregory thought she looked just like Jacqueline Kennedy and said as much to the amusement of her siblings, who then referred to him as JFK. The worry he had felt about not fitting in was gone. In its place was a feeling akin to either longing or regret for a family who looked happy, fun and normal. Gregory glanced over at Maura and could tell she felt it, too. It made him sad to think that no matter how hard he worked, he couldn't give a moment like this to his sisters. He was thankful that one of them was here to share it with him.

The five minutes of picture-taking at the Lyons' house ended up taking twenty-five minutes to accomplish. But it was time well spent. Gregory swallowed the anxiety that arose when Walter had pulled him into the kitchen for a brief but serious talk about respect and his desire to see Valerie have "a nice prom experience." He ended his sermon by telling Gregory he admired him for having done such a good job keeping his family going, paying the rent on time and, in general, being a hard worker. It was more words than they had exchanged in all their monthly rent transfers combined. He and Valerie were then paraded into Mike's car, both feeling relaxed and not the least bit shy with each other after that fiasco. On the way to Lombardo's they decided to spend the night referring to themselves as Mr. and Mrs. Kennedy. Their chauffeur was happy to comply.

*

Lombardo's was the first nice restaurant Gregory had been inside since his move to America. There had been many opportunities before this one, most of which he had declined because of work or money. He and his sisters didn't go out much. They occasionally went to Upham's Corner and saw a first-run movie at the Strand Theatre or sometimes a double horror flick at Uphams Theatre across the street; a little rundown movie house with ripped upholstered seats and a bad smell. After the movie, Gregory would take the twins to sit at the counter at Sawyer's Drug Store and let them order a milkshake or a root beer float. If he was feeling particularly generous, the girls got to pick out something from the refrigerated vending machines at the automat section of the market, maybe an egg salad sandwich or a piece of lemon meringue pie. The Costas didn't have money to waste on a meal that wasn't going to stretch halfway through the week.

Walking into Lombardo's immediately brought Gregory to a time when dining in the best trattorias in Sorrento was a weekly occurrence, and eating at a fine banquet hall happened at least five or six times a year. All his social graces came back to him in a rush of memories. The crystal chandeliers, white linen tablecloths and floral centerpieces made Gregory feel more at home than he had at any time in the past four years. He decided he was more like James Bond than JFK. He was a man who had pulled off the caper of the century. Valerie Lyons was suddenly not just the pretty girl who made him laugh in science lab. She was a rich and beautiful socialite, a woman who any man would be proud to escort into a room such as this. *This is my real world.*

Gregory checked the table list, easily finding their names and table number. With the confidence of a man who knew that he would someday be living the life of his dreams, Gregory stopped Valerie en route to their table. He turned her to face him and kissed her with an intensity normally reserved for the end of prom night. She kissed him back with equal fervor. Those around them clapped heartily. Valerie pulled back, her Irish complexion the color of the red carnation in Gregory's lapel.

"What was that for?" Valerie exclaimed breathlessly.

"I wanted to get our first kiss out of the way," he said with a grin, "so I could relax and not worry about it all night."

"Well, I was more worried about the *second* one," said Valerie, ever the wisecracker. Then she stood on her toes and pulled his face down for another kiss, seemingly oblivious to the whoops and clapping going on in the background.

Mr. and Mrs. Kennedy are off to a good start, Gregory decided. He had never been happier.

*

The end of the night was nearing. Like Cinderella, Gregory didn't want it to end. The food had been delicious, the band fun, and Valerie, amazing. She wasn't the least bit jolted when he told her that he had never danced before. She pulled him onto the dance floor and began a lesson that didn't look like a lesson to those who were watching. It looked like a blast. Before long everyone was doing Gregory's stilted version of the Mashed Potato.

"How come you're so good at this? Do you go to a lot of dances?" Gregory was suddenly worried that Valerie had a full social life.

"No!" She laughed. "I have eight brothers and sisters! We set up the basement of our house as our own dance party. We have tons of records. That's how my father keeps his eye on us, he locks us all in the basement! I've never even been to a dance!"

"Well, you have now!" Gregory yelled over the band's rendition of Marvin Gaye's *Ain't No Mountain High Enough*. Then he saw Mike Donohoe coming toward them, his wife trailing close behind. The looks on their faces created an intensely familiar feeling of dread in Gregory's stomach. He stopped dancing.

"We've got trouble," Mike said with no fanfare. "Your mother's in the hospital. Linda's gonna drive Valerie home and we'll go straight to Carney. Maura's already there."

*

"I checked on her ten times!" Maura screamed into the hospital corridor at her brother. "You know Ma! She always looks bad. She never talks! Don't blame this on me!"

"I'm not blaming you," Gregory said, accusatively. "I'm just trying to get to the bottom of this. Have you heard *anything* from *anyone* about your sister?"

It was eight o'clock in the morning, two days after the prom and Maria was still missing. They had called everyone they could think of. Gregory was almost at the point of getting the police involved, a move he would use only after exhausting everything else. *Police take orphans from their families* were the words rolling around Gregory's head. Mike and Linda had assured him that they would never let that happen. But the list of situations over which Gregory had no control, a list he had unconsciously begun at the age of three, had been steadily increasing in length over the span of his teenage years. He was not going to take the chance that the police would do the right thing. *No one is going to break up my family!*

*

Nine days had passed with no sign of Maria. Gregory decided he had no choice but to get the police involved - although he was certain they wouldn't do anything he hadn't already done. Some of the kids from the twins' classes had plastered the area with copies of Maria's sixth-grade school picture, which showed her more as a little girl than the woman she had become. Gregory cringed the first time he saw the telephone pole near his house with its stapled copy of his sister's face. All the wonderful memories of his special night with Valerie had been reduced in his mind to one image, one slap. Ashamed, he hadn't told anyone about it. The most he had said was that they had fought about her going out that night. If Maura knew more she never let on, making this the first of a number of guilts that Gregory would carry alone.

*

It was five o'clock in the morning, too early for family members to visit. But the Intensive Care Unit at Carney Hospital had been making a lot of exceptions for Gregory and his sister. Two days before, the charge nurse had told him that based on his mother's blood work and her failure to regain consciousness she wouldn't last long. So they transferred Louise out of the intensive care unit and into a private room on the third floor; a place to die. He

222

and Maura were going to stay there tonight. But for now, his plan was to make a quick stop in to see how her night went, and then go to the Boston Police Department to report his sister missing.

Gregory had learned to avoid using the elevator any time before 8 a.m. Taking the back stairs put him out of the way of the receptionist, whose job it was to block visitors from coming in before or after visiting hours. It was easier on all counts. His mother's room was the first one on the right at the top of the stairs. When he got there, the door was slightly ajar. He quietly pushed it open, as if waking his mother was a concern. Maria was sitting at the bedside, holding her mother's hand. *Santa Madre di Dio!*

"Jesus! Maria, where have you been?" Maria turned around to look at her brother with sunken eyes and a tear-streaked face.

"I was home, hiding in our basement. I came back the next day and read the note you left me about Ma. I couldn't face you. It's my fault," Maria sobbed. "I wanted her dead. I killed her!"

"Maria, she's not dead. You didn't kill her. There was nothing any of us could do." Gregory grabbed his sister and hugged her with all his strength. "If it's anyone's fault it's mine. I shouldn't have hit you." Partially unburdened by both her homecoming and his apology, Gregory broke down.

*

Maria had never seen her brother cry. His anguish broke her out of her own tears. His apology opened her heart to him. *My brother needs me.* She held him and let him cry in her arms, as any comforting mother might, while their own mother, lying quietly in a coma behind them, slipped from this life.

*

Just as Louise had hoped, it was a burst appendix. The surgeon determined from the level of sepsis, it had probably ruptured a day or two before. After two operations to flush and debride the abdominal cavity, they decided there was nothing left to do except hope that the antibiotic would kick in and kill the bacteria spreading throughout her body. *Per favore, Dio, non permettere che accada. Please, God, don't let that happen.*

Louise drifted between worlds, desperately reaching for the one she had yet to see, and her blessed relief. She hung on for nine days, feeling her body become a bloated, yellow replica of the woman she once was, a woman whose physical appearance had already experienced epic change in the two years since her husband was arrested. By the time she died, she bore no resemblance to the lady who had lived a beautiful life on the coast of Italy. *Grazie Dio, per questo Benedetto sollievo.*

*

The simple service at St. Mark the Evangelist Parish was surprisingly well attended. Gregory's popularity at school had skyrocketed over the past two weeks. Students with whom he had never spoken came by to give their final farewell to a woman whom they had never met. Dozens of people from Marino Construction came, along with Valerie's entire family. Walter and Valentina Lyons had insisted on having the after-funeral event at their home. Al Marino fulfilled the last of his unpaid debt to Joseph Costa by going to the funeral home behind Gregory's back and paying for the casket and the embalming of Louise's body. Gregory wandered through the day of the funeral letting others do what they would to make the event happen. He smiled, shook hands and said a prayer without knowing he was doing so. His sisters stayed by his side and did the same, neither having to be told what to do or what to say.

From the outside, the Costa children looked grieved and united. Their grief was real. But little did they know, they would not be united for long.

1968

ROME, ITALY

ELENA COSTA GAFFURI had always been jealous of her younger brother, Joseph. He was handsome, athletic, and at ease in every situation. After college he married the woman of his dreams, proceeded to have three beautiful children, and had the ear of both his mother and his father. In Elena's eyes, he lived an undeservedly charmed life. She, on the other hand, had worked just as hard and had gotten nowhere. Her husband, Baldo, couldn't keep a business going to save his life. She had met and married Baldo Gaffuri on his best day, then watched as he plummeted slowly downward, level by level, until he was, in her view, a barely functioning human being. One after another, she had given birth to his sons, each with her own small, narrowly positioned eyes and their father's lack of drive. She was four months pregnant when her sister-in-law, Louise, gave birth to the twins. The sight of those perfect, if underweight, baby girls was more than she could bear. Five months later, Elena gave birth to her fourth son, who also represented the last time she would ever have sex with her husband, Baldo. As a focus of her postpartum depression, Elena honed her antithetical hatred toward her brother and sister-in-law and never spoke to them again. The Costas appeared not to notice.

When Joseph was arrested and brought back to Italy, a little spark ignited in Elena. She couldn't decide what she wanted as her role in this drama. Her choices were clear: she could be the supportive sister and proclaim his innocence; that was something she could work with. Maybe it would parlay into a newspaper interview or a memoir. But there was a huge risk with that position. If Joseph was found guilty (as she suspected he was), she would become one more person who had supported a criminal and a liar. Unless she was the betrayed wife or the person who had been swindled, a guilty verdict left her with no story to tell. Elena decided on role number two: the sad daughter who was bearing it all bravely for the sake of her parents. *How horrible that my parents*

225

have to suffer through my brother's bad choices, Elena practiced in her head. She told everyone who would listen that she *wanted* to visit Joseph in prison, but the strain of it was too much. Those close to her knew that she hadn't seen her brother in over eleven years. Those who didn't know her nodded their heads in sympathy.

The minute her father had gotten the phone call from America, telling him Louise was dead, Elena's delicate inability to see her brother vanished. She couldn't wait to get to the prison and tell him the news. *My dreams are coming true.*

*

"I live in a convent of God," Joseph whispered to himself every morning, as he choked down the tasteless fette biscottate.

Regina Coeli Prison in Rome was named for the original use of the building, a convent. Housing primarily political prisoners, Regina Coeli was not the worst prison Joseph could have found himself in, but it wasn't the best. His crime, the theft of government monies, was political in nature thus providing him with this better choice for his incarceration. *As if I have a choice.* But he knew that Rebibbia Prison would have been much worse.

By the time his sister came to visit him, two years and one month after being imprisoned, Joseph's trial was finally underway. Her visit marked the only time he had been called to the visitor's room to receive anyone other than his attorney. He was surprised and disappointed to see Elena sitting on the opposite side of the table to which he was being led. His first thought was actually a hope that by some miracle she was there to visit another prisoner. Joseph wasn't that lucky. When he sat down, Elena didn't bother asking him how he, or his trial, were faring. She cut right to the chase.

"Louise is dead and your kids are all alone in America." Joseph already knew this. Her statement didn't warrant a response; he remained silent.

"I would take the girls, but not Gregory. He's too much like his father," Elena's cruelty was unnecessary. *Gregory is eighteen. He doesn't need to be taken.*

"What do you want, Elena?"

"I'm telling you, Joseph, I would take care of your girls, treat them like my own," Elena said, ignoring the look of disgust on her brother's face. "I would do that for you… and Louise… if only I had the money."

There it was. *My bitch of a sister is looking for money.* Joseph weighed his options. He hadn't heard a word from his son since he was deported. His attorney had told him about the letter of inquiry that Gregory had filed two years ago, but that was it. He wondered what his mother and father knew. He had tried writing to them on several occasions, but had never received a reply. He knew his sister had intercepted the post. *I hope that reading my letters gave you the joy that your miserable life doesn't provide.* Elena looked smug, like she had everyone exactly where she wanted them. If Joseph had one shred of hope that this trial would go in his favor he would tell his sister to go fuck herself, wait to be released and then go to America and get his kids. But it wasn't looking good. Maybe this was for the best. If Maria and Maura were here in Italy, at least he would be able to see them and keep track of how they were doing. *Of course, she wants money.*

"Before we left for the States, I had my lawyer change the beneficiaries on our life insurance policies from each other to the kids, split three ways. Louise's policy was worth one hundred thousand American dollars." Joseph let his words sink in a little. He could almost hear her crunching the numbers in her head.

"Maybe I could take the boy, too. He's probably changed a lot, grown up," his sister said, obviously feeling her way through the money. Joseph couldn't believe the magnitude of the hatred he felt for her.

"I have my conditions," he said, ignoring Elena's attempt to include his only son in her plan. "The girls will visit me here every two months. You will personally bring them. It will be a temporary legal guardianship, until I am released. My attorney will provide the documents."

"Temporary? No, Joseph. I'm not willing to disrupt my husband and children's lives with something that may only be temporary. It's a lot you're asking of..."

"Don't worry, Elena," Joseph interrupted, seeing how little his sister had changed in over a decade. "You'll get to keep all their money whether they stay with you for six months or six years. If I were you, I'd pray for my release. It'd be the easiest money you ever made."

Joseph signaled the guard and got up from the chair, knowing the deal was done. He would speak to Xuereb tomorrow about the paperwork.

1992

BOSTON, MASSACHUSETTS

THE LIGHT IN Gregory's harbor-facing apartment had dimmed to a warm sunset glow. Teres had watched the sun lower itself in the sky for the last hour from the solid enclosure of Gregory's arms. There had been many times during his story when Teres had wanted to ask a question, or even stop him from telling this painful tale when she saw the anguish it was causing him. But she didn't. It was like listening to a spider web in the wind; one puff in the wrong direction could dismantle everything. The web of his story would vanish and Gregory would close up that part of his life to her forever. The perfection in timing of the orange sphere slipping below the horizon and Gregory's family slipping from his grasp made Teres no longer able to bear his story silently.

"What happened to the girls? Did they go back?" Just as she knew it would, her question pulled him out of the past and into the present.

"Oh, they went back, all right." Gregory said, with his customary anger creeping past the sadness in his voice. "They hated me for it, but I had no choice. Maria wanted us to run away, where no one could find us. But I couldn't support us if I left Dorchester. And our inheritance was only going to be released to my aunt and uncle once the girls were back in Italy."

"Have you kept in touch with them?"

Now his voice was bitter. "My aunt turned them against me. She told the girls that I could have kept them, but I chose the insurance money instead. I've seen Maura twice, but Maria won't see me. I try every couple of years. Elena died of pancreatic cancer five years ago and I'd hoped her death would change things. But it didn't."

"What about your father?" Teres asked, fearing she was asking one question too many.

"The evidence collected by the Pubblico Ministero suggested my father's case was considered a war crime and his trial was moved from

229

Tribunale Court to Corte d'Assise. He was found guilty of crimes against his country and sentenced to thirty years. I saw him for the first time two years ago when I picked him up from Regina Coeli Prison. He lives in Sorrento in a tiny apartment that I rent for him. Having my sisters turn their backs on me made me think hard about what ignoring my father probably did to him. I guess what goes around comes around."

Gregory was quiet for a moment. Teres shifted, thinking she must leave soon. Gregory had more to say.

"So, there you have it. That's what turned me into the twisted man you see before you." The bravado was back in his voice. "I moved in with Mike and Linda, went to college, then medical school and dated any woman who would let me. I've recreated the childhood that fate had robbed from me and thought only about myself for twenty-three years, until I met you... and now him." Gregory looked down at the ultrasound picture he had been holding in his hand throughout his story. "I would never have risked losing something so precious to me again. You can read about my commitment phobia in any psychology journal. It's classic, the reason I've stayed unavailable. And then I saw you that night in the hospital, and it was like my past came rushing up to meet my future..."

Teres touched his face. "I know, Gregorio. It all makes sense to me now. But still, this..."

"This was meant to be!" Gregory said with passion, "You, me, this baby. I know it's a painful decision, Teressa. But having our family is worth somebody else's pain."

1992

SCITUATE, MASSACHUSETTS

ON THE MORNING of February seventh, Danny's sixtieth birthday, Teres received a telephone call from Dr. Aarons' office confirming that all her blood work was completely normal and pointing to a healthy baby. She took the call in the kitchen, as she was fixing a special birthday omelet for her husband who was sitting at the counter directly in front of her.

"What was that about?" Danny asked. Teres could feel her own heartbeat accelerate in rhythm and volume, but she couldn't detect one hint of suspicion in her husband's voice.

"The physical I had a couple of weeks ago, my PAP smear is fine. My blood tests are normal."

"Good. Only one of us can be a physical mess at a time. And since I'm taking the first twenty years of our marriage, you'll have to wait for the second twenty." Danny's wisecracking rescued her from having to conjure up a fictitious list of perimenopausal and hormonal tests which a good doctor would routinely run on a thirty-nine-year-old woman. She had even been ready to fabricate a story about her thyroid. And here he was, talking about the next twenty years of their life together. Teres could have taken the knife she was using to cut up Danny's low sodium turkey sausage and plunged it into her own chest. *God should strike me dead* had become her daily mantra. She put down the knife, walked to the other side of the breakfast bar and stood behind Danny, putting her arms around him and kissing the top of his head where his hair had thinned out enough to allow her lips to touch skin.

"Daniello. You haven't been so much trouble. You always get better? I have been a handful, I know. Always push, push, push. I don't know how you have put up with *me* all of these years."

"It's been easy, sweet girl. You've kept me alive in more ways than you know," Danny said. Teres was certain this time she detected a note of sorrow in his voice. She had to rush away from him, before this moment turned into a pivotal one, with her on the floor crying and her husband's life shattered to pieces.

"Bagel or Tuscan toast with your omelet?" Teres grabbed a paper towel and dabbed her eyes. "These damn onions, they always make my eyes water," she lied, hoping her husband wouldn't notice that the sweet Vidalia onion was sitting, uncut, on the handmade butcher-block cutting board. The board was in the shape of a lighthouse; a gift from Danny to celebrate their new Scituate gourmet kitchen. *God should strike me dead.*

*

Danny drank his second cup of coffee slowly, knowing it was the last one for the day. Two cups were his limit. He used to drink coffee all day long. Sometimes, when he worked a double or an overnight, he'd log in eight or nine cups, all with cream and artificial sweetener. "I guess that wasn't a good idea," he mumbled to himself. He could have said it out loud. He was all alone in the breakfast nook. Teres had rushed off to get dressed. She said she still had a million things to do before his birthday party. He wished he had said no when she first mentioned the idea of a big bash for his sixtieth birthday. But that had been over six months ago, when they were both happy that he had lived through the surgery.

Danny still couldn't believe how awful the surgery and recuperation had been. If he had it to do over... *If I had any of this to do over, what would I have done differently?* His mind went back seven months, to the day of his second heart attack.

1991

SCITUATE, MASSACHUSETTS

DANNY WAS IN love with the golf course at Scituate Country Club. It was founded in 1919, its clubhouse having been built as a residence in 1779 by the Welch family. Not only was the property of historic significance, it was also an oasis of real estate. Each hole had something different to offer: marshlands, ocean views and rolling fairways with meticulously kept greens. The layout was as challenging as it was beautiful, with a first hole that was considered the toughest of any course on the South Shore. He had come to know every inch of it like the back of his hand, maybe even better than his mentor and golfing partner, Ron Watters, did. Danny felt like thanking Ron for introducing him to the game of golf every time he held a club in his hands.

*

It hadn't taken Ron any time to realize that he had created a monster. Danny had height and strength, and his stiff left leg seemed to help his swing, rather than hinder it. Before long, his friend could hit the ball a ton. Within a couple of years, Danny had refined his short game and become an intuitive putter.

They had been playing every Thursday for almost ten years. When there was snow on the ground, they used fluorescent orange golf balls. Ron liked the fact that Danny was as obsessed with the game as he was. Playing golf with Danny was the highlight of Ron's week, *even if I have to admit that he's better than me.*

*

On the morning of his second heart attack, Danny was kicking Ron's ass again, with his friend taking it somewhat less philosophically than was usual.

"You fucking sandbagger! This isn't even fair anymore! You live right around the corner! What do you play, like ten rounds a week? Jesus, Danny! You're killing me!"

"Ha! You're just jealous... and the student is schooling the master!" Danny chanted after birdying hole six. He reached down to retrieve his secret weapon, a long distance Pinnacle golf ball. When he bent over the hole, Danny felt something let go in his chest.

Let go was the only way his mind could describe the sensation. It was like feeling the sound of a pop. This wasn't the same as the oxygen-deprived tunnel vision Danny had experienced almost twenty years prior. This was a sudden stab to the heart and then he was down. Before his heart stopped beating entirely, he had two thoughts: *It's been a good life*, and *Teres is gonna be pissed at me*.

*

Teres was at work when she got Ron's phone call.

"He's had a heart attack. I did CPR, kept him alive, but it doesn't look good. We're at South Shore Hospital. Have whoever's on bring you in by ambulance."

*

The ride from Accelerated Ambulance in Quincy to South Shore Hospital in Hingham takes twenty-one minutes, fourteen in the middle of the night when there's no traffic. Teres arrived there in eleven minutes during a Friday morning rush hour. *Thank God it's Doug*, she thought to herself. Doug was calm and fearless, two traits she wished all her paramedics possessed. As he rammed the ambulance through the impossibly small spaces of pushed aside traffic, he spoke reassuringly to Teres.

"Danny's a tough guy, Teres. You think of him as a delicate flower, but he's not. They'll go in and do a bypass, maybe a full cabbage, and you'll get another thirty years outta the guy."

Teres hoped he was right. But for now, she needed to know if her husband was alive. She picked up the mic and pressed for the dispatcher.

"Boston Control, this is C-Med 3-4-5, C-Med 3-4-5, looking for a patch to South Shore Hospital." Teres requested.

"C-Med 3-4-5, putting you through to South Shore on channel six, that is channel six," they responded within seconds. Teres tuned to six and spoke.

"South Shore, this is C-Med 3-4-5, C-Med 3-4-5."

"South Shore ER. Go ahead C-Med 3-4-5. What is your emergency?" The words clipped out from the speaker in the dash. Doug took the mic out of his boss' hand.

"South Shore. This is Doug with Accelerated Ambulance. We're carrying next of kin for patient Daniel Muldaur with an ETA of two minutes. Can you clear a path through the back door for us?"

"You got it, Doug. General bay two, South Shore out."

"They wouldn't have told you, anyway, Boss," Doug said gently. "In a couple of minutes we'll know the whole story." Teres nodded her head and began to cry, fully giving over to her position as next of kin.

*

"The blockage is in his left main artery. The left anterior descending is probably occluded as well, but we can't tell because of the main blockage. So we're looking at a double bypass, maybe more." The cardiologist at South Shore wasn't painting a good picture. Danny's heart attack had been the serious kind.

He suggested Danny undergo surgery within the next few days and then left Ron and Teres alone to decide on the next step.

"If a blockage of the LAD is considered the widow maker, a blockage of the Left Main Artery is the mother of all widow makers." Ron didn't mince his words. "He's only alive because he plays golf with an ER doc. It's like some kind of bad joke."

"Who do we want for a surgeon?" Teres asked Ron.

"Gregory Costa. I went to Tufts with him, top of his class in all categories. Now he's chief of Cardiothoracic Surgery at Beth Israel and their program's getting nothing but praise. I'll call him." Ron gave Teres a quick hug and made his way out of the Coronary Care Unit. Teres headed back to Danny.

"Daniello, we are going to fix this." She put her face close to Danny's cheek. Although he had been unconscious when she had reached the hospital, he had resurfaced on and off since then. It was as though the event had simply made him too tired to stay awake for more than a minute or two. As long as the zigzag lines on the cardiac monitor stayed steady, Teres was content for Danny to remain relatively unresponsive. There was nothing she could do about it anyway. She wondered if she should leave Danny for a few minutes and make some calls. She decided there was no one on the must-know list except Martha. The emergency room nurse had suggested she call her children.

"I don't have children," she had answered.

"Well, perhaps you should call your husband's children. You never know in these situations," the nurse urged.

"*We* don't have children," Teres had responded, barely holding it together. It drove her crazy when people assumed that she was Danny's second wife. She wanted to yell at them, but she could see their point. Anyone who didn't know the Muldaurs might think Danny was a rich man with a successful ambulance company who had succumbed to a midlife crisis, trading in his first wife for a younger model. It made her want to scream. Especially when it came to their ignorance of who was the driving force behind Accelerated Ambulance.

Teres sometimes worked their wedding date into the conversation, or perhaps a joke about how he got her to marry him by running over her, twenty years ago. But the truth was that she looked younger than her age and Danny sometimes looked older than his fifty-nine years. She knew she was fortunate to have what she referred to as "a lucky gene pool." The women in her family had beautiful skin, which Teres had taken good care to see stay that way. Danny always laughed at her bedtime ritual of "greasing up," as he referred to it. But Teres had just turned thirty-nine and people often mistook her for someone in her twenties.

It was also true that Danny had worked hard to get himself into good physical condition after his accident. Although he never went back to running, the weights, stationary bike and the golfing had put her husband into great shape for a man his age. And to give Danny his due, he worked pretty hard in the bedroom as well. Thinking about all this made her furious. *Why now? Why did this have to happen just when everything was going so well?*

Teres tried to shake off fate's questions and concentrate on what it would take to get her husband well again. She forced herself to mentally visualize the arteries of the heart. She had taken Anatomy and Physiology so long ago. But since then she had gotten her EMT's certification which had included an EKG class and later, her ACLS. Teres knew a lot about the heart. She knew they were going to have to crack open her husband's chest and use blood vessels from somewhere else in his body to create a new pathway for each of his blocked arteries. The surgeon would go around the blocked areas of his heart. In her head it sounded simple. She knew better.

Teres decided to set a goal. She realized this was foolish and presumptuous of her. Here her husband was, seriously ill, barely conscious, and facing major open heart surgery and she was busy setting a goal for him. But setting goals for her and Danny had always made Teres feel like they were going in a positive direction. This was July. Danny's sixtieth birthday was in February. That would give him, and her, exactly seven months to get this behind them and get Danny back in shape. Teres knew she could make it happen. With that decided, an emotional exhaustion sank in. She pulled the reclining chair closer to Danny's bed, settled it into a comfortable position and then fell asleep, holding her husband's hand while listening to the reassuringly steady beeps of his heart monitor.

*

Gregory had one more patient to see for the day. If he weren't doing it as a favor for an old classmate, he would have just looked over the test results that South Shore had forwarded and then dealt with it in the morning. There was really nothing to see when it came to hearts, heart attacks or coronary blockages. The tests and medical history gave the whole picture. If there was anything further to know, he'd find it out once he had the guy open. But Ron had told him that this guy was his best friend, his business partner. *What the hell?* Gregory cursed. *Who heads south toward Cape Cod on the Friday of a Fourth of July weekend? Ron is going to owe me big time!*

Gregory was regretting his decision to be a good guy. The traffic was bumper to bumper, even with the breakdown lane open to travel. He scooted his Mazda Miata over to the right lane, taking the next exit. He would figure out how to get to South Shore Hospital using the back roads. *How hard could it be?*

Two hours later, Gregory pulled into the physicians' parking lot at South Shore Hospital. He was in a foul mood. This good deed, along with one wrong turn, had cost him a night of socializing at Union Oyster House, his favorite go-to place for a Friday evening after a long week of saving lives. It was already 8:30. If he hurried, he could be back there by ten. Gregory parked the car, grabbed his briefcase and glanced back at the Miata, deciding he hadn't left anything worth stealing in the little convertible. His mood lightened when he saw his new license plate *WILLOW DOC*. He chuckled to himself, thinking about how evasive he was every time somebody asked him what Willow stood for. *Let 'em guess all they want.* No one needed to know that he was paying homage to his humble beginnings on Willow Court in Dorchester.

*

Gregory strolled into the CCU of South Shore Hospital as if he had been there a million times. He introduced himself to the unit clerk, asked for Mr. Muldaur's chart and stood reading it for a moment. He looked around the unit. The evening shift was on. There was something universal about hospital shifts. Sadly, Gregory always thought of the evening shift as the one with the least potential for meeting a woman. The shift was filled with wives who were splitting the care of their children with husbands who worked days, and overweight matrons with no evening social life and plenty of cats at home. He liked the night shift the best; eleven p to seven a. Because third shifts were the most difficult to fill, all the young nurses with no seniority ended up working them. Sure, there was a downside as far as patient care was concerned, but not as far as meeting a pretty young nurse who would think herself fortunate to date a successful, rich surgeon. Overnight shifts reeked of intimacy and temptation. Gregory had experienced the pleasure of seeing more than one critical case end up in a romance by the time the sun rose, breakfast being a perfect first date. But then there was the subsequent awkwardness of working with a woman after you've dumped her. That's why it was preferable to date nurses from other hospitals; that, plus not having to curb his flirtatious behavior while strolling around his own hospital.

He walked across the unit. Everything was peacefully humming around him, giving the impression that patients were either asleep or critical. He quietly pulled back the curtain to Mr. Muldaur's cubicle. What he saw in the darkened space made his own heart misbeat in disbelief:

The wild, curly, dark hair, the young hand holding an older, lifeless hand, the side of a tear-stained face: *It was Maria!* He took a step back, bumping into a blood draw cart that a phlebotomist was pushing past the enclosure. The sound of the glass tubes smacking together woke the woman in the chair. She turned to look at him with confused, hollow eyes.

"Maria?" Gregory said, before he could stop himself. In seconds he realized the ridiculousness of his mistake. "I'm sorry," he sputtered, still not quite in this moment. "I'm here to see Mr. Muldaur. I'm Dr. Gregory Costa. Dr. Watters…"

Gregory's hand was outstretched. The woman took it. Her touch created an electric current to his past. The grasp was gentle, but sure. She used Gregory's hand as her assist in standing up from the recliner. She made it look effortless, as if closing the foot rest and standing were one movement and not many. The action contributed to Gregory's impression that she was a vision and not real. He remained uncharacteristically speechless. The woman spoke for him.

"Thank you, Dr. Costa, for coming tonight. I didn't think that we would see you until tomorrow. My husband…"

Gregory stopped understanding words at that point. *My husband* she had said with a hint of Europe in her voice. An undefinable feeling of loss and failure shot through his body. The sensations came so rapidly and namelessly that Gregory felt confused by them. He let go of her hand and became more himself.

"Yes. Ron is a good friend, an extremely good friend to get me to come in this direction on a holiday weekend. I've gone over Mr. Muldaur's tests and I feel he would be a good candidate for coronary bypass surgery, his only option really. What that means, Mrs. Muldaur…"

"Teressa. Please call me Teressa. And thank you, Dr. Costa…"

"Call me Gregory." *Call me Gregory? What am I thinking? I don't let my staff doctors call me Gregory!*

"Thank you - Gregory. I am familiar with the procedure. Do you know when you can do the operation?"

Hearing this woman say his name made Gregory wonder why he had worked so hard to rid himself of his accent. Without considering how difficult it would be to secure an operating room on the Monday after a major holiday, he said, "I can do the surgery on July sixth, three days from now."

"That would be good. I'll make arrangements to have my husband transferred to Beth Israel. I appreciate this. Ron said that you are the best at what you do."

Her compliment, although true, left him feeling flustered and unsure of how to end the conversation.

"Yes, I am. I will see you on Monday." Gregory ignored Mrs. Muldaur's extended hand in favor of a head nod. Then he turned on his heel and left.

*

Teres wondered what had just happened. She had fallen asleep at Danny's bedside and was dreaming about Greece. In her dream, she was adrift in a small wooden sailboat that looked to be homemade. The sail was just a triangle of material sewn from her wedding dress. It was too small and too sheer to handle the winds. She was by herself and couldn't remember how to sail. Just when the boat was ready to capsize, she heard the sound of breaking glass from somewhere above the storm clouds, in the heavens. She awoke with a start, unsure of where she was. Standing in front of her was a beautiful man. He called her 'Maria' and then the dream was over.

Gregory Costa. He had stood there as though he were part of her dream. But he appeared to be looking at her like he had seen a ghost. *Who is Maria? Did I say something in my sleep that caused him to call me Maria?* Teres trusted Ron, but it wouldn't hurt for her to research this heart surgeon, *Dr. Gregory Costa.*

*

Danny's surgery had been going on for six hours. Gregory had told Teres that he expected it to take three to four hours. Both Ron and Martha offered to sit with her, but Teres insisted they stay at work, assuring them she would need their help much more after surgery. She wished that she, too, could have had work as a distraction. Teres was alone and out of her mind with worry by the time Gregory walked into the family waiting area.

"Is he alive?" She wondered how many times she had asked this about her husband. *If Danny is alive I can do the rest to make him better. All he has to be is alive.*

"Yes. He did well. But there was a lot to repair. We ended up doing four grafts, two more than we anticipated. But everything went perfectly."

Teres stood and hugged the man who had just saved her husband's life. "Gregory, thank you for being his doctor and doing this surgery. I have nothing to give you that would properly repay you for this." Teres knew that her thank you wasn't making complete sense. *I will pay him in chickens* she thought and then laughed at herself through her tears.

*

Gregory Costa avoided unnecessary displays of emotion from his patients' families. He achieved this in a number of ways. He never spoke more than a brief sentence or two in the patient's room prior to surgery. His surgical assistant was well trained in preparing both the patient and their family for what to expect during and after surgery. And he always sent his surgical resident out to talk to the family directly after surgery, which was the point in patient care most likely to induce tears and hugs. Because Beth Israel was a teaching hospital, Gregory had no lack of eager learners to do his dirty work, as he referred to the task of family liaison. Even when a patient died on the table, which rarely happened, Gregory would first send a minion out to tell the family, and then make a brief appearance, himself.

The fact that he had voluntarily gone out to speak with Teressa Muldaur was a mystery to everyone, including himself. He rationalized that he was doing this for Ron Watters. But he knew he wasn't. *I'm doing it to see her.* And now she had hugged him and made a dramatic statement about never being able to repay him. This would have been the perfect scenario for a follow-up conversation leading to a date; *if* she weren't already married, and *if* he weren't already enchanted by her. Gregory felt confused again, unsure of what to say. It was not like him. He opted to joke his way out of it.

"Don't you worry. When you see how much I bill your insurance company you'll think that I've been adequately repaid for my favor to Ron." She laughed. The tension was broken, or so he thought.

"Please, Gregory," she said, putting her hand on his arm. "Let me do something special for you. Perhaps we can all go out for dinner once Danny is feeling better? You, me, Danny and Ron. I want my husband to get to know this doctor who has saved his life."

She was looking at him with such intense sincerity that Gregory momentarily forgot the number one reason why he became a surgeon: surgeons rarely have to see the patient or their family ever again. It's normally a one-and-done proposition. Gregory returned Teressa's direct eye contact. It may only have been for a second or two, but it created a flood of warmth to his stomach.

"That sounds perfect," he said, against his will. "I'll have the nurse come get you when your husband's out of recovery." And then he fled to the safety of the next surgery.

*

It had been three days since the surgery and Danny's recovery was going along like clockwork. He was alert and making much more sense than he did when he initially woke up. His first words to Teres had scared her enough to make her ring for the nurse.

"You were right. I feel much better when I'm working out." Teres couldn't wrap her mind around it. She was certain that those were the same words he had said when he came to after being hit by the car. She leaned close to him.

"What, Danny? What did you say?"

"I'm glad you're back from Greece, Teres. I missed you so much," Danny said with tears running down his cheeks.

Oh God! He's lost ten years of his life! The panic rose in her chest. She pushed the call button for the nurse. Within seconds the nurse came to the bedside, full of reassurances. After relaying a number of stories about the things that patients had been known to say upon waking, Teres felt better.

An hour later, Gregory arrived.

"The nurse told me you had some concerns," he said, rather formally.

"Well, no, not really. I just panicked when Danny woke up and said things that were from a decade ago."

"Some confusion is normal. If it continues, I'll put in for a neuro workup."

"Oh my God! Do you think that he has brain damage?" Teres was immediately alarmed.

"No. I think this is normal. I just wanted to come by and let you know that so you wouldn't be needlessly worried," Gregory replied.

"The nurse's assurances stopped my worrying. You have made me scared about oxygen deprivation. Did something happen during Danny's surgery?"

"Teressa, he's fine. Nothing happened."

*

Teressa. She had told him to call her Teressa, but this was the first time that his lips had done so. He was making a jackass of himself with this woman. How ridiculous of him to leave a note on Mr. Muldaur's chart to alert him of the smallest concern or detail. He was relatively certain that all his patients experienced mental confusion upon waking. He really didn't care, so long as they woke up. How they functioned after surgery was their primary doctor's concern, not his. *Where am I going with all of this?* The noise of Danny's alarms broke though Gregory's thoughts. *Oh, shit! Her husband's crashing!*

Because Beth Israel's coronary care unit had recently been outfitted with telemetry units, the code blue was called on Danny before Gregory even managed to read meaning into the monitor's worsening configuration above his head.

"Code blue, CCU, room two-three. Code blue, CCU, room two-three," the generic voice bellowed efficiently over the public address system of the hospital. Danny's room filled with staff.

"Teressa, get out of the way! I think your husband's having a heart attack," Gregory yelled as he sprang into action. Teres jumped from the chair and ran from the room.

*

He found her an hour later in the Chapel. Her head was hanging down between her arms, both hands gripping the pew in front of her. She looked up from her distress as though she had known it would be him standing there.

"I cannot do this. It is killing me. I would rather not love him. It would be easier."

In her simple statement, Teressa had summed up Gregory's life. Her anguish anchored him to her as a kindred soul. Gregory pulled her up from the chapel's bench, in full sight of a God who had abandoned him in Italy, and held her tightly while she cried. And then Gregory said the strangest thing. He whispered it into her hair.

"He's alive, Teressa. Your husband's alive. I'll help you get through this, Il mio piccolo gattino." *My little kitten.*

*

Accelerated Ambulance ran itself when it had to. Other than phone calls throughout the day, Teres hadn't stepped foot inside their business since Danny's heart attack. Martha had taken over the day-to-day operations, with the support of the entire staff. Everyone at the company loved Danny. He worked his few hours a week with good humor and a hands-off approach to management. On those rare occasions when he was needed to fill in as a driver, he was everyone's first choice for co-pilot. Most of the calls that Teres fielded while Danny was in the hospital were just excuses to check up on him.

One day was beginning to blend into another for Teres. They all consisted of waking up exhausted, taking a shower, grabbing a yogurt or an apple, then heading to the hospital, where she stayed until Danny was resting comfortably for the night. Most nights she didn't get into her own bed until after midnight. It was taking its toll.

*

"Did you eat dinner?" Ron asked Teres.

"No, she did not." Gregory interjected on his way into Danny's room. "She hasn't eaten dinner since I operated on her husband."

"Quiet! Both of you!" Teres whispered harshly. "He just fell asleep. This arrhythmia thing is making him too nervous to settle in." Danny had developed another complication in the form of atrial fibrillation. It was too soon after his surgery to risk a cardiac ablation, so they were working at trying to find

246

the right medication to control his irregular heart rhythm. So far the current med wasn't working. Teres had upped both her vigilance and her research. "I'm fine. I eat food from Danny's tray. I do not need a babysitter."

"Clearly, you do," said Ron.

"I'm done for the night. Why don't the three of us grab dinner?" Gregory suggested.

Teres stared them both down for a moment, ready to refuse.

"I'm in," said Ron, encouraging her to cave.

"Fine. But, Ron, you have to drive. And Gregory, I will pay for dinner and you will validate my overnight parking."

"Agreed," Gregory replied. "I'll meet you both downstairs in twenty minutes."

*

Going to Legal Sea Foods in Cambridge was Gregory's idea. He liked the restaurant because of its impeccable service and its resemblance to the old-world restaurants of Europe. The bar was the perfect place to dine when he was alone and the seafood was always fresh. He also liked the idea of being the one to choose the restaurant. Gregory had come around to the viewpoint that life was all about good choices. He had stopped believing that fate was the driving force in life. Since the day he put his sisters on the flight back to Italy, he had worked at choosing only those things which led to a better life for himself, and he exclusively trusted his own judgment. With every successful decision, his confidence had grown to the point where he was used to being unchallenged, which was why Teressa's comment about the restaurant choice made him testy.

*

"Danny would hate this place!" Teres laughed, sipping a crisp, white Verdicchio wine, which Gregory had insisted she try. "He would think that it was a plot to make him eat better. He is not a fan of fish."

"There's a delicious filet mignon on the menu, and I think a Porterhouse," Gregory defended.

"It wouldn't matter to Danny," Ron stated. "He'd say, 'If you want steak, go to a steakhouse. If you want fish, don't take me!'" Ron and Teres laughed at their joke. Gregory didn't find it as funny as they did.

"I could tell by the condition of his heart that he was a meat-and-potato man." There was a moment of silence while everyone decided how they were going to take this comment. Teres broke the moment.

"Well, that was mean," she retorted. "But how mad can we get at you? You did save the man's life!" And then she and Ron cracked up again.

It was obvious to Gregory that Teressa was exhausted and punch drunk on her one glass of wine. He also marveled at how close she and Ron were. They thought alike and finished each other's sentences. He wondered briefly if they had ever slept together. Maybe it was wishful thinking on his part, but he couldn't detect a bit of sexual tension between them. *No*, he decided, *this is a best friend kind of relationship.*

"How did you two meet?" Gregory asked them. They started laughing again. Ron answered for them.

"The same way that you and Teres met, over Danny's practically dead body." Then they continued to laugh.

Gregory wasn't sure what to make of this duo. They had gone from ready to fall apart over Danny's health to laughing about it over dinner. It began to make more sense once Ron decided that it was time to tell him the story of Danny. For the next twenty minutes, Ron recalled, in humorous detail, every minute of Danny's life from the moment they had met: treating him for the first time in the ER after his seizure, his short-lived attempt to become a runner, the trash truck accident, opening up the ambulance company together, accidentally teaching Danny to play better golf than him, going behind Teres' back about the food and drinks they shared after golf, going behind Danny's back about everything else he and Teres schemed for their company and Danny's well-being. It became obvious to Gregory that Danny didn't try to be the center of attention, he just was.

Gregory watched Teressa's face while Ron told his stories. The wine had relaxed her to the point where every emotion played across her like a movie: pride, humor, love. He wanted to think that she didn't love her husband, but it was clear that she did.

"What about you, Teressa? How did you and Danny meet?"

"I was nineteen years old, living with my family in Nea Makri, Greece. One day, while I was riding my bicycle down the mountainside, Danny hit me with his car." She could barely get the words out of her mouth when they all began laughing again.

"And it was love at first sight." Gregory said, rather sarcastically. Teres became serious.

"Yes. It was that rapid. I knew the moment I saw him that he was important to me."

Oh, God! Why is this happening? Gregory asked himself. He would have laughed at the notion of love at first sight before he had met her. He sensed that he was about to make a host of bad decisions. He had already made a few when it came to this woman, like being here at this table and watching her face; delighting in its expressive beauty.

Ron's pager went off. Everyone at the table checked their pagers. Ron excused himself to call the hospital. Gregory and Teressa sat in silence, as if needing their mutual friend present in order to speak. Gregory cleared his throat. "You know we'll get this arrhythmia under control, right?"

"Yes," she answered simply. "You are the best at what you do." Ron returned.

"Thank God I only had one glass of wine. They're swamped in the ER, and begging me to come in. Is it okay, Teres, if Gregory brings you home?"

"Yes."

"Good, because I've already told them that I'm on my way. And the meal was fabulous and the company great. And the bill is not my problem. I'm off!" Ron kissed Teres on the head, shook hands with Gregory, then ran for the door. They watched him go.

"Would you like dessert?" Gregory asked his remaining dinner partner.

"What is your favorite dessert?" She wanted to know.

"Biscotti and a good espresso," he answered. "But since they don't serve that here I normally get the Boston cream pie."

"I'll pass on all accounts," Teres said. "I am beyond tired and I think that you need to get me home."

Gregory put his hand in the air and signaled the waiter. "Check, please." The waiter came with check and pen in hand. Gregory signed the check with a flourish.

"What are you..." Teres sputtered.

"I run a tab here. Don't worry, Mrs. Muldaur. I'm just going to write it off as a business expense."

*

The ride home in the Mazda Miata began quietly. Teres' only comment upon getting into the car was, "I hate small cars. They are a death trap."

So much for impressing her with my cool car. She'll really hate the one I'm getting next week, Gregory thought wryly. Teres gave him the basic directions to her house and then reclined the seat and shut her eyes. It struck Gregory as kind of sexy, being so thoroughly ignored. *This is all in your head, stupid,* he reminded himself. He finally decided to speak.

"Is your husband jealous of Ron?"

250

Teres' snort of laughter caught Gregory off guard.

"You went all through medical school with Ron and you never guessed that he was gay?"

It was Gregory's turn to snort. "You're kidding!"

"Ha! Danny had the same reaction. I was almost afraid to tell him that his best friend, the man he wanted to spend every extra minute with, was playing for the other team. It was a great conversation."

"I'll bet." And then for reasons he will never understand, he said, "I think I love you, Teressa." It was dark in the car, and intimate, and close. His hand was partly on her side of the seat, planned, but casual. Gregory could feel her, even though he wasn't touching any part of her. He heard her take in a deep breath. It was the kind of inhale that could precipitate a tirade, although he knew one wasn't coming. He felt the air flowing slowly out of her body as she took his hand.

"I know," she said. And for Gregory, the beating of a human heart took on a whole new meaning.

*

Teres would love to think that Gregory had just worn her down with his persistence. In part, it was true. She knew she had opened the floodgates by acknowledging his love for her. She could have done so many things to shut him down that night: laugh as though his comment were a joke, pretend that she didn't hear him (like she had pretended when he called her "my little kitten"). Teres relived the dialogue from that night in his car a hundred times in her mind. She knew that she was the villain in this drama. She was married, not him. Hers were the vows that were broken.

It was three months before they slept together, three months of Gregory doing everything that he could to right Danny's heart, while doing everything he could to wrong hers. *That's not fair.* Teres would not make this his fault. She had known what she was doing. While Gregory was obsessively pulling her into the deep end, she was hesitantly feeling her way through every emotion. She hated herself. That was one emotion which never left her for more than a minute. But to feel butterflies in her stomach that were not attached to the dread of her husband's health was new and intoxicating. It made her find ways to run into Gregory, be alone with him. The fault was on her. When Gregory began taking Tuesdays off, her day on the road, the die was cast.

Teres had promised herself that the first time they made love would be their last. She even swore to God she would stop in exchange for Danny's health. But then the next time happened. Each Tuesday was going to be their last.

*

It was on Christmas Eve morning that Teres found out she was pregnant. She had purchased the pregnancy test the day before, certain by the ache in her uterus that she wouldn't have to use it. She was wrong. The ache was not the result of an impending menstrual period. It was the ache of a uterus expanding ever-so-slightly to accommodate and protect the embryo which had recently attached itself to the uterine wall. A miracle had happened. She was having a baby. She had wanted to rush into the other room and tell Danny. That was when the full force of her guilt hit her. *I want to tell my husband I am pregnant because he is the only one who will truly know what this means to me.* She couldn't make herself leave the bathroom.

When Danny had come to check on her an hour later she told him that she was sick, but feeling a little better. The truth was that she was sick and feeling worse, almost to the point of ending her life. There were enough different medications in the Muldaur medicine cabinet to kill a small army. Teres had taken them down, one by one, analyzing each one's effectiveness as a life ender. But to kill herself would be to kill the life that was growing inside her. An abortion and ending her affair would also resolve her problem. Neither Gregory nor Danny would ever have to know. *But I will know and my life will be over.* Teres put the medications back onto their shelves. She knew she would do nothing to harm this baby.

She decided the only thing she could do was to take a shower, finish the preparations for Christmas dinner and then allow herself to think about the tiny being that her deceit had created. It was the best she could do in the way of a plan.

She would have plenty of time to reflect on the miracle of her pregnancy while sitting in St. Mary of the Nativity, where she and Danny went to Mass every Christmas Eve to celebrate the birth of Christ.

1992

SCITUATE, MASSACHUSETTS

EVERYTHING WAS ALL set for Danny's party: seventy guests, dinner and then dancing to a live band. Teres had chosen to have the event at the Mill Wharf Restaurant, right on Scituate Harbor. Although the waterside eating establishment was technically considered a seafood restaurant, it had Danny's one hundred percent approval based on the fact that the chef somehow always managed to save him an end cut from the perfectly cooked prime rib of beef.

Scanning the room with one last look before going home to dress for the party, Teres decided that the Mill Wharf had outdone itself. White linens, beautiful table lanterns and twinkling white lights decorated every corner. It was going to be a beautiful night, which her husband truly deserved.

That happy thought took the wind out of Teres' sails. She fell into the nearest chair. A waiter came running to see if she was okay. "I could use a glass of water," she said, prepared to stay in the chair for the rest of her life. She was exhausted. The emotional combination of being a liar and being pregnant was straining her to the max. If she hadn't ruined everything, this would be the happiest day of their lives, especially after last night.

*

Danny had woken her in the middle of the night with purposefully tantalizing hands and a very erect penis. They had made love slowly, almost apologetically. His gentle, tentative thrusts caused her to forget for a moment that he didn't know about the baby. She almost told him that it was okay, their baby would be fine with this lovemaking. When her orgasm ruptured through her, she called out his name and clung to him, crying.

"I know, sweet girl. It's been a long time and I'm sorry for that." he whispered in the darkness. "I'll try to make it up to you." Danny held her and

254

she fell back into a dead sleep without uttering a word. She awoke in the morning, still wrapped in his arms and trying to decide if the night before had been a dream. The grin on Danny's birthday boy face let her know that it wasn't.

*

Teres sat in the chair for a few more minutes, realizing that it was ridiculous to put herself through any more of this. Waiting until the end of February was a stupid idea. Nothing was going to change. She needed to make a decision today. If she was staying with Danny, she'd have to confess everything. If not, why prolong the agony? Teres stood up, feeling a little lighter. Having a plan always made her feel better. Even if her plan was to blow up her life sooner, rather than later, at least it was a plan.

*

The party was a success. The look on Danny's face said it all. Teres had never seen her husband happier. The cocktail hour was going beautifully, with the open raw bar being as big a hit as the guest of honor. Teres had deliberately set up the night in a nontraditional way by having Danny there early to greet his guests as they came in, rather than bombarding him with a room full of people. Teres had promised her husband that she would stay by his side and not let him fumble over a forgotten name or have the conversational ball dropped into his lap. He was already a wreck over the idea of saying a few words of thanks to his friends.

The cocktail hour was almost over when Gregory walked in, looking handsome and confident. Danny spotted him before Teres did.

"Well there he is! If it isn't the man responsible for this wonderful night!" Danny walked away from Teres to greet the good doctor. "I'm so glad you made it." The two men shook hands, with Danny pulling Gregory into an embrace.

"I'm sure Teressa would take offense at your giving me credit for all of this," Gregory said, as he swept his arm across the scene of Danny's party. "It looks like she nailed it."

Danny looked over at his wife with pride. "She did. This is more than I ever imagined, having seventy friends…"

"I said that there were seventy guests, Daniello. I did not say anything about them all being friends," Teres joked, grabbing her husband's hand and offering her cheek to Gregory. "Thank you, Gregory, for coming. It looks like there were no emergencies to stand in your way?"

"I left a few people dying on the table, but I did tell Danny I would be here no matter what," Gregory stared her down with a smile on his lips that didn't reach his eyes.

"No! I don't want anyone dying over my big night," Danny joked, without a clue how close to the truth his words were treading. More people made their way toward them. Gregory saw Ron in the distance and excused himself to go say hello.

Thank God that moment is over Teres thought as she greeted the next guest.

*

Dinner was over and the band was in full swing. Martha had pulled Danny onto the dance floor. Gregory was standing to the side of the room, taking in both the action and his fourth glass of wine. Teres decided that the time had come to talk to him.

*

The look on Teressa's face as she walked toward him told Gregory everything he needed to know. *She is ending it.* No matter what happened with the baby, she was ending it with him. *Why are you making this decision tonight?* He wanted to scream the question at her. She was clearly emotionally unstable and would regret her decision in the morning. There was too much nostalgia in this room for her to do anything but choose Danny. Gregory counseled himself not to say anything rash tonight, or even tomorrow. He would give Teressa as much time as she needed to change her mind.

"I have made a decision, Gregorio." She held a sealed envelope out to him. He didn't reach for it, knowing its contents cemented her decision and his life. "Please promise me that you will not open this letter until you get home, tonight." She put the envelope in his front suitcoat pocket, letting the top stick out like a folded white handkerchief. He wanted to hand it back.

"You don't have to make this decision right now," he said to her. "I'm not opening this letter." *But, of course I will.* The music stopped. He searched her face for a clue leading in his favor and saw nothing.

"I have to give a toast," she said abruptly, and left him standing there. Gregory wasn't certain that he could listen to her tribute to Danny. But he stood there, involuntarily glued in place, watching another precious piece of his life tear itself away. He already hated her for the moment he was about to witness.

*

"Thank you, everyone, for coming to celebrate Danny's sixtieth birthday. I was hoping to persuade Ron Watters to do this toast, but he insisted that he is far too shy." Anyone who knew Ron laughed heartily, especially Danny. Teres took a deep breath and began:

"My husband is a special man to many people. He is a man who spent twenty years serving his country as a medic in the Navy. Just when he thought that he would be retiring to a carefree life, he met me. And I have run over that calm life he had planned for himself, much like a Sherman tank. But to be fair, he ran over me first." Teres waited until the laughter subsided and she resumed.

"He has put up with my bullish behavior with grace and patience. I have dragged him into adventures, made plans that he hated, and then stomped around like General MacArthur when he didn't see things my way. My husband, as you all know, is a true gentleman. He is quick with a smile, a joke or a shoulder, a man with modest wants and needs. Danny is happy if the people he cares about are happy. He is the same man that I married nearly twenty years ago."

Teres began crying in earnest. She took another deep breath and pulled it together. The waiter handed her a glass of champagne from his tray. She turned to her husband and raised the glass. "Please raise your glasses in a toast to my husband, Daniel Muldaur. This day is for you, Danny! Happy Birthday, my sweet man. I love you!" And she downed her glass of champagne in one long gulp to the cheers of everyone around them.

*

Danny had made up his mind on the day before his birthday that he would behave as if nothing could change the life that he and Teres had together, not even her pregnancy. His first step toward that thought process had been to accept that she was pregnant. The evidence was mounting. In the mailbox there had been a surge of junk mail with coupons directed at new mothers. Danny knew that most doctor's offices sold their patient list to vendors in exchange for free samples for their office. Teres was pregnant. He was going to hang onto the fact that she hadn't already run off with somebody as a sign that she planned to stay with him. Danny wasn't certain where all of this was pointing to, but he knew that she loved him. And her speech was more proof of that love. Nothing was as true or as touching as her toast had been. *I just want her to be happy.* Tears were streaming down both their faces when he kissed her. Then she handed him the microphone and he was somehow expected to speak. Out of necessity, he made it short and sweet:

"Thank you, my friends. I'm speechless. This means so much to me. Sixty years is a long time. And to think that the best part of it only began twenty years ago when I fell in love with a little tyrant of a girl who has filled my world with more happiness than I had any right to hope for. I love you, Teressa. My life would be nothing without you." Danny raised his glass to his wife, while his friends clapped wildly. Then he grabbed Teres in a hug and the band began playing his favorite song, Louis Armstrong's *What a Wonderful World.*

*

Teres was relieved when she looked around and didn't see Gregory. She hoped he had left before her speech. Soon he would read her letter and they would figure out the details of what she had planned. Everyone was either on the dance floor or lingering around the bar area. Teres headed to the coat closet in order to retrieve the checkbook in her coat pocket. She would settle the bill and then try to enjoy the rest of the night. *One last perfect night.* She stepped into the back hall and jumped when she heard Gregory's voice behind her.

"Jesus Christ, Teressa! Did you ask me here tonight so you could torture me? I get it! He's amazing! You love him!" Teres reached for his arm.

"Gregory, I don't want you to be in pain, and I do have feelings…"

He angrily ripped his arm away. "Just stop talking! I don't want to hear about your feelings!" Gregory pulled her letter out of his pocket and threw it onto the floor at her feet. "You think that you can wrap this up in a letter? It's my baby, too! I will fight you in court for this child! Fathers get custody all the time these days!" Gregory grabbed his coat from the rack and stormed out the back door of the restaurant, leaving Teres standing there in shock.

Oh my God! He wouldn't dare! Teres reached down and picked up the letter. He hadn't even opened it. If he had, he would have seen that Teres planned to tell Danny everything, beg his forgiveness and offer joint custody to Gregory. She was tired of the lies and she wanted it all out in the open. And now Gregory had run off, with a threat to take her baby! She needed to get to him and make him open the letter for himself so he would know that she wasn't trying to take anything away from him. If this escalated into a custody fight, Gregory was not a man who she wanted to battle in court. He didn't know how to lose.

Teres grabbed her coat and was heading for the back door when she realized that her car keys were in her purse on a table near the dance floor. It would take too much explaining to walk past Danny and out the front door with her coat on. But it was freezing cold out and starting to snow. Her sleeveless satin dress wouldn't make it to the car. She threw her coat out the back door onto the steps, then rushed to grab her purse. She would pretend to be going to the ladies' room, keep walking out the front door, then slip around back to grab her coat.

*

Danny needed a break from socializing. He had consumed one beer too many and really had to pee. *Where is Teres?* He couldn't leave his guests without a host. The urge of his bladder suggested that maybe he could.

*

Danny rounded the corner as Ron was exiting the men's room.

"Nice speech," Ron began.

Before he could come up with a smartass reply, Danny looked through the full-length glass doors behind Ron and saw Teres speeding across the parking lot. He caught a glimpse of her face as she flew by. She looked frantic.

Without analyzing his next move, he barked to Ron, "Give me your car keys!"

Ron did as he was told, pulling the keys from his pants pocket and flipping them to Danny, who raced out the door, in hot pursuit of his wife.

*

He caught up to Teres in a matter of minutes. She was driving fast and the road conditions were worsening. *What would make her drive so recklessly?* Danny was becoming anxious for her safety. *Maybe something is happening to the baby. Maybe she's having a miscarriage.* His mind didn't have a list of possibilities, just the thought that his wife was in danger. He decided that it would be too risky to try to get alongside her car and flag her down. He would just stay close behind and see her safely to wherever it was she felt she had to go. It was all he could do. Danny concentrated on the road. The level of adrenaline pumping through him negated the relaxed effect that having his first couple of beers in months had created. He was acutely focused on the car in front of him.

Teres was driving north on County Way. It looked to Danny like she was heading for 3A, maybe Quincy or Boston. The roads were becoming more slippery. Ron's car, an '89 BMW 325i, was holding the road pretty well. Teres' Lincoln seemed to be slipping around more than it should for a car of its weight and price tag. As they approached the junction to Route 3A, he looked down at the speedometer and saw that they were doing over 50 mph. *If she's gonna make that turn, she'd better slow down!* Danny felt a rise of helpless panic in his throat.

Teres appeared to see the crash at the same time he did. She braked hard, pulling into a spin. Danny swung around both his wife's car and the wreckage of the red sports car, rotating in a 180-degree turn and finally coming to a stop with his headlights focused on the accident. Before he saw the license plate, he knew it was Gregory Costa. He figured the Ferrari must have lost control, fishtailed and then flipped a couple of times before coming to rest on its side, up against an electrical service box. He looked over to his wife's car. It was off the road, but in no apparent danger. She was out of it and coming toward the accident. Danny got there first.

Gregory was hanging out the smashed driver's side window. His scalp was half pulled away from his skull and blood ran out onto the snow in a steaming hot puddle. Danny saw his wife approaching. "Teres, are you hurt?" he yelled.

"No!" she screamed back at him.

"Don't come any closer! Get back in your car and drive to the police! It'll take you two minutes. Drive carefully!" Danny felt Gregory's neck for a pulse. It was thready. He put his hand under the doctor's head and gently lifted the scalp back into place in order to slow the bleeding. It was tricky business to apply pressure without moving Gregory's neck, which looked like it might be broken. He felt a shadow in the headlights coming close to him. It was Teres.

"What are you doing? Get back in your car and go! We need to get him to the hospital!"

Teres stood there, her eyes frozen on Gregory's face.

"Teres, don't look at him. Look at me. Whatever it is you've got going on can wait. It'll be okay. We've got to get Gregory to a hospital." Danny had spoken calmly, as though she were a child. It worked. She ran back to her car and took off toward the Scituate Police Department. Gregory made a gurgling sound, as if he were trying to talk. His eyes fluttered open.

"It's okay, Doc. Help is coming," Danny said, calmly. "Don't try to move. I've got you."

"Danny," Gregory struggled to speak.

"Shh. It's okay, it's gonna be fine," Danny said, soothingly.

"Please… please… take care of the baby. Promise me… the baby is… yours." And then he was gone. Danny checked his pulse again. Nothing. He heard the sirens in the distance and tried to assess whether or not there was more he could do. CPR would mean dragging Gregory through the broken window to get him on the ground, impossible since the door was bashed in and facing the sky. Plus, there was nothing around for Danny to use as an airway.

"Jesus, Doc!" Danny cried in anguish. He was sobbing, shaking and still holding the deceased man's head when the ambulance arrived a few minutes later. Gregory was pronounced dead at the scene. Danny was taken to the hospital in a severe state of shock.

PART III

2015

SCITUATE, MASSACHUSETTS

"DID YOU HATE my real father for ruining your life?" It had taken four days for Costas to bring himself back to the house to talk to his mother. He had been furious when he had left. But it was difficult to stay mad at a woman who was dying. He already felt ruined with guilt for wasting those four days. "Did you end up hating my real father?"

She was sitting in his father's chair in the sunroom. She looked delicate, still beautiful. The home health aide had just left after seeing to her personal care and then tidying up the house. Costas couldn't believe how much thinner she had gotten in just a few days. He began to cry. She had told him once that she loved the way he was so easily moved to tears, like his father. He wondered now which father she had been referring to. As if she could hear his thoughts, she said: "Danny."

And then she answered his question. "I could never hate Gregory. He saved my husband's life... and he gave us you. I pray for him every day." She stared at her son, making him see the truth of her reply. "Everybody said that you looked like me, but you look just like your father. We both had dark looks. I resembled his sister."

Wait? I have an aunt? I have family? Do I have brothers and sisters? Costas realized that he had spent so much energy brooding on the revelation of his real parentage that he hadn't even considered the possibility of more family. He was going to be an orphan soon. The family in Greece was his only family. They had all reached out to him. Papus and Yaya were too distraught to come and see their daughter, but Theo Nicky and Thea Irene had been to Scituate twice in the past six months and his two cousins had emailed him. Costas didn't need more relatives.

"My father's sister?" he finally asked. His mother's smile was sad.

"Two. I never met them. There was so much…" She searched for a word to fit his dead father's family, "strife in his life, in his family. Costas, I'm sorry I waited until now to tell you this. It was wrong." His mother looked exhausted. He thought again about the four days and what his absence had done to her. He thanked God that Julia had talked some sense into him.

"Your father thought that Gregory was a genius, a savior. If there is a villain in this story, it is me." Teres leaned over in pain. Costas couldn't decide if it was physical or emotional.

"Mom, do you need something? Your pain meds?" She shook her head no.

"Get me my white shell jewelry box on the bureau."

Costas went into her bedroom and came back with the box. He had never seen her open it before, and up until now could not have cared less about its contents. His mother struggled to remove the necklace with the key from around her neck. Costas helped her unclasp the chain.

"The memories in this box are things that have changed my life, sent it in different directions. Some of them are reminders of my moral compass… and then not."

His mother pushed the key into Costas' hand, and smiled. "It was quite a journey to get to you. I'm so tired, my sweet boy. But later tonight I will answer all of your questions. I promise." She shut her eyes and he kissed her forehead, not realizing it would be the last kiss he would give her.

*

When he went to check on her an hour later, she was already gone. He stood staring at her with a mixture of relief, despair and disbelief. She had been in pain for so long that Costas didn't fall apart at her passing. He fell apart instead because he had missed the last four days of her life. He hated himself for it. And then he hated himself even more for making his mother's death all about himself, so he cried a little harder. He pulled it together long enough to call Uncle Ron. Then he cried some more, simply because his mother had died and she had been the world to him. And his world had fallen apart, first with her revelation, and now with her death. *How am I going to get through this without her?* And then he called Julia.

*

The perpetual motion of the funeral arrangements happened with minimal movement on Costas' part. Ron went with him to the funeral home, where they made plans for a service and cremation. Martha and Julia handled the food and flowers for the Makaria. Every time he stopped to dwell on her death, someone asked him to make a decision. Do you like A or B? Shall we go with black or white? *Nothing is black or white* his mind screamed. *It's all gray from here.* Costas made choices because it was expected of him. He didn't care about the details. His mother was dead. And her death had begun a whole new life for Costas, a life he didn't want to enter.

It would have been tempting to forget about what she had told him. Nobody knew the truth, not even Uncle Ron. It was a truth that *he* didn't want know. He regretted telling Julia and blamed her for some of the angst he felt. She held him to the responsibility of that knowledge. She implored him to get to the bottom of it, find out everything he could, explore his feelings on the matter. It was Julia who pointed out the bravery of what his mother had done. She could have gone to her grave with this information and no one would have been the wiser. Costas wished that she had.

Julia suggested they go through the family albums and pick out pictures for the service. There wasn't another thing in this world that Costas wanted to do less than to look at pictures of parents *who have perpetrated a lie onto my life*. But once he opened the first album, he was hooked. He pored over the pictures, telling Julia he was trying to pick out the perfect ones. But he knew he was looking for any sign that Danny was disappointed about his birth. There was nothing. For the first two weeks of his life, his father was in more pictures than his mother. And like his mother had said, Danny's face was always wet from the tears streaming down his cheeks.

"Maybe they weren't happy tears," Costas had said to Julia. But he knew that they were. He remembered the stories. He had been born on their twentieth wedding anniversary, a gift from God they always told him. It had been a difficult delivery. He remembered his father reliving the anxious day of his birth during one of his teenage birthday dinners. Costas had stopped his father from continuing, stating that it was gross dinner conversation and no kid cared about how they arrived into the world. He realized too late how untrue that was. All he wanted to know now was every detail of his birth.

He had been a C-section, that much he knew. His mother had stayed in the hospital for ten days and ended up having a hysterectomy six months after he was born. He wondered how his father had felt, holding him and knowing his wife was not doing well. Maybe he had feared that he would be saddled with another man's child to raise, and no wife? But Costas had to admit, all the pictures pointed to a happy little family. All his memories pointed in that same direction. Sure, every once in a while, his mother had gone on the warpath about something. But it was nothing that anyone else's mother hadn't done a million times. Their household was pretty calm compared to other friends of his. He had only seen his father lose his temper once. It had been over a car. That same incident also ranked as the only time his mother had ever hit him.

*

Costas had gotten his driver's license and he wanted his own car so badly that arguing his case had become part of his daily routine. Teres told her son that buying a car was unnecessary since Costas could drive his father's car, an older model Ford Explorer, which Danny rarely drove. As always, his father had backed up his mother's decision and Costas, realizing his case was futile, temporarily gave up the fight.

A few months later, he came home and told his parents that he had found the car of his dreams, a 1999 Ford Mustang GT. His friend was selling it for a price well under Kelley Blue Book value. It was a red convertible with only 88,000 miles on it. After getting a firm "no" from his mother, Costas went to the sunroom to work on his father.

"Pups, it's a steal! The mileage is so low, less than ten thousand miles a year! It's in amazing..."

"No! Absolutely not!" His father had shouted.

"This sucks! I get that you're an old man and you think..."

Costas didn't have the sentence out of his mouth when his mother came flying around the corner and attacked him, first with a slap across his face and then with banshee-like blows to his head and shoulders which he tried to deflect with his raised arms.

"You fucking, little, ungrateful son-of-a-bitch!" She had screamed at him during the pummeling. "If I ever hear you refer to your father with..."

His seventy-seven-year-old father had leapt to his feet and pulled his mother off him. "Teres! It's okay! He didn't mean anything by it!" Costas retreated to the corner of the room and watched, in confused awe, the scene taking place in front of him. His mother was hysterical and appeared unable to calm down. His father had folded her into his arms, covering every inch of her little frame in a way that Costas had never witnessed before. He was cooing into her hair and trying to quell her shaking sobs.

"It's okay, Teres. It's okay, sweet girl. He just wanted the car. He wasn't trying to be disrespectful, he doesn't know everything. He's just a kid. I won't let him get hurt. He'll be fine, baby girl. Come on, let's go lay down for a few minutes..."

Costas stood, ignored, as his father led his mother out of the room and into their bedroom, shutting the door behind them. They didn't come out for the rest of the night. He eventually went into the kitchen and turned off the oven when he smelled their dinner burning. None of the Muldaurs ever spoke a word about that day. Costas got his first car at eighteen, as a high school graduation present. It was a brand new, bright red 2010 Jeep Cherokee, complete with an off-road beach sticker for Sandy Neck Beach on Cape Cod. By then, his father had been dead for almost a year. Costas could never bring himself to drive the new car, favoring his father's Ford Explorer instead. It sat, unused, for three months. His mother eventually sold it after he left for UMass Amherst that fall.

*

The wake was packed. And like his father's showing five years earlier, Costas didn't know half the people in attendance. But, unlike his father's wake, his mother wasn't there to prompt and guide him through introductions. Ron Watters stood by his side throughout the evening and did what he could to take the burden off him. Martha acted as the hostess and Julia somehow managed to skirt between his needs and the needs of the event. His girlfriend was amazing. *So why am I being such an asshole to her?* Costas had managed to hurt her feelings a number of times during the days following his mother's death. She either appeared not to notice or just gave him the benefit of the doubt. They made love in his bedroom that night after the wake. He was immediately upset when it was over, insisting that what they had done was disrespectful.

"Love and sex are appropriate emotions to have in the face of death," she told him, in an attempt to soothe his guilt.

"What do you know about death?" he shot back at her, mad that she had two living parents in their late forties.

"Nothing. I'm sorry," she said. "Why don't you tell me how you're feeling?"

"I'm feeling like the butt of a joke. I'm feeling like I'm having a complete breakdown. I'm feeling like you're happy that you're in on this somehow. I don't want you to be in on this! I want to make this whole thing about my father go away and I can't do that if you know about it. I get it, Julia! I have to deal with this. But I don't want to." There. He had said it. *I'm mad at you for knowing the truth. What else do you know about me? What did she tell you in the last few days while I sulked and you took your turn at her bedside? Whatever it is, I don't want to know,* thought Costas, desperate to know more.

"She loved you more than life."

"That makes me feel worse," he spewed, "because my love for her is mixed up with some pretty hefty hate right now."

"We can figure it out. There are probably answers in that box…"

"This is not your problem, Julia! It's mine! There's no *we* on figuring this out!" Costas turned his back to her and pretended to fall asleep. He thought he heard her crying, then felt her crawl out of his bed an hour later. He was unable to make himself stop her from leaving.

He didn't see Julia until the next morning when she came to his mother's funeral service, as a guest, seated with her parents.

*

Ron gave the eulogy. It was sad, funny and slightly longer than appropriate. He told stories about Teres' natural abilities when it came to running a business, brainstorming, cooking, decorating and socializing, which complemented her husband's amazing golfing skills and… "Nope. That's it," Ron had said, laughing in front of the church full of people at St. Mary of the Nativity. "Danny had golf covered and Teres had everything else covered. Wait, that's not true. They had each other covered, and their son. They were a family to be envied."

Hearing Ron talk about them made Costas feel like his life had been less of a lie. The rest of the service was a blur. Once all the mourners had left, he and Ron sat in the sunroom and drank beer. The late afternoon sun streamed through the windows. It was May fourteenth, his mother's sixty-second birthday. "At least she didn't die on her birthday," was everyone's consoling words. *As if that could make losing my mother any sadder.*

"I've decided I'm going to take Mom's ashes and spread them in the places she loved, Greece, Scituate, Quincy…"

"Just don't let any of them drift over to Houghs Neck. She'll come back to haunt you," Ron cautioned him. "Your mother hated that place with a passion."

"Oh, I know. She gave that look of hers every time the town was mentioned. You know everything about my parents, don't you, Uncle Ron. Tell me about when they found out they were having a baby." Costas didn't admit to himself that he was beginning a journey with his question.

"It was a wonderful event, born of a horrible time. I don't know if you've ever heard of Dr. Gregory Costa, the heart surgeon who operated on your father. He died the night of your father's sixtieth birthday party, a tragic car accident. I went to Tufts Medical School with him. That's how he ended up being your dad's doctor. Gregory left the party that night and your parents came upon the accident. Your dad tried to save him." Ron paused. Costas couldn't decide if he was collecting the memory or deciding what to tell.

I'm going to the same medical school as my real father? How do I feel about that? Manipulated. I feel manipulated. Ron continued his story.

"Neither of your parents went to his funeral. They were too devastated. They had become good friends since the surgery. The next thing I knew, I got a call from your dad asking me to handle the business for a couple of months. He was taking your mother away for the rest of the winter, or perhaps she was taking him. They came back in May. She was six months pregnant by then. Your father announced the news cautiously. It had been a difficult pregnancy.

271

We were all overjoyed when you finally arrived, healthy as a horse. And the rest is history," Ron laughed with his famous wrap-up. "Your mother never let you out of her sight and your father worshipped the ground you walked on. *And* you were lucky enough to get me as the best godfather ever."

"They named me after the doctor who operated on Pups?" Costas pushed a little.

Ron hesitated for just a second. "Well, I don't know about that. Maybe. But isn't Costas a Greek name? It means sturdy?

"Something like that." He stopped himself from asking Ron more questions about Gregory. If Ron doesn't know the truth, the last thing Costas wanted to do was to become so emotional that he blurted it out. He had made up his mind that he wasn't telling another soul about any of this until he decided whether he could live with the knowledge himself.

*

Just ask me, Costas! I know that you want to. Ask me if I know the truth about your father. Ask me so I can honestly say, "No, I don't know the truth!" Because really I don't, not for certain and definitely not the details.

In spite of all of his experience in the emergency room, Ron had no quick treatment for the type of heartache that his godson was experiencing. But, yes, in his own heart he knew the truth.

1992

SCITUATE, MASSACHUSETTS

"GIVE ME YOUR car keys!" Danny barked at Ron.

Ron pulled the keys from his pants pocket and flipped them to Danny. Before he could ask what was up, Danny was gone. Ron turned and looked just in time to see the back of Teres' car speeding from the parking lot, then Danny chasing after her in his BMW.

What the hell is going on?

He hadn't given it a thought when Gregory flew out the door without so much as a "goodbye." He assumed it was an emergency. Although, Costa was a guy who might not have bid his adieus even if his reason for leaving wasn't life or death. *But not Teres and Danny?* Ron's thoughts raced to the uneasy feeling he had been pushing toward the back of his mind.

Please God, don't let it be what I think it is.

*

The writing had been on the wall well before the dinner at Legal Sea Foods. *I should have driven her home.* Ron had seen Gregory reel in a lot of women over the years, but this looked different. True, it still had a predatory feel. But it was softer, more genuine than Costa's typical set of bait and tackle moves. If Ron hadn't known the guy as well as he did, he might have even called it love. He found himself examining Gregory's face whenever Teres was in the room. *It certainly looked like love.*

Gregory's behavior, he was used to. *But Teres? No way.* Never had he met a woman more devoted to her husband and her marriage. He was nauseous watching it unfold. *Maybe I'm wrong* was his hopeful wish for the sake of Danny, their business and the perfect friendship they had created.

*

"We're having a baby," Danny had said to him on the day he and Teres returned from Europe. Ron's stomach sank. *Way to drop the bomb.* It had been three months since Gregory Costa's death and this was the first time that Ron had seen Danny. He still hadn't seen Teres.

"Wow! That's amazing news! We are happy about this little miracle?"

"Yes." Danny's smile contained no hint of anything but sincerity, bone-crushing sincerity.

Ron clapped his friend on the back. "You old dog! Congratulations! How is Teres feeling? When is the baby due? Will she be back in the lineup at work, or is she sitting out the season until after the birth?"

Danny's look turned serious. "I'm trying to talk her out of going back to work. She's..." He appeared to be at a loss for words. Ron jumped in and helped his friend out.

"Well, there's plenty of time to decide about that. I'm glad you're home and I'm thrilled about your news. Give Teres a big, fat kiss for me. Tell her if she needs anything," and this is where Ron became serious, "I mean *anything,* I'm just a phone call away. And that goes for you, too, Danny."

And then Ron waited. He wasn't sure what he was waiting for: the other shoe to drop, the telltale signs of a marriage in trouble, or maybe the rumor mill to start production. He didn't know. But as the months turned into a baby and the baby turned into a man, none of the terrible things that Ron had waited for ever happened.

2015

SCITUATE, MASSACHUSETTS

UNTIL NOW.

"He is going to need you, Ron."

"I know, Teres. You know I'll take..." She put her hand up to stop him from speaking. The gesture was so slow and painful that Ron almost cried. But since he had managed not to cry in front of her yet, it seemed wrong of him to start now. "What is it, honey?"

"I told him something, something that I should have told him a long time ago."

I love you, Teres, but please don't say another word. I am not ready to hear this, not now, maybe not ever.

His best friend heard his thoughts and stopped talking. The deep breath that she took made him wince with her pain. He waited to see if she was going to continue. She shut her eyes. When she opened them again the rims were red, as if from crying, but tearless from dehydration. Ron lifted the glass of water from the table beside her and attempted to bring it to her lips. She waved it away.

"I know you will take care of him. You have been our family, the closest and dearest person in our lives. We love you."

"I love you, too, baby. He'll be okay. I'll make sure of it."

*

Instead of pursuing Costas' conversation about Gregory, Ron had let the moment pass. *I promised her I'd take care of him. How the hell am I going to do that if I can't even talk to him about the one thing he wants to know?* They had both panicked and changed the subject. And now Ron was disgusted by the relief he felt.

275

*

"Thanks, Uncle Ron, for everything that you did this week. I would have been lost without you." Costas stood up and gave Ron a hug. He was grateful that Ron took the embrace as a signal that he was ready to be alone.

After Ron left he would open his mother's box. He needed to know all of it.

2015

THE BOX

THE LID SPRANG open so quickly when he turned the key that Costas half expected a snake to jump out of the little box. It was jam-packed with stuff. *A lifetime's worth of stuff.* Danny's obituary was on the top. Costas had read it a million times. He read it again. He would have to put his mother's obituary in the box when he was done. Below the obituary were a number of envelopes, labeled with his mother's distinctive handwriting. The first one said *Danny.* Just about everything in it was something that he already knew about his father. It contained his discharge paperwork from the Navy along with an official report of the car accident that prompted his parents' meeting, a laminated Massachusetts state board license for his job as a respiratory therapist, a golf score card from the first time his father had beaten Ron, his one and done road race number, and a receipt from lunch at the Governor Bradford in Provincetown, dated July 8, 1973. Costas had no idea why it had been saved, but it didn't seem odd. Every hospital ID bracelet that Teres had ever cut off her husband's wrist was tucked into the bottom of his father's white envelope.

The last thing in his envelope was a folded lab report. It looked to Costas' pre-med eyes to be a sperm analysis, an extremely bad sperm analysis. *Well, that explains it. Maybe they made a sperm donor deal with this Dr. Costa?*

Costas packed everything back in Danny's envelope and went on to the next one. It was marked simply *Costas.* He wanted to open it and have all his questions magically answered. He suddenly wished he hadn't been such a shit to Julia. He could use some Dutch courage right about now. Costas spilled the envelope's contents onto his mother's bed. There was hardly anything in it: a pregnancy test in a baggie, an ultrasound picture dated February 4, 1992. He looked more closely at the image and saw that the last name at the top said Giannopoulos and not Muldaur. He found his original birth certificate, naming Daniel Muldaur as his father and then two birth announcements, one from the

Scituate Mariner and the other from the Boston Globe. All his other important papers, like his Baptism certificate and high school diploma, were already in the top drawer of his bureau.

The next envelope was titled *GAC,* with a newspaper report as its first item:

Prominent Cardiothoracic Surgeon Gregory A. Costa

Dies in One Car Accident on Icy Roads of Scituate.

The article included Gregory's history as a leading heart surgeon and Chief of Staff at Beth Israel Hospital as well as the details of the accident with speculation that it was caused by high speeds and bad road conditions. He was pronounced dead at the scene.

Then there was Gregory's obituary, which gave his birthplace as Sorrento, Italy and listed his parents, Joseph Costa and Louise Costa (deceased) as well as two sisters, Maria Delvecchio (Costa) and Maura Russo (Costa). *And a baby on the way.*

Clearly, he had been named after his father. Yet, they never once mentioned the man to him, not even in passing as an old friend. "Costas" his mother had told him, meant persistent, like the waters to the shoreline. She said that it reminded her of the two coasts that she and Danny were from, Nea Makri and the Quincy shore, and later Scituate. Costas decided he could now add the coast of Sorrento, Italy to that list.

There was a stained cocktail napkin from Legal Sea Foods and the program from a Christmas Eve Mass at St. Mary of the Nativity, dated December 24, 1991. All in all, it was not much to go on.

He shuffled through a number of other things that he didn't take the time to really look at: the adoption denial letter (which he knew about), a letter from his Grandmother, written in Greek, and one from his Great-Grandfather. He would need a translator. Costas wished that he had worked harder at learning his mother's native language. She was never amused when he would joke, "It's all Greek to me." He suddenly realized how serious his mother was. Yes, she could have fun, hit a baseball, make a joke. But she was so determined to ensure a good outcome for the Muldaur family, that her intensity overrode her joy in every situation, except when it came to his father.

Danny could make Teres laugh. Most of it was ridiculous. Costas never understood what she thought was so funny about his father. She laughed every time he told her he was waiting for her so they could decide about dinner. There was nothing funny about that. Even after his father stopped driving, he would ask his wife, "Do you want to take the blue car?" She would smile as if her husband were hilarious. But he also never quite understood his father's protective nature when it came to his mother. Costas would have pitted her against a thousand men. She was a force to be reckoned with and could definitely hold her own. But his father had treated her as though she would break at any moment. He wished that he had paid more attention to what went on between them, noticed all the little signals. *But what kid cares about their parents' marriage?*

The last item in the jewelry box was a sealed envelope. *Gregorio* was the only word, written in her hand. He held it up to the light. It was clearly a letter to his biological father. *Was it a thank-you letter? Thank you for your donation of...* Costas couldn't open it. He was done for the night. Whatever was in that letter would have to wait.

2015

GREECE

YAYA WAS EIGHTY-EIGHT, and Papus, a year older. The death of their daughter had taken its toll. Costas had insisted that they not come for his mother's funeral. He would bring his mother to them. He hadn't realized what would be involved in doing that when he had made the promise.

*

The airline had requirements when transporting the ashes of a loved one. Those requirements had become stricter after 9/11. At the last minute, Costas was running around trying to fulfill those rules. *Thank God my phone is charged!*

"Ron, I need you to go to the house and get a copy of Mom's death certificate and either fax it to me, email it or send me a picture. The airport security won't let me on the plane without it. I thought I just needed the cremation certificate." Costas looked up at the airline attendant at the counter in front of him. "What's your fax number?"

"Six-one-seven, five-five-five, six-six-four-nine. And I hope that's in a container that can be X-rayed." Costas lost it.

"*That* is my mother!" He nearly yelled the words. He could hear Ron on his end of the phone telling him to calm down. He thought about how much calming down he had needed over the past month. But Ron had this covered. He was already at Accelerated Ambulance and there was a copy of the death certificate on file for the changeover of ownership. Within minutes the fax came through, security passed him along and Costas became one of a sea of nameless, faceless fliers on their way to who knows where.

*

Although Costas had told his Theo Nicky that he planned on renting a car at the airport, his uncle was waiting for him when his plane landed in Athens. The moment that Nicky eyed the container in his nephew's hands he began to cry. Instead of saying something consoling, Costas blurted, "I know! This is so awful!" And then the two men cried through the baggage claim and halfway to Nea Makri. They only began to laugh when Nicky told him that Yaya had dinner waiting for them, and she had made his mother's favorite Paximadia in his honor. Everyone knew that Yaya was a horrible cook and a worse baker.

*

After more hysterics with his grandparents, Costas devoured every bite of the food offered to him. Afterward, Irene pulled out a bottle of wine and the five of them began to relax and reminisce, with his uncle interpreting everything that Costas didn't quite understand. When the time seemed right, he reached into his backpack and pulled out his grandmother's letter.

"Yaya. Do you remember writing this?" he asked, handing it to her. She opened the letter, reaching inside for the poem. She cried again, a torrent of words gushing out in Greek. Nicky translated.

"That's the letter and the poem that your Yaya wrote to your parents after they lost the baby."

Lost the baby? What baby? Costas couldn't believe he was hearing another big piece of news about a mother and father who he apparently knew nothing about. *How could they have conceived a baby with his father's sperm count?*

He had brought his father's lab results to a friend from school who was just finishing his lab science degree. They both agreed that it was virtually impossible to father a child with an analysis that bad. *More shit to process.* Every answer seemed to lead to more questions. He asked Yaya if it was all right for Nicky to translate the poem for him later. She nodded yes. He pleaded exhaustion and went to bed.

*

Julia had just fallen asleep when her cell phone rang beside her on the bed. *One a.m. would be seven in the morning in Italy? It's Costas.* She had already decided she would pick up the phone if he called. She was powerless to do it any other way. It wasn't that she needed him so desperately; it was the opposite. Costas needed her. He was his own worst enemy. Being on his side meant fighting anyone against him - plus him. She couldn't leave him out there with no one, even after their last fight, which had been epic.

*

"Great! Go by yourself! Maybe you can find a Greek girl to fall in love with! At least with a language barrier it will take her a while to figure out what a self-absorbed prick you are!"

This bore no resemblance to the rational argument that Julia had rehearsed in her head before coming over one last time to talk him out of going to Europe by himself. *I'm supposed to be the calm one in this relationship,* she thought as she readied herself for his full-out temper tantrum, which was well overdue. Ever since his mother's death, she had looked on in awe as Costas restrained himself from giving over to the tirade brewing inside him. She was certain that it was going to spill out now. She was wrong.

*

"That's something I need to find out," he said quietly in the face of her anger. "I need to know if my real father was a self-absorbed prick. It would explain a lot." Then he walked out of his mother's kitchen and into the woods behind their house, leaving his girlfriend to let herself out.

*

Julia answered right away. Her voice sounded sleepy. He knew she would have looked at the caller ID and known it was him. In spite of his behavior, she had picked up the call.

"My mother had a miscarriage when she was first married," was what he had wanted to blurt out to her. He hadn't stopped to think about whether he was calling her because he loved her or because she was the only person who would understand this latest revelation. It hit him that he should have already decided which one it was *before* he dialed her number.

"Costas?"

He couldn't make himself speak.

"Costas? Is that you?"

He still didn't answer. He knew she could hear him breathing. *Say something!* He pleaded with himself. Then it was too late.

"Fuck you, Costas! Don't call me again!" And she hung up on him, just as he thought she should.

"Now you have no one. I hope you're happy," he whispered to himself, as miserable as he had ever been in his life.

*

Greece was an oasis. Costas spent the next six weeks hiking, swimming and partying with his cousins. The two girls knew how to party. They took him to the Gazi district in Athens, where he danced and drank to a level he had never achieved in college. Their favorite places became his. Kitty Cat and Enzzo de Cuba were always filled with locals and great music.

283

Calista and Stefanie were thirty-three and thirty-one. If either one of them was dating somebody, Costas had yet to see him. They partied with everyone. Calista worked as an event planner for a large computer software corporation and Stefanie was the beloved black sheep of the family, choosing to become a physical trainer, rather than finish college. Neither had a problem with the fact they were still living at home and hadn't established any new branches for their family tree.

"Papa said that you were coming to Greece with a girl. Where is she?" Stefanie had asked on day two of his visit.

"Yeah. No. It didn't work out," Costas wanted the subject dropped. But they were women and used to prying.

"He said she was pretty, and nice. She reminded him of your mother, the way she took charge of things. Papa tried to make us feel bad because we didn't have husbands."

Calista laughed with a snort. "Who wants a husband?" she asked. "I told him I'd be happy to give him a grandchild or two, but I wasn't ready to get married." She laughed again. "He declined my offer."

Being with his cousins was like a tonic for Costas. They wanted nothing more than to show off their American cousin and make sure he was having a good time. And much to his surprise, he was. Even the day they spread some of his mother's ashes into the waters off Nea Makri had been joyous rather than sad. His uncle had rented a thirty-five-foot Tobago Catamaran for the occasion. Unlike Costas' vision, the event turned out to be more of a party than a funeral. Papus and Yaya seemed relaxed and happy to sit on the deck of the catamaran, drinking mimosas and eating the calamari and shrimp that Irene had packed to go along with their brunch. With no industry in sight, the waters around Nea Makri were cleaner and more beautiful than any water Costas had ever seen. He wondered how his mother had left a place so beautiful. *Well, she's back here now.*

*

Costas, Ron, Martha and Bemus had already spread his mother's ashes in three different places. They had chosen Wollaston Beach, right around the corner from Danny and Teres' first apartment on Sea Street, as well as the Scituate Lighthouse, where Teres first fell in love with the town. The third place Costas had chosen was inside the little stone-walled clearing behind their house. Teres had been making that space into an oasis for as long as Costas could remember. After his father died, she had constructed a cobblestone labyrinth to go with the meditation pool. Whenever he couldn't find his mother, it was the first place he would look. Spreading her ashes there was difficult for Costas. He had been going out to the clearing a lot since her death. It was easy to feel her there. When he closed his eyes he could see her in those woods, praying, meditating, or just enjoying the silence.

With each ash-spreading ceremony, one of them chose to speak. At the clearing Martha had read a passage from the Book of Revelations:

And I saw a new heaven and a new earth: for the first heaven and the first earth were passed away; and there was no more sea.

2 And I John saw the holy city, new Jerusalem, coming down from God out of heaven, prepared as a bride adorned for her husband.

3 And I heard a great voice out of heaven saying, Behold, the tabernacle of God is with men, and he will dwell with them, and they shall be his people, and God himself shall be with them, and be their God.

4 And God shall wipe away all tears from their eyes; and there shall be no more death, neither sorrow, nor crying, neither shall there be any more pain: for the former things are passed away.

5 And he that sat upon the throne said, Behold, I make all things new. And he said unto me, Write: for these words are true and faithful.

*

Costas had to hand it to his grandparents. Before he had arrived in Greece, he was unaware that cremation was forbidden by the Orthodox Church. But Papus and Yaya seemed happy to have a little piece of their only daughter back with them. His grandfather said prayers before letting some ashes slip from the urn that he held in his hands. Later, Costas would realize that Papus had recited the same verses that Martha had: Revelation 21, 1-5. After the prayer, the little Giannopoulos family bowed their heads in a moment of silence, finishing with a toast of ouzo in Teres' memory. Costas had expected that the boat would then turn around and head home, but Nicky had rented it for the full day.

"I hope you brought your sunscreen," Calista said to Costas. "For a Greek boy, you've got some pretty Irish skin!"

Little do you know was the comeback in his head.

They spent the remainder of the afternoon cruising around and stopping whenever the heat forced them into a swim. They would dive off the back of the catamaran into the cool, blue waters of the Mediterranean until they had their fill of swimming and then pick up anchor and move on. It was paradise. Leaving his Greek family would be one of the hardest things he would ever have to do. It would have been so much easier to ignore his admission to Tufts, stay in Greece and take over the family jewelry business, like Theo Nicky had jokingly offered. But he had worked too long and hard toward his goal of becoming a doctor to give it up on a whim.

Greece will still be here when I'm finished with medical school.

But before his return to Boston, Costas had one more stop to make: Sorrento, Italy, to visit his grandfather, Joseph Costa.

2015

SORRENTO, ITALY

JOSEPH COSTA WAS eighty-nine years old and still living in the little apartment his son had rented for him after his release from prison, twenty-five years prior. Having had no beneficiaries, Gregory had assigned his father as his next of kin, making him a wealthy man upon his son's untimely death. The pain of losing a son, whom he had so recently found again, almost killed Joseph. He put the money into safe funds, setting up trusts for his two daughters and their families, the size of which would keep them secure for a lifetime. And then he purchased his little apartment in the old portion of downtown Sorrento and tried to find meaning in his life by growing tomatoes on his back windowsill and volunteering at the church. Receiving Daniel Muldaur's phone call three months after his son's death had been quite a shock. A week after the call, Joseph met with Daniel Muldaur in a little café around the corner from his apartment. The next day Muldaur brought his wife, Teressa.

*

"You are beautiful," were Joseph's first words upon meeting Teressa. "You look like my daughters." The woman had no reply to that. Joseph got straight to the point. "Your husband tells me that you're carrying my son's child. I have to admit, I am both overjoyed and confused by this news." The woman was still silent. "He also assures me that you are not here to seek money…"

"I don't want anything from you. If anything, I owe you a debt. My husband and I could not have children. Your son, Gregory…"

The pain on her face at the mention of his son's name was pure and obvious; a pain he had felt for thirty years at the sound of Gregory's name. *She either loved him, or… no, she didn't hate him*, that much Joseph could see. And maybe the guilt he saw was a reflection of his own guilty pain.

"Your son and I lived a lie for a short time, a lie that gave me the gift of this pregnancy. I, we, couldn't let you live out your life not knowing that this child had been conceived." Teresa Muldaur began to cry, which caused Joseph to do the same. Her husband took over the conversation.

"We've chosen not to tell our child about Gregory. The baby will be brought up as my child in every way, including my heart. If that's something you can live with, we'll send you pictures and letters, keep you informed about his life."

"If it is too painful for you, we will understand," added Teressa Muldaur through her tears.

Joseph noticed that the man had said "our child." When he had met Daniel Muldaur the previous day, he sensed that he was a good man. Daniel had told him that his wife had been through enough and warned Joseph that if he said anything to upset her, their meeting would be over. Joseph had already made his decision.

"I am grateful for whatever you will share with me of this child's life," Joseph said. "It's more than I deserve."

*

Costas was thankful that he had read all the reviews about driving to Sorrento before making his plans. He would have been dead in a hundred different ways if he had been driving these winding coastal roads. As it was, the bus looked like it was about to careen off the side of a mountain at any given moment. His stomach was in knots, and not just from the motion sickness. If Joseph Costa hadn't already been expecting him, he would have turned around and headed for home. Costas was terrified of this next step. He didn't need more relatives. He had a perfectly good family in Greece.

Finding Joseph had been relatively simple. Calling him on the phone had taken courage, but in the end the old man had made it easy.

"Hello, this is Costas Muldaur. I'm calling to speak to Joseph Costa." There had been a moment of silence that Costas mistook as an international delay.

"I wondered if I would ever hear from you," the old man had said and then began to choke up, coughing and unable to speak.

"I'm sorry," Costas had said. "I didn't mean to startle you."

"No, no. Please, it's okay. Don't hang up." The man sounded panicked over the possibility of losing their connection.

"I won't hang up. Take your time, if you need a bit of water, I'll wait," Costas reassured Joseph, feeling the importance of this moment. He waited while his grandfather cried for a bit and then got it together. Joseph first asked about Teressa. *He knows my mother.* Costas told him she had died of stomach cancer. He said how sorry he was.

"Mr. Costa? I'm coming to Sorrento in a few days. Can we... would you like to meet me?" The silence was deafening.

"It would be the happiest day of my life."

*

Joseph would like to have met his grandson outside, at the bottom of the apartment stairs. But the stairs had been taking a toll on his heart of late. He had told the boy to ring the apartment buzzer and then come right up to the top of the landing. His apartment was on the left. When the buzzer rang, Joseph almost had a heart attack. The moment between the ringing of the bell and seeing Costas' face was a lifetime; more than a lifetime when he saw how much his grandson resembled Gregory.

"You are your father, your face, your hair, your eyes. I have seen it in the pictures, but didn't realize how much." Joseph grabbed Costas in a wiry hug, the kind only an old man can give.

"Hello, Grandfather? Is that what I should call you? Grandfather?"

289

"What about Nonno? Is that good?" Joseph's eyes were filled with everything: tears, gratitude, and some pretty substantial cataracts which he had not gone through the trouble to fix. Now he wished that he had. He grabbed the dish towel hanging over the porcelain sink and wiped his eyes. "Let me look at you. You're so handsome, like your mother. She was beautiful."

"You met my mother?" Costas was shocked.

"Just one time, and I met your father, too. Daniel was a good man. Are you hungry?" Costas nodded. Joseph went over to the counter and toasted up bread, slathered it with mayonnaise and then layered the bread with his homegrown tomatoes. While he did this, he told Costas that he would tell him everything he knew about the circumstances of his birth. He figured he knew more than anyone else, alive or dead. And it was all in the form of letters.

*

After he finished his sandwich, Costas helped his grandfather pull out the big box that was stored in the bottom of the bedroom wardrobe. They carried it over to the parlor and placed it on the coffee table beside a picture album. Costas sat down on the sofa, expecting his grandfather to sit beside him. The old man chose a chair across the room from him.

"I want to look at you. I'll be right here. Take your time. When you're done, I would like to tell you things about Gregory."

Costas began with the album. It was a complete journal of his life through photographs and keepsakes. Every birthday party, baseball game and golf match were in that album, all titled in his mother's neat little scrawl. She had even sent Joseph a copy of his nursery school diploma. His mother had made copies of every report card and accomplishment, including the acceptance letter from Tufts University School of Medicine. It was surreal to find out that a complete compilation of his life existed, let alone that it was in this stranger's apartment. *Not a stranger, Nonno,* Costas reminded himself.

"Your mother was a good letter writer. There are some letters from your father, Daniel, too. His are short. In the back of the box is a card to me from Gregory, telling me that he was going to be a father. When your parents came to see me, I let them think that I didn't know about the baby - you." Costas was taken back by Joseph's openness. He had to keep reminding himself that this man had known about him for twenty-three years. He opened Gregory's card first. The front had a picture of a small sailboat sitting alone in the water. The note was short:

Pa - I met a woman. She's important to me, but it's so complicated. I finally know what you meant when you said that not all of life's decisions are black and white. We're going to have a baby. I'll let you know more later. Happy New Year! Love, Gregory

Another piece of the puzzle was solved for Costas. *My biological father wanted me and loved my mother.* Costas didn't know why that made him feel so much better. It shifted things, though. This was definitely no longer a case of his parents asking a friend to help them have a child. He felt better about Gregory, but worse about his mother.

The letters from his mother were too numerous to read in one sitting. She mentioned Gregory's name a couple of times in reference to Costas' likeness, or sometimes his stubbornness. The first letter from Danny was written after his mother's hysterectomy. It had been a while since she had written and Danny had wanted to assure Joseph that the baby was doing well. Every letter created a new set of emotions. It was draining and he was exhausted.

In spite of his grandfather's request that he spend the night, Costas called a taxi. It was a little after midnight and he had a raging headache from all the turmoil in his mind. He promised Nonno that he would be back early the next morning and they could go to church together. But for now he needed a hot shower and a good night's sleep.

*

The day's events had made him miss Julia even more. He had been such an ass. Costas knew that being an ass was kind of a thing for him. Actually, it was their thing. He was a jerk, and she made it okay. Her goodness sort of made up for his selfish, bad behavior. Costas had told her once that like many couples, he would be the one to cancel out her vote at the election polls. She was used to him pulling the rug out from under her. But maybe this time he had gone too far. He really missed her and could have pictured her on Nonno's couch beside him. He forced himself not to call her and went to sleep, wondering what tomorrow would bring.

*

Jesus! I can't believe I overslept! Costas raced into his clothes and decided it would be faster to run to his grandfather's rather than to wait for a cab. It was only a few miles. He was sweaty and ready to pass out from the ninety-degree early morning heat when he reached the apartment. He rang Nonno's bell and quickly began his ascent up the stairs. In the darkness of the hallway, he saw his mother rushing toward him. He somehow managed to stop himself from falling down the staircase.

"Costas! I'm so excited to meet you!" It was his Aunt Maura, and she was a dead ringer for his dead mother.

*

By the time Costas calmed down and stopped hyperventilating, it was too late for church. Instead they spent the day outside in the park near Nonno's apartment. Maura told him everything she could remember about her brother. Some of it was too much for her father to bear. Costas noticed that he would get up and throw his breakfast roll at the pigeons whenever she spoke of the Costa children's time alone in Dorchester. When she was done talking about her brother, she told him about herself. Maura was sixty years old. She had grandchildren of her own and a very happy life. She credited Gregory for that life, both the early years and her current financial comfort. She never mentioned her sister and Costas didn't ask.

After eating dinner at Joseph's favorite trattoria, Costas walked them back to the apartment, kissed them both goodbye and promised to plan another trip to Italy so he could meet all his relatives. He left Nonno the album, but took the letters with him.

*

The next morning, at the break of dawn, Costas walked to the docks. In his backpack was the urn with the rest of his mother's ashes. He planned on walking to the end of the pier and sifting them into the water. He had decided to do it early, while Sorrento was still asleep and his chances of being alone were good. As he strode down the ramp, he spotted a little wooden boat tied up to the dock. It was being washed down by a teenaged boy.

"Hey, kid! Any chance you speak English?" Costas yelled.

The boy eyed Costas suspiciously. "Yes. What do you want?"

"Will you row me out a ways so I can throw my mother's ashes into the sea?" Costas pulled out the urn and walked toward him while he spoke.

"Your dead mother is in there?"

"Yup," Costas replied.

The boy grinned, "This will be a first. Hop in." Costas hopped into the Gozzo Sorrentino, the boy's pride and joy.

2015

SOMEWHERE OVER THE ATLANTIC

EACH DAY, FOR exactly three months, Costas had told himself that this would be the day he would open the letter his mother had written to Gregory. And every day he chickened out. That letter was the only piece of communication that existed between the two people whose short-lived affair had created him. He was terrified of its contents, more so now, knowing the rest of the story. *Not all of life's decisions are black and white* Gregory had written in his letter to Joseph.

In two hours he would be landing in Boston. Summer was nearly over. It was time to put all this drama behind him. Costas knew he had a choice to make. He could let the issue of his genetics forever color his view of the world or put it in perspective and get on with his life. He took his mother's letter out of his backpack and carefully pulled it open, trying not to tear the envelope. As he unfolded the pages, Costas took a deep breath and then began to read:

February 7, 1992

My Dearest Gregorio,

This is the hardest letter that I have ever had to write. You have been so much to me these last few months, a savior in so many ways. Whatever the reasons for what we have done, it has appeared to be out of our control. I'm not making an excuse for my part in this. I wanted to be with you. The pull toward one another was more like a remembering than a meeting. It could not be stopped.

As if the debt that I already owed you for saving my husband's life was not enough, I now owe you my soul for the creation of this little being growing in my womb, whom I already love and cherish more than my own life. I know, Gregorio, that you feel the same way as I do about this baby. You would give your life to make certain that your child is well.

But Danny doesn't deserve any of this. He is a good man. He is the only man I have ever loved. I know that it's difficult for you to hear me say that. It was difficult for me to admit. What I feel for you is a connection and a love, but I am not in love with you. I know the difference.

Tonight, after Danny's party, I am going to tell him everything, and beg for his forgiveness. Whether or not he forgives me will not change my reasons for ending our relationship. We are over as a couple, but we are just beginning as parents.

I don't want this to be done in secrecy. If you are willing, we will tell the world that this baby is yours and let them think what they want. It won't matter to me. We have created a life. I'm willing to suffer whatever arrows are slung my way in return for this baby's health and happiness.

Please believe that I never meant to hurt you and I am forever grateful to you for the life that I am carrying. I plan to contact a lawyer to make a legal agreement of joint custody between us. I have every confidence that you are going to make a wonderful father.

With love and shared devotion for our child,

Teressa

*

Costas read the letter three times, each time feeling more loved than he had ever felt in his life. *Not all of life's decisions are black and white.* He suddenly couldn't wait for his plane to land so that he could drive to Lowell, tell Julia everything and beg for her forgiveness.

THE END

BOOK CLUB DISCUSSION

1. *Baklava, Biscotti, and an Irishman* began as one question: Is it soul recognition that determines who we love, thereby making human relationships somewhat out of our control? What do you think about this concept?

2. Teressa is the common thread between the main characters in this novel. Do you feel that the principal story is hers?

3. For centuries, and in many cultures, women have looked the other way when it came to infidelity. In this case, it's a man who looks the other way. Other than love and loyalty, what factors allowed him to do so, even before he knows the entire story?

4. Was the glimpse (given through Joseph Costa's eyes) into the three months that Teres and Danny were away enough for you to imagine the conversations leading to the choice they made.

5. The déjà vu of history repeating itself throughout the story is a common thread. If you can look back into your own family history, have there been situations and scenarios where you can see a pattern of repetition or in the case of good fortune, serendipity?

6. "God, I hope no one ever judges me by my worst day or my worst deed," is what Mike Donohoe says when Gregory tells him

about his father's crime. It's a powerful statement. How does that apply to the way in which we view mistakes and misjudgments in today's world?

7. *Baklava, Biscotti, and an Irishman* is written using interweaving timelines, each in chronological order to its individual character. This allows information to dribble out in a manner chosen to create the most impact on the overall story. Can you recall an example where an incident made more sense to you *later* in the story, because you became privy to a scene that took place *earlier* in time? Did you enjoy this style of writing?

8. There are many types of strengths showcased in *Baklava, Biscotti, and an Irishman.* Costas sees his mother as "a force to reckon with" and questions why his father treats her "as though she would break at any moment." Teres is accused of thinking of Danny "as a delicate flower" when it comes to his health. Do you see the trading of strengths as a normal part of any relationship? What about between Costas and Julia?

9. There are no accidents. Did *reading Baklava, Biscotti, and an Irishman* cause you to rethink the concept of fate and destiny?

10. Teres and Danny's friends play small but important roles in the novel. Ron Watters is particularly vital to the story. Would you have wanted to know more about him? Did his desire to be "solving someone else's problems" rather than "thinking about his own" make you curious all along to know what those problems may have been?

11. Gregory's history evokes a lot of sympathy. Did knowing about his life cause you to vacillated when considering your own desired outcome for the story. What was your desired outcome for the story?

12. Danny and Gregory would appear to be opposites, but in what ways were they similar?

13. Both Teres and Gregory have affluent early lives and then a period of struggle. Danny's life is structured in the opposite, having come from parents who didn't have much. Danny appears to resist an affluent life. Do you think it's more common, or less common, for a person to seek the lifestyle they knew in their early years? How do you feel that Danny's ego (or sometimes lack of ego) factored into their success?

14. The role that religion plays for at least two of the main characters is obvious. Although Teres remains particularly devout, it appears that her devotion transfers from religious to spiritual. Do you think she views her Greek Orthodox religion as having failed her or she having failed it? Or is it neither of those things?

15. Even without Julia's persuasion, Costas' need to know the truth is apparent. What do you view as the main question that Costas needs answered?

16. Thirteen times the word "miracle" is used in the novel. Only four of those times have nothing to do with the conception of a child. Do you think everyone views birth as a miracle or is it viewed as more of a miracle when the desire to have a baby is unfulfilled?

17. Gregory admits he is good at "compartmentalizing" in order to achieve his goals. In what ways were the other characters also compartmentalizing their lives?

18. If you haven't already, did reading *Baklava, Biscotti, and an Irishman* make you wish to visit Italy and Greece?

ABOUT THE AUTHOR

Kathy Aspden lives with her family on Cape Cod, Massachusetts and is a freelance writer for the Cape Cod Times, where her column has had the distinction of being the most read blog. She has written a number of screenplays including features, *An Inconvenient Miracle* and *Only Words*. Her movie short, **The First of the Month** was chosen as an official selection for the **15 Minutes of Fame Film Festival** in Orlando, Florida.

www.KathyAspden.com

Made in the USA
Middletown, DE
14 September 2017